DOUBLE DARE

by

Michael Madigan

Adventure Publications, Inc.
Cambridge, Minnesota

Cover design by Lora Westberg
Book design by Jonathan Norberg
Edited by Brett Ortler

10 9 8 7 6 5 4 3 2 1

Published by Adventure Publications, Inc.
820 Cleveland Street South
Cambridge, MN 55008
1-800-678-7006
www.adventurepublications.net

Printed in the U.S.A.
ISBN: 978-1-59193-434-9

DOUBLE DARE

ACKNOWLEDGMENTS

It would have been a mistake for me to attempt to write about the Dolores River without first meeting "Ranger Rick" Ryan, retired from the Bureau of Land Management's Dolores office, and I was lucky enough to have discovered that before I started writing. His time and experience were invaluable to me. Here's hoping the surf is always up for the old long-boarder. The BLM's Tres Rios Field Office provided valuable geocaching assistance. Toni Kelly of the U.S. Forest Service also pointed me in the right direction several times.

My decision to mold Cutter into a disabled character was based on tremendous admiration and respect I have for physically challenged heroes in all walks of life. More specifically, I owe legendary climber Malcolm Daly for his inspiration, and former *Rocky Mountain News* reporter Jody Berger for writing about him. I leaned heavily on the expertise and patience of Jeff Boonstra, a Certified Prosthetist at the Advanced Prosthetics Center in Dakota Dunes, South Dakota, who showed me what was possible.

I based the kayak scenes on my own experiences. Jason Beausoleil, a Front Range instructor, guided me through more difficult waters.

Whatever I now know about helicopters is due almost entirely to the generosity and experience of Mike and Regina Fyola, owners of TYJ Global of Broomfield, Colorado.

The Dolores Library was a resource for me. I leaned on two of its publications in particular—*The River of Sorrows*, published by the U.S. Dept. of the Interior, and *Where Eagles Winter: History and Legend of the Disappointment Country*, by Wilma Crisp Bankston. *The Dolores River Guide*, published by the Southwest Natural and Cultural Heritage Association, is the bible of the river. My awe for wildlands firefighters and my understanding of what makes them do what they do was greatly deepened by John N. Maclean's *Fire on the Mountain* and his other works. The archives of the late *Rocky Mountain News* remain a mother lode of Western history, and I respect and appreciate the privilege of access that I had. Any errors in the book are my own and no one else's.

Evidently, it's true that all good things do come to those who wait: I found Adventure Publications. I can't thank Publisher Gerri Slabaugh and her team enough. In his very first email, Editor Brett Ortler told me that *Double Dare* was my story; he just wanted to make it better. And, he did.

Before Brett, there was a Murderer's Row of unofficial editors whom I must thank:

The first to read *Double Dare* was my wife Julie, a discriminating reader and my toughest critic. She inspires me every day. Jeannie Patton, former literature professor, longtime skiing and river buddy, who shares a love of the West, edited the first draft with knowing grace. Clearly, she cut in front of me in line when the Big Chief was handing out writing skills. Friend and fellow author Denny Dressman performed editing triage once again; we take turns carving and suturing up each other. Petra St. George, Tim Madigan, Patricia Madigan, Mike Patton, Larry Strutton, Dan and Patsy Ginsberg and Michael Brotzman read early drafts of the manuscript and encouraged me to keep at it. Melanie Dressman is always in my corner, no matter the subject. Kathleen Madigan contributed her mapping skills. The Tall Girls Book Club shared the unvarnished reactions of real readers with me, which was timely and positive. My Rocky Mountain Fiction Writers critique group—Nancy Williams, Ron Heimbecher, Vicki Rubin, Dave Jackson, Jodie Ball and Deb Quadrani—were ruthless and caring. And thanks to Mark Stevens for being my publishing wingman.

Finally, my thanks to the family and friends who allowed me to borrow bits of their personalities as stand-ins for some of the characters of *Double Dare*. Despite the occasional family fracas we may have from time to time, Radic Vuko is not based on one of them.

—MM

DEDICATION

In memory of Lloyd "T" Madigan and Vernard Keeney, the earliest adventurers in a young boy's life.

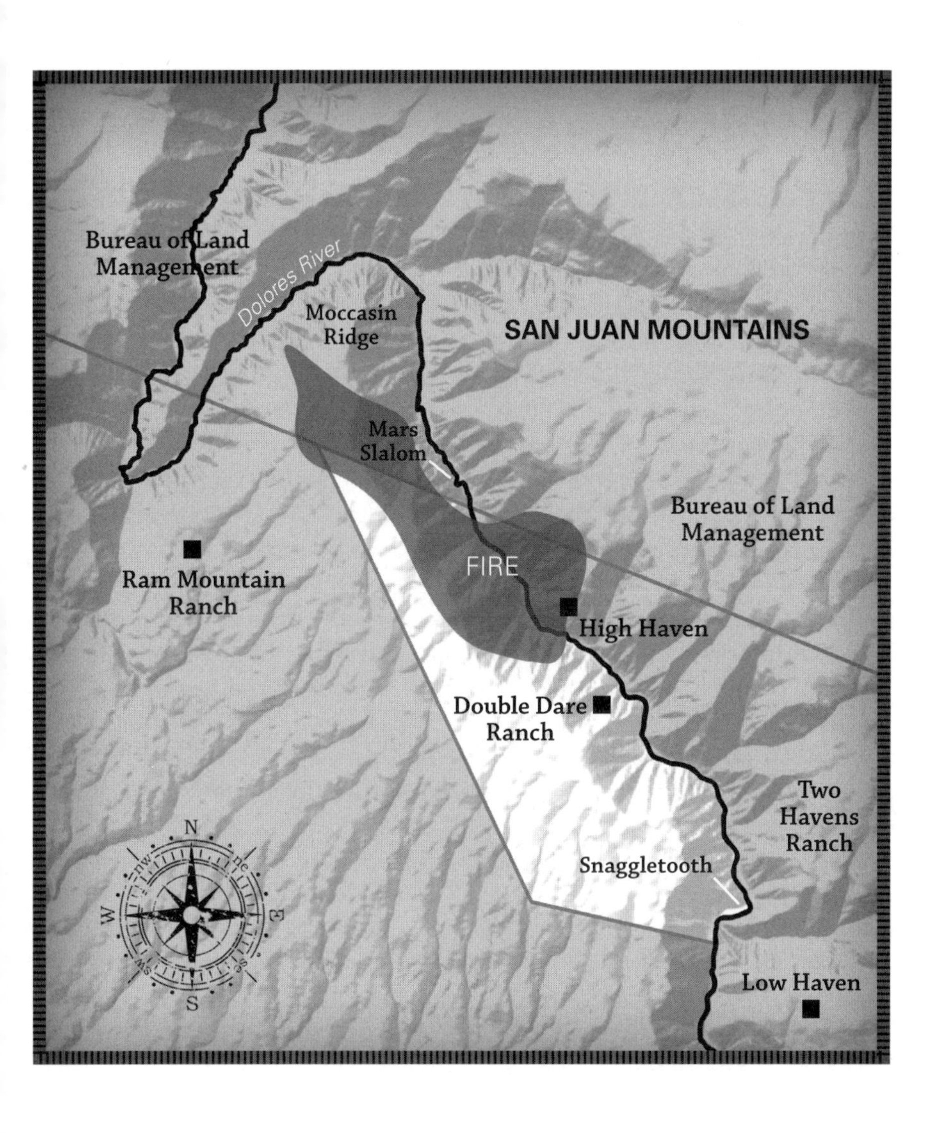
Bureau of Land Management
Dolores River
Moccasin Ridge
SAN JUAN MOUNTAINS
Mars Slalom
Bureau of Land Management
Ram Mountain Ranch
FIRE
High Haven
Double Dare Ranch
Two Havens Ranch
Snaggletooth
Low Haven
N
W
E
S

Chapter 1

The wave train attacked Serena's kayak, swarming her in frothy whitewater. As the icy rapids of the Dolores River slapped her face, she broke out in an exultant smile.

She gasped and tried to catch her breath. *So this is what Double Dare Ranch is all about.* The smell of sage rushed her from the riverbank.

The West's adrenaline junkies had been anxiously awaiting the opening of a new breed of wilderness resort—described by its creator as an "adventure ranch"—for more than a year. The man behind the project, Blake Cutter, promised backcountry challenges that would "test the best, and teach the rest." A glitzy advertising campaign pummeled TV viewers and newspaper readers from Austin to Yellowstone, beckoning them to the ranch, which sat at the foot of the remote San Juan Mountains in southwest Colorado.

"This is no dude ranch," Cutter told Serena when he greeted her at the compound with a go-get-'em grin that made her pulse quicken. "This is a *do* ranch."

With broad-shouldered paddle strokes, she powered the kayak through the roiling, milky-green spume. Staring downriver, she fought the glare even from behind polarized Oakleys, reading the water but at the same time probing the banks and every nook and eddy. She was searching for a prize.

She was waist deep in her first Double Dare challenge, but the sky-blue day and the pleasure of a solitary physical task lulled her to distraction. It almost made her forget that she'd left her career—her real career—back in Denver in tatters. *Almost*, she thought bitterly. She scolded herself for dredging that up now, then drove off the black mood.

Her mind wandered back to Cutter. *That one might be worth an extended stay. He didn't look handicapped to me. I wonder how he . . .* The lurid fantasy in the middle of the watery chaos made her laugh out loud. *What if I wanted to choose between him and the crazy business proposition that brought me to Double Dare Ranch?* She remembered her disappointment when he abruptly ran for a pile of equipment and left the ranch, his pickup spraying gravel behind it. What could be so urgent?

There!

Serena caught a flash of crimson and the twinkle of metal. But in the split-second it took to alter her stroke, the river swept her past the prize. The next instant, a four-foot tumbler broadsided the kayak from the right and erased her from the surface, rolling her over and under the frigid water. Her cherry-red helmet and the bottom of the red fiberglass boat suddenly exchanged places. *Cold. Think. Hold that air.* She'd executed Eskimo rolls hundreds of times, but she still always struggled to get her brain right about it. Submerged and upside down, the current flushing her downriver, she positioned her paddle parallel along the left side of the kayak. She cocked her left hand under her left glute, then she dug the paddle into the water on her right with all her strength and at the same time snapped her upper-body weight from left to right. She popped to the surface like a freed fishing bobber. The flow flushed her out into a placid eddy.

Pay attention, you dumb blonde. Now she had to fight her way back upriver to get what she came for.

"Nice combat roll." Mouse Patton's compliment echoed off the sheer rust-tinted walls of the canyon.

Serena stole a peek behind her at Double Dare's river master, her spotter for her challenge. About forty years old, she guessed, the former U.S. Olympic kayaker patiently back-paddled his twelve-foot-long, bright yellow inflatable raft. Behind him, mounted on a contraption that looked like a mini TV tower, perched a stuffed mouse, its mouth agape as if in mid-insult. *They definitely do things differently at Double Dare.*

He nodded at her, waiting.

Serena gauged the current and rapids in this part of the Dolores River as Class III on the international whitewater scale—two-foot-high waves, regularly spaced, no holes or obstacles. Nothing compared to the Class V water ahead.

She pointed the shark-nosed kayak back into the current and muscled her way back to a semi-submerged, silicone-smooth boulder. Just past it, her aching arms and the Dolores' flow reached a shaky compromise and she neatly pivoted the boat downstream. As she turned, the kayak's bow nudged onto the boulder, as she planned. The scarred underbelly of the boat tenuously gripped the slick rock long enough for her to snatch her trophy from the trapped tree limb where Mouse hung it that morning.

Some trophy.

She clipped the common climbing carabiner, with a cheap red calico neckerchief knotted around it, to her flotation vest. It clinked against an exact replica, the first she had recovered. They were called "challenge coups"—prizes that few could claim. It meant that she was playing the game correctly. She possessed enough skill and stamina to pull off what she had set out to do. That was the mantra of Double Dare Ranch.

Serena was no Olympic-class kayaker, but she was an expert. She'd run the Grand Canyon, the Salmon and Snake Rivers, and most of Colorado's best whitewater numerous times.

She paddled the kayak through the riffles and slid backwards into slack water along the bank, nestling up against the willows but still safely away from the thickets of fading-red poison ivy that lined the Dolores' banks. A river otter, a species now thriving in the canyon after reintroduction, ducked beneath the water.

"Now I'm really stoked," she shouted at Mouse, jingling the two carabiners together. "One more to go. This baby's mine."

For all her bravado, she expected Mouse to save his nastiest trick for last. But sometimes the absence of an obstacle or a surprise was part of the wicked fun at Double Dare, leaving players to psyche-out themselves if they didn't trust their abilities or instincts. Indecision could cost you a challenge; a poor decision could cost you a body part. She couldn't imagine the kid-like river master missing a chance to unleash more mischief.

She also knew she was tiring. She had been alternately playing and fighting with the Dolores River for nearly three hours. Even in late September, usually one of the mildest times of the year in the southwest corner of Colorado, the water gushed at a bone-numbing 50 degrees. The neck-to-ankle neoprene rubber wetsuit and spray skirt combined to keep the water out and her body heat in. But over time the river's cold mass seeped in, took her muscles hostage and began the stealthy process of sapping her energy.

She turned back into the current. The most dangerous rapids on the Dolores, the Grandfathers, lay only a half mile or so ahead. If they weren't worrisome enough, a twenty-foot waterfall nicknamed Snaggletooth awaited, crowding Serena's thoughts.

The Grandfathers were massive, log-cabin-sized blocks of rust and burnt-purple sandstone that had been calving off the walls of the Dolores Canyon for centuries. The walls rippled for miles and their angular, wise-looking faces all but spoke of the Ancestral Puebloans who inhabited the region over a thousand years ago and adopted "grandfather rocks" as beloved symbols of the elders of their world. The rocks loomed as high as one thousand feet above the river, and when they crashed into the river bottom they divided the Dolores into a labyrinth of rolling, undulating lanes of water.

In this stretch, the river also lost elevation more rapidly, and the combined effect propelled the kayak forward like a torpedo. Below the Grandfathers a slot rapid, left high and dry for the last five years owing to Colorado's drought, now brimmed with the last runoff water from the record snowfall last winter. An unprecedented late-summer release of water from McPhee Dam added to the high flow. Angling off from the Dolores' main channel, the rapid churned into Snaggletooth. It marked the end of today's challenge for Serena. If she could get that far.

From studying her river map she guessed that Mouse had hidden the third coup among the Grandfathers, guardians of the channel into Snaggletooth. This was Class V water—the most dangerous, one step below virtually impassable. She knew the dam release on the Dolores generated currents too fast, too big, too deadly for her to fight back upstream if she shot past the third coup. In such violent water, she'd risk being swept backwards over Snaggletooth. That would be suicide. She possessed the whitewater skill to get through the course, but no amount of coaching by Mouse assured her of picking up the final coup.

Hoping to give herself the most options and enough time for decision-making, she chose the centermost rapid into the Grandfathers and dove into the trough. Breaking out, she executed a couple spins and paddled upstream for a few strokes to take some of the speed out of the river. But the surge was undeniable, and she turned and set up for a sweeping hairpin that passed between two more Grandfathers the size of recreation vehicles. She read the river expertly, taking satisfaction as the tiny craft glided through the channel as if it were riding on honey. It rode so smoothly, within seconds she hurtled directly at one of the huge boulders stained black by the river's spray. Using her paddle as a rudder, she dug its tip into the water, barely scraping the rock, then bolted downstream.

She was getting close now. She scanned the sides of the few remaining Grandfathers below, the only conceivable places Mouse could have stashed the third coup. Once past them, she would have to veer right into Snaggletooth's slot.

A twinkle of titanium and a flash of red caught her eye. It was the coup, about one hundred feet directly in front of her between two boulders. Hanging in mid-air. That made no sense. There were no logs or limbs trapped by the river to support it. But there it was, the telltale red neckerchief suspended four or five feet above the black-green water that poured through the gap.

"What the . . .?" Serena muttered. She came up on the dangling prize fast, and she still couldn't figure it out.

She grinned. "Mouse, you are so bad," she yelled back at the river master, her words lost in the canyon's tumult.

Fishing line.

Stretched between the last two Grandfathers. Ingenious, devious, pure Mouse.

She had no more time for playing tourist. The coup bobbed dead ahead, though not in a particularly nasty part of the Dolores. The river dipped steeply—very fast—into a trough directly below the neckerchief, but it looked straight, uncomplicated. Once through it, she'd have only seconds before the current carried her over the waterfall. Snaggletooth foamed only fifty feet beyond the coup, so there would be no second chance.

Serena shot forward, readying her upper body for a slight stretch above her head to grab the coup. At the same time, she loosened her left hand on the paddle, her bare fingers aching after hours of being curled around the metal tubing. Her timing needed to be perfect.

She raised her left hand just as she entered the silky slide. But as the kayak rode the current, the tip of the paddle dipped into the river and clipped a submerged rock and her grip slipped. Even as she instinctively grabbed for the paddle with her left hand she knew she'd blown it. Her mind barely computed what had happened before she rocketed past the coup, which remained swaying, untouched, taunting, above the river.

Then she disappeared over Snaggletooth.

"Shhhiiii-iiiittttt."

Serena's screech of disappointment seemed to hang in the air as she dove past slick, black walls into the roaring white cauldron of foam. Hoots and cheers from a half-dozen friends from Double Dare and local whitewater fans perched on rocks around the aspen-lined grotto barely registered with her as the kayak knifed into the mist. Within seconds she shot to the surface, rolled, and paddled over to the rocky bank.

"Great run, Serena," a young woman shouted, leading a chorus of compliments as the kayak kissed the bank.

The two coups scraped together on her vest as she popped the black spray skirt that sealed the top of the kayak around her and squirmed out of the boat. About the same time, Mouse's raft crunched onto the gravel shore after he'd followed the river's main flow into the grotto.

Serena locked her eyes with Mouse's. Most everyone else's, especially the males in the crowd, were fixed on her. Just negotiating the toughest stretch of the Dolores was something to be proud of, she knew. Plus she'd recovered two of Mouse's coups, one short of the challenge goal. Her eyes bore into the boatman as she sought some acknowledgment of what she'd done.

The mildewed rodent on the back of his raft mocked her.

"You almost had it," the river master said, running one hand through thick, unruly, black-going-to-gray hair. "You need to work on your focus. You got distracted a couple times. But it was a nice effort for your first challenge run."

That's it?

Tucking her paddle inside the boat, she grabbed the rim of the seat, hefted the kayak to her shoulder, and strutted past him. As she passed Mouse, she stuck out her tongue at him and kept going. The river people around them laughed, taking it as a flash of good-natured, girlish moxie.

It was oh-so-much-more than that.

She'd show him. She'd show them all.

Chapter 2

"Let's go, let's go, move it," Cutter shouted as loud as he could, barely able to hear his own hoarse croak above the wind and the jet-engine roar of the wildfire.

A dozen Double Dare emergency firefighters—"EFFers," they called themselves—ran with him to the firebreak, filling gaps between others already on the line. Together, backs bent, yellow hardhats bobbing, they frantically hacked at knee-high grass, sage and scrub to clear a zone between flames thirty feet in front of them, and the taller, even more dangerous fuel at their backs. Early fall gusts off the San Juans pushed the flames toward them and fanned choking, blinding smoke into their faces.

Cutter nodded his greeting and understanding of the situation to a soot-coated Mexican urging on his own small crew—a mix of Mexican immigrants and local ranch hands. Manuel "Manny" Cepeda was top hand at Ram Mountain Ranch, the largest property in the Dolores Valley, a fraction of which burned in front of them.

"Cutter, thanks for coming, *amigo*," he yelled. "If the fire reaches that PJ in back of us, we're in big trouble. We've got to cut it off here. Hotshots are on the way."

PJ—pinyon pine and juniper trees—thrived across the Colorado Plateau. It grew as tall as a bunkhouse and, in drought years, was drier than dirt. Sagebrush acted like a fuse, conducting fire across the ground, until it reached the PJ, which could explode like a Roman candle. The EFFers called it "flashy fire."

The drought that had smothered the West may have finally relented, at least in Colorado. But it hadn't rained much in five weeks. The tops of mountains and mesas stood wispy-dry from the constant hot breezes that rode over the Four Corners region. The prolonged dry spell left behind stunted grasslands and forests strewn with dead timber. The wildfire showed no mercy.

Cutter looked again behind them. Stands of PJ climbed nearly to the top of the low ridge guarding their side of Little Cahone Canyon, which ran roughly north-to-south between Ram Mountain Ranch and Double Dare Ranch. Ram Mountain Ranch was closer, about three miles west, but was probably safer from this fire due to the prevailing winds pushing east. Double Dare's border lay in the next valley on the other side of the ridge, some five miles away, but it was downwind. As suddenly and unpredictably as the Plateau winds could shift, both ranches had a stake in controlling the burn. Just across the Dolores River from Double Dare, Cutter's next-closest neighbor, Two Havens, spread for miles farther east.

The whine of chainsaws bit into the smoke-filled chaos, adding to the urgency.

Ushered by the stubborn wind, the flames crept forward to within only a couple feet of the hastily cleared ground, backing the firefighters into the PJ. The more experienced EFFers began picking up shovels, Pulaskis and other tools, staging an orderly retreat. Twenty feet to his left, Manny shouldered his equipment.

"Cutter," the Mexican foreman yelled, worry in his tone but delivered with a grin, "your pants are on fire."

Double Dare's boss returned the grin and waved his shovel, taking the warning as a fire line joke exchanged between two friends.

"No, man, really," Manny shouted with genuine concern, pointing to Cutter's leg. "You're on fire!"

Cutter looked down. Shreds of lining from the inside of his pants leg flapped around his right ankle, smoking, with almost imperceptible tendrils of fire curling around the edges. Surprised, he calmly swatted the flames out with his gloved hands. He looked back at the Mexican and gave him a thumbs-up.

Manny gave him a puzzled look and shook his head.

He must not know about my leg, Cutter thought.

It wasn't the job of the local EFFers to stop a wildfire. But the volunteers could sometimes hold it at bay until professionals like the San Juan Hotshots and Bureau of Land Management firefighters arrived.

"Carlos, get out of there," Manny yelled at one Ram Mountain hand who continued to beat at ground fire with water-soaked burlap sacks in each hand. "Everyone, get back."

Cutter added his voice to Manny's.

"The break isn't wide enough. C'mon, out, get out. The fire's going to jump it. And get away from the PJ!" He grabbed the back of one firefighter's blood-red Nomex jacket and dragged him back.

With a searing WHUMP! a patch of pinyon-juniper to the left of Carlos erupted in a riot of orange-red-blue flames. He flailed the sodden sacks as he tried to back away. In seconds, the wind accelerated and spiraled, arcing fire into another, larger grove of PJ behind the man.

"Carlos!" Manny screamed. "Carlos!" He dropped the Pulaski on his shoulder and shot toward the man, who tried to beat out the tendrils of flames licking his arms and long black hair.

Too late. A wall of flame and thick smoke enveloped the doomed volunteer.

Cutter hurled himself forward with Manny. But the blasting heat forced them both back, their Nomex fire retardant clothing smoking. In his last seconds Carlos was a mute, wind-milling maniac. Then he disappeared.

"Carlos!" Manny howled as Cutter struggled to hold him back. The Mexican stared in disbelief into the inferno until finally his will and muscles gave out and he went limp in Cutter's arms. It happened so fast. Manny sank to his knees. In uncontrollable, wrenching sobs, he cried, "*Mi hermano. Mi pobre hermano.*"

My brother. My poor brother.

Not for the first time, Cutter remembered how early explorers described this land when their desperate search for water ended in a dry creek bed.

They called it the Disappointment Country.

. . . .

The boy burst into the Double Dare ranchhouse, one hand still on the door handle, breathing hard.

"Hey, you guys," he gasped, "Cutter is back."

Serena broke away first from the noisy knot of guests and staff crowded around her in the high-peaked foyer of the ponderosa log building. Bodies collided as the rest fought to get out the door.

Outside on the plank deck she saw people in every direction drop what they were doing and head toward the big house. She was reminded this was a ranch, alright. But not like any ranch she had ever experienced.

Men and women of all ages were crisscrossing the yard on mountain bikes and skidded their tires to turn toward them. Other riders, huddled around the backs of sport utility vehicles, tuning every model and color bike imaginable, jogged over. A well-worn path behind the ranchhouse led to a grassy bluff where Double Dare's own unique game of softball was played, and a herd of players ran and elbowed their way to the main yard.

But as each group arrived, their laughter faded. Wide smiles tightened and shouts and greetings were soon hushed.

Serena guessed more than a hundred people crowded around a grimy, silver pickup as it arrived just ahead of a flume of road dust.

From the truck bed, a half-dozen men and women, their faces and clothes blackened by a soup of soot and sweat, began passing down shovels, rakes, Pulaskis, axes, hardhats, goggles, oxygen tanks, water bottles and fire shelter packs. Serena recognized the bright yellow or red Nomex pants and matching jackets. She guessed how long many of their owners had lived in wildfire country by the number of holes in the gear. Most had gear that was singed and patched, often crisscrossed with gray duct tape.

She watched Cutter swing down from the pickup bed. He landed most of his weight on his left leg, she noticed, and seemed to settle on his right leg. When he hit the ground a tiny, muffled "ugh" escaped him. Motes of dust and ash loosened from his clothes and hair hovered around him. The owner of Double Dare Ranch didn't look physically imposing. Six-foot tall, maybe. Rangy-lean. But he exuded a sense of owning his space in the world easily, without feeling he had to defend it daily or add to it. He looked to be in his mid-thirties. Not exactly Hollywood handsome. But even beneath the coat of baked-on smoke, one could pick out sharp, high cheekbones in his grimy face and penetrating gray-blue eyes that seemed to scan everything at once.

. . . .

"How bad?" asked an immense Native American man, who approached Cutter through the milling crowd like a storybook giant. Grateful Bobby Long Water was head foreman at Double Dare. Cutter turned away and grabbed his knees as he endured a coughing fit.

"Ramworthy lost a man," Cutter said. "Manny's brother."

"Oh no," Bobby moaned. He and Manny were friends, and despite their bosses' differences, they depended on each other for help at times like this.

"Manny's crew made it into the canyon first and most of his people worked in the worst spots. Some of them didn't have the best equipment. They were soaking their neckerchiefs with water to use as masks. The smoke . . . well, you know what that PJ and sage are like when they get lit up. The fire jumped behind Manny's brother—Carlos was his name—into the PJ, and it just ate him. Manny and I tried to get there, but . . ." Cutter shook his head. "There was no way."

He bent and hacked again, trying to spit out the smoke.

"The fire came through Little Cahone Canyon in back of Ramworthy's property and went through a corner of his hayfield in about four seconds." Cutter showed a grim smile. "Then the wind caught it and it really got interesting."

Three days earlier they had spotted the gray and white plume of smoke from miles away and its appearance was soon followed by a phone call. It sent Cutter and as many workers as he could safely spare on a weekend, when the ranch was full, scrambling for their gear.

Vernard Ramworthy, the second-generation owner of Ram Mountain Ranch, was Cutter's neighbor, though they weren't close. In fact, Cutter and Ramworthy had tangled a few times. But feuds over land use and water rights were momentarily forgotten when wildfire threatened anyone living in the scoured ridges and valleys that formed the southwest ribs of the San Juan Mountains.

This fire was sparked by yet another autumn lightning strike. It was the third time this season Cutter and his workers had rushed over old logging roads and hunting trails to reach a fire line. Usually, if enough men and women from the surrounding ranches and haciendas got there quickly enough, they could put out a fire before it got rolling. But this one gorged on ground table-set with crew-cut hay and PJ. And, right on cue, the afternoon freight train of wind pulled in to instantly blow the grass-high flames into a blaze. And then into a killer.

Cutter straightened his hunched back and bent backward with a grimace until he thought he heard something like gristle rubbing together. "We couldn't leave after Manny's loss," he said. "They dropped in smoke jumpers the next morning, and it was pretty well under control when we left."

A stunning young woman with coal-and-satin hair that cascaded down her back stood in front of Cutter, face upturned. He bent slightly to kiss her, then she started to help him with his gear.

"Thanks, Lexi," he said, handing over a backpack that reeked of fire smoke.

"What now? How long will the fires keep breaking out?" she asked with a hint of an accent.

"Are you worried about Double Dare, Cutter?" piped up one of the guests at the same time, a woman with two braids peeking from beneath a bike helmet.

"This threat isn't going away soon, folks," he replied. "Even with some rain. It's been too dry for too long. We live in it. We've got to deal with it. Be smart. Take precautions. And fight the hell out of it when we have to."

As the subdued crowd began to disperse, Cutter looked around the ranch as if to reaffirm his belief that it was all worth it.

"Bobby," Cutter said as the mahogany-skinned giant, at least a head taller, reached over and clapped him on the back, sending a puff of fine ash into the air. "Thanks for watching over things."

"You know it, man," the foreman said, meeting his eyes.

Workers, friends, bike riders milled around Cutter, stopping to shake hands or offer encouragement.

A woman approached him. Tawny blonde hair, bobbed short, swayed with each step she took. Tanned and toned, about the same height as Cutter, she was a stone-cold beauty. She wore buckskin-colored shorts and hiking boots and a cutoff Telluride T-shirt that showed off her taut stomach.

"Serena, I hear you almost won your silver kayak paddle."

She reacted with surprise that he knew about her river challenge.

"Yeah, if it hadn't been for that sneaky Mouse," she replied, periwinkle-blue eyes flashing. "I had it. I had the third coup almost in my hand. I was in control. I knew exactly what my next move was into Snaggletooth." Her face became stern, and her voice quickened. "If I just hadn't let my paddle slip. I was so close. I—"

"Whoa, ease up," said Cutter, shifting his weight. "Good thing kayaks don't have gas pedals."

A hint of a smile escaped her. She took a deep breath, and looked up at him.

"Don't be so hard on yourself. It wasn't your strategy or your skill. You just made a mistake. That's what Double Dare is all about—testing our skills so we have confidence to react instinctively when challenged. But," he added with a nod, dropping his hands, "we're always going to make mistakes."

"I suppose. I'll get it for sure next time. I'll be back."

"Are you flying to Denver tonight? Must be nice to have a private jet."

She nodded. "I've got some business calls to make on the way. I've got a busy week trying to pull together a . . . umm, a new defense project. The plane—it belongs to a friend."

"Nice friend."

She looked down and her face pinched imperceptibly, as though some concern had taken her hostage for an instant. Then she straightened and lightly squeezed his arm. "I'll see you in a couple weeks." She turned toward the vehicles parked in the yard. "Don't play with the fire," she said, shooting a cover girl pout over her shoulder.

Cutter followed her with his eyes. With a weary sigh, he looked to the deck of the log ranchhouse just in time to see Lexi turn away. Cutter realized she must have been watching him talk to Serena.

Even from a distance, her high cheekbones and sculpted jaw stood out more prominently than ever, and her stony gaze bore straight ahead.

Chapter 3

The private jet shot from the tiny Dove Creek airport into the darkening sky. Serena placed a satellite phone call to a dimly lit office in one of Denver's tallest downtown buildings two hundred sixty miles to the northeast.

"Hello, Radic," she said, intending to be all business.

"What you see there? What goes on?" the harsh, guttural voice of the man answering asked, dispensing with some words that his heavily accented English found expendable. "What's happening at ranch?"

"Well, thank you, darling, I'm just fine," Serena said, ice in her tone. "You know, I'm down here doing your dirty work, and you act like I'm just another one of your sales sluts."

"*Ser-e-na*," he softened, stretching out the syllables, "of course, I want to hear about weekend. I am sorry, only very anxious to learn if we are closer to business objective. How things? I heard there was wildfire?"

It always surprised her how much Vuko seemed to know about what went on at Double Dare. And so quickly. It worried her, too, that it might diminish her value in his eyes. After all, they did have a deal.

. . . .

Six weeks before, Serena stormed into the downtown Denver YMCA for her regular night workout class—"Kick Him Where He Lives: Personal Defense For Women"—intent on dealing out some serious whoop-ass.

Less than an hour earlier, she'd been fired from a job she thought she excelled at: a corner-office executive for Xtent, one of Denver's mammoth telecommunications firms. The director of the Human Resources Department had informed her that he had recently received a third complaint from one of Xtent's gold-plated Homeland Security contractors. She was accused of verbally emasculating a project manager that reported to her. With that brief explanation, he escorted her out of the building. Following HR best practices, he waited until the end of work Friday to deliver the devastating news, the thinking being that a nice, calming weekend lessened the possibility of someone like Serena showing up the next work day with an Uzi.

Scorned, humiliated and jobless, Serena fired her Via Spiga stilettos into the back of the metal YMCA locker. When one innocent high-heel shoe dared to bounce out, she grabbed it and hammered home another strike.

"All this counseling I'm getting is really doing wonders," she muttered sarcastically as she finished dressing and headed for the gym. "You better be here tonight, Vuko." Serena worked out more than Chuck Norris in his prime.

The first night of the class, the instructor told the twelve women that his rough, bruising accent was Croatian.

"My name is Radic Vuko," he began, "and I going to make you hate me." He didn't waste any time.

It quickly became apparent that Vuko's reputation as a former military instructor and merciless personal trainer was well deserved. He didn't abuse anyone, but he demanded that the women take his instruction seriously, and he worked them into exhaustion three nights a week. He was certainly fit, especially for a man who looked to be mid-fiftyish. In his demonstrations, Serena noticed firm, well-defined pecs, thick shoulders and a tight butt beneath his standard workout uniform—a black, sleeveless Under Armour singlet and loose black shorts over black knee-length spandex.

The man wasn't unattractive—except for one ear. Or rather the lack of one. It looked like he had shaved off his outer ear cartilage and his entire left ear. It was just gone.

Two weeks after the first class, only five women had showed up. This night she found herself one of four. Vuko must have been waiting for some space to hit on her. Just for a drink, he said.

"You very focused tonight in counter-attacks. Very aggressive," he said as he lifted a pint of dark ale to his lips. "I like it." Marlowe's restaurant-bar on the 16th Street Mall was half full with patrons making the most of the mild late-summer evening. Outside a few stragglers from the Capitol chased the setting sun down the sidewalk as they ran for the shuttle bus.

"Let's just say I came to class highly motivated tonight," Serena replied. She paused to set her glass of chardonnay on the bistro tabletop, then glumly dropped her chin into her palm. "I was fired from my job today."

Vuko seemed unmoved. "What did you do?"

"I told one of my project weasels to get his head out—" she started.

"No, I mean what was job?"

"I worked for Xtent Telecom. Mostly I managed our underground installations and sub-contractors on Homeland Security projects," Serena replied.

Maybe it was her imagination, but Vuko seemed to lean forward slightly.

"What sort of projects?"

"If I told you, I'd have to kill you." Serena smirked as she delivered the tired, but appropriate, cliché.

He smiled back.

"Serena, I have my eyes on you in class. You not only smart and attractive. You tough—physically, I mean. And you ballsiest one in the bunch. I mean that as compliment."

Serena thought he was trying too hard.

"Rad, tell me the story of what happened to your ear?"

"There, see what I mean about ballsy." He looked down as if contemplating an event he'd rather not revisit. He hoisted the tall glass, sucked down two gulps, and licked some froth from his lips. Still he hesitated. Then he seemed to make up his mind and his eyes, angry and flashing, bolted up to hers.

"I tell you if you sleep with me tonight?"

Serena almost blew wine through her nose.

"No . . . Thanks . . . Sorry. I just wanted to learn more about you."

"It happen in one of little wars I have been in," he said, his voice rough and hard. "I don't really like talk about it." Then his eyes went as dark as the beer he drained. He signaled the waitress for another ale. Serena held her hand over her half-full glass and shook her head.

"I have other question for you," Vuko said. "A different proposition. I was going to ask you tonight anyway, so now is good . . . There's a business in southwest Colorado that I'm getting ready to take over. Unusual business. I've been looking for someone to study it for me, take inside look. Go visit regularly as a guest for me. Report back what you see. I want evaluation of its potential, if it is success, all the details you can have. Call it professional snooping. It's a good deal."

"What kind of business? What's the name of the company?" she asked, curious.

"It perfectly suits your experience and interests. They call it outdoors recreation resort. Name is . . . uh . . . uh . . ."

"You can't remember the name? You're going to take over this place and you can't remember its name?"

"I know name. It's . . . it's . . . it's near a little town name of Dolores, very isolated. They call it 'adventure ranch.' It's—"

"Double Dare Ranch?" Serena blurted. Her voice shifted into a higher gear. "Really? I've been wanting to go. All my friends who mountain bike or kayak, or are into orienteering, or who like to take on outdoor challenges, are talking about it. All the adventure magazines are raving about it—"

"Yeah. That's it."

"You're going to take it over? It just opened this summer."

"I want it," he said harshly. Any pretense of charm evaporated. "It should be mine."

He can't say the name Double Dare? What's with that?

"So you want a spy, huh? That could be illegal." Serena paused as if she needed to consider, but she was already planning her Double Dare reservations. "It'll cost you."

"No," Vuko said, shaking his head. "No fee. I pay all expenses, and once ranch is mine, you run it as my general manager. You used to make pay of one hundred-and-seventeen thousand dollars each year at Xtent; I'll double that when you run my ranch."

Serena stared at him. She didn't know if she was more shocked by the offer, or by the fact Vuko knew what she had earned.

"Why do you want this ranch so much? What's so important about it?"

"That's fair question. It's small ranch. Not much. But it is next to B-L-M land? I say it right?"

"Yes, Bureau of Land Management land. It's owned by the government, but it's public land, anyone can go on it."

"Hundreds of thousands of acres of BLM land there. I will use some of it for training men."

"Training men?" Serena blinked. "Training them for what?"

"Security. Bodyguards. Providing special force is one of my businesses. Also, I owe ranch owner for something."

"Owe him? Owe him what? You mean payback."

"Enough questions," Vuko said abruptly, shifting in his chair. "Oh, and don't forget other thing," he added, the wisp of a smile on his lips.

"You stay with me at LoDo apartment tonight."

Serena stared at him for a moment. Then she stood, gathered her workout bag, and bent over the only ear she assumed Vuko could hear with.

"I'll be your spy. I'll be your general manager. I won't be your whore," she hissed. "You put the rest of it in writing—the basics, the business deal—and I'll consider it."

She turned and walked out of the bar.

Serena had always wanted to run her own business. She didn't have a job. What could she lose?

. . . .

"What . . .?" she mumbled, coming back to the present. To the jet cabin. To the phone at her ear. "Oh, I hardly saw Cutter. He was fighting the fire the last three days. The ranch is really taking shape. He's got some good, capable people helping him, and business seems to be picking up. The front yard was full of mountain bikers.

"Rad," she said, almost cooing, getting even now, "I really wonder if Double Dare Ranch might make—"

"Don't call by that name!" he spat into the phone. "Don't ever call it that again, or . . ."

She could hear him breathing heavily, fighting to regain his calm. She smiled. *I thought that would prick a nerve. That's the second time he's gone off like that about the stupid name.*

Seconds passed before either spoke.

"Come back," he said in a casual tone. "We have dinner and we talk more. I want your perspective of things there."

"Maybe," Serena said. She paused. "Rad, you didn't ask about my kayak challenge?"

"You breathing, aren't you? You are in jet, probably sipping my Dom Perignon. I am sure you got what you wanted, and you be back sleeping under satin sheets tonight."

Serena's eyes ignited. "Not under *your* satin sheets," she said, and slammed the phone into the receiver.

She sipped the champagne, considering her brief relationship with the man she hung up on and would see in an hour. She would still talk to Vuko. He was certainly nothing like Cutter. Vuko was not to be trifled with. She sensed a mean streak in him. She hadn't slept with him, but he was asking for it nearly every time they met. Finally, she acknowledged to herself that she and Vuko both had at least one trait in common. They both knew what they wanted and how to get it.

Chapter 4

Her skin still damp and supple from their shower, Lexi watched as Cutter hopped on his left leg toward the bed, toweled himself dry while standing on one leg, and then collapsed face-down on their bed. She straddled his back and began digging strong, expert fingers and knuckles into the knots in his body. Her lips softly followed the warm trail of her hands.

Neck. Shoulders. The spine of his back. Irish-pale buns. Down the hogback of his right hamstring. Then she lightly pecked the angry-pink stump some five inches below his right knee. The exertion on the fire line must have rubbed it wrong, she thought, as she studied his amputated limb. Kissing the taut scar, acknowledging it, was her way of expressing absolute acceptance. Lexi didn't know exactly when she had fallen in love with Cutter. She hadn't intended to love him.

She'd been given firm instructions not to become emotionally involved with him.

"How's the leg?" she asked, careful not to massage the tender-looking tissue too roughly.

"Sore."

"Any more phantom sensations?"

"Not so much."

She could barely hear him, his exhaustion complete, his voice muffled in the down comforter. Deep sigh.

"Working the fire line, the grinding from the constant stooping, turning, running makes the stump sensitive. Working makes the muscle shrink, and I didn't have time to change to a thicker sock to make the socket fit better. I'll be glad when I get my new foot, too. I've worn this one out. It's clicking and wobbles around in my boot, so I slipped a couple times."

Lexi kneaded and nibbled, sensing Cutter drift away.

. . . .

He glanced over the edge of the massive aspen-log bed frame.

Leaning against the wall across from his side of the bed was the rest of him—a mud-colored resin foot shell that looked like a loafer with toes, molded over a carbon-fiber foot blade. From the foot shell rose a shiny, blue-tinted titanium shaft. He noticed a smudge on the metal shaft, charred he guessed, by the flame on his pants leg during the fire. Topping it off was the bullet-shaped, black carbon fiber socket that pulled over his stump. In his first bitter days of rehabilitation, he disdainfully began thinking of the whole contraption as his "Sasquatch" leg.

What? Had it already been twelve years since the accident?

. . . .

He lay alone on a rock-and-ice ledge on the side of 12,500-foot Kahiltna Dome in Denali National Park, his right leg shattered and useless.

He and his ice-climbing partner had been picking and hacking up the final pitch of their target route, working on beautiful blue ice that held their axes and crampons. Cutter was leading and then, in an instant, falling, scraping down the ice face, pulling loose his embedded protective gear. After plunging more than ninety feet, it was a miracle that he somehow crumpled onto the ledge and didn't pull his partner off the wall with him.

Two years and six surgeries later, he still couldn't walk without excruciating, spiraling pain. The surgeries succeeded in repairing two compound fractures in his lower leg. But they failed, again and again, to fuse together the puddle of cornmeal that remained of his right ankle. The fall had crushed his talus, the connecting bone between the leg and foot that assists in pointing and flexing the foot. So he decided: *"I'd rather have no foot than a useless one."*

It was during his introduction to the world of an amputee, as he journeyed down the seemingly endless tunnel of rehabilitation, when he resumed his aborted college career as a mechanical engineering student at Colorado State University in Fort Collins, and also rediscovered his passion to play. That occurred on, of all places, Radic Vuko's ropes course.

The business used rope catwalks and mesh ladders and rigging, mostly strung thirty feet over a former rodeo arena, to train law enforcement personnel in climbing and rescue techniques. But it also offered tamer classes for private citizens. Cutter's introduction to the course was a revelation. He personally experienced an unimaginable physical challenge every day—living as a legally disabled person. Success on the ropes course was grueling, but it transformed him.

And he wasn't alone. Day after day, he observed what such physical challenges did for others—young and old, weak and strong. As a result, he walked with the newly discovered satisfaction of being one of them.

Once he realized that, scarcely a day went by that Cutter didn't think about how to turn his new dream into reality. Into Double Dare Ranch.

The name for the ranch, though, didn't come to him until much later. After another life-altering experience.

. . . .

Half asleep, eyeing Sasquatch—Cutter could never think of it any other way—he marveled once again at how the loss of his leg changed his life. Now the sleek, spring-pinned limb was part of an elegant "quick-change" prosthetic system that he helped design and that had transformed the industry. Simply put, he designed useful "feet." To run, climb, work, swim, bike, drive, ride horseback, ski, skate. A complete line of exotic, high-tech Sasquatches gave athletes and war-wounded soldiers and kids born with unfair diseases a new quality of life.

Lexi's voice brought Cutter back.

"It's so sad about Manny's brother. To die like that, right in front of him."

"It was awful. I felt so helpless. We had our eyes on him, we knew the fire was running fast. Then he was just gone. Taken over. I swear, Manny would have gone after him if I hadn't held onto him . . ."

Abruptly, she reached for a glass of red wine on the nightstand. "Serena seems to be getting to know her way around the ranch."

In Cutter's head, Lexi's remark might as well have set off a warning klaxon like the one at the Dolores fire station. He wondered if she felt every one of his muscles she had just soothed go instantly on Red Alert. He did what any caring, concerned lover would do in the same situation: he chose his words carefully.

"Well, she's been a paying customer here now two or three times." He tried to sound casual, hoping that was that.

"Um-hmm," he heard behind him.

Lexi had been with him nearly a year, since Double Dare began construction. Sunday nights normally were their time to catch up on each other's news, make plans, and patch up any slights in their relationship. The fact that he had been out on the fire the last three days certainly could add to the gulf after an already grueling work week. The ranch's first season was nearly over. Cutter tried to focus his mind on Lexi, but his thoughts pinballed from concern to contemplation. There was one thing he couldn't figure out: *It's hard to believe it's by total chance that this beautiful creature from the other side of the world happens to be at Double Dare.*

. . . .

Sitting in the sun-basted kitchen of the loft in Denver's trendy Lower Downtown, or LoDo, Cutter looked down and read one more time the Help Wanted ad he'd written for the Spring 2004 issue of *Gourmet* magazine:

HEAD CHEF, DOUBLE DARE RANCH
Experienced, international background required. Ability to create eclectic, five-star menu, finest ingredients, for year-round resort. Train/direct outdoor guides/staff to prepare/serve. Must pass owner's personal Chef's Challenge. Refs, resume required. Salary, perks neg. Apply DD Ranch, Dolores, CO 81323

The loft's intercom chirped softly, signaling the arrival of Cutter's first applicant for a job he considered one of the most important at the ranch.

"It's me—Lexi," the woman identified herself, the intercom adding a tinny electronic hum to her voice.

Cutter knew from his phone interview with her that Alexis Skupo—the full name on her work visa—was born and raised in Croatia. That jarred him, for a second. The only other Croatian he'd ever met was Radic Vuko, his ropes course boss nearly a decade ago, and they hadn't exactly stayed pen-pals. Curious, Cutter checked U.S. Immigration statistics and learned that in the year 2000, the year Lexi left home, America accepted some three hundred immigrants from Croatia.

His pre-screening service reported that his want-ad had attracted more than two hundred inquiries, from San Francisco to St. Petersburg, Russia. The service approved ten chefs for him to screen personally. Lexi currently worked as executive sous chef at Aspen's private Caribou Club, so she had the pedigree. He chose her and two others for his first one-on-one interviews. And the Chef's Challenge.

Once again he couldn't help but fantasize about the person behind the exotic-sounding voice.

Cutter opened the door, prepared to be welcoming, friendly, but all business. The young woman walking toward him carrying a brown grocery bag made an instant impression. *God—please, please—let this angel be able to cook.*

Alexis Skupo transformed the hallway into a New York City Fashion Week ramp. She wore a glamorous black leather jacket and mini-skirt above knee-high black boots. As Cutter helped her slip out of her jacket, he couldn't help but notice she wore a low-cut white satin blouse.

"What a beautiful loft," she said, looking past him at the professionally decorated foyer that opened into the floor-to-ceiling, glass-walled living room and kitchen.

"It's owned by a friend named Michael Antonini," Cutter replied. "He's also my attorney when I get into trouble at Double Dare."

"Trouble?" she asked with concern.

"No, no." He rushed to reassure her. "Not real trouble. I mean, when I need advice. His counsel."

"So tell me about this adventure ranch, please, Mr. Cutter? Where will all these athletes be coming from? Are there horses and cows? How large a kitchen?"

He couldn't suppress a soft laugh at her wide-eyed curiosity.

"Please, call me Cutter. It's what everyone calls me. Why don't we both share our stories over lunch. Are you ready for the most important part of this interview? I explained on the phone. To make it interesting, I call it the Chef's Challenge."

"Your Double Dare Ranch is all about challenges, isn't it . . . Cutter? I know some things about challenges. How should we begin?"

Cutter couldn't resist turning even a simple interview for a chef into a game. It was more fun, and more revealing for him, with something at stake. The winner got the job.

He showed her into the kitchen lined with stainless steel appliances. On the clear acrylic cutting board, he had set out a modest array of cooking ingredients.

"The rules, as I told you, are simple. I've provided ten common high-quality ingredients: a lemon, sea salt and fresh-ground pepper, a clove of garlic, eggs, balsamic vinegar, olive oil, bread crumbs, spinach and feta cheese. You brought the main ingredient, one complementary ingredient, and," he paused for effect, "hopefully, your creativity. It's all yours. Ready to cook me lunch?"

The young woman glanced casually at the goods before her. From the grocery bag, she unwrapped two gleaming fresh mountain trout, about twelve inches each, and a package of Orzo pasta.

Seeing the fish, Cutter plucked a bottle of Ferrari-Carano chardonnay from Antonini's wine chiller and poured them both glasses.

As casually as if she had been entertaining him in her own kitchen, Lexi began slicing, dicing and talking.

"You know I grew up in Croatia," she began, dark eyes darting up at him, then back to her work. "In a place known as Krajina."

Cutter thought she teared up a bit at the thought and she blinked rapidly several times. She never ceased her preparations.

"The whole country was like one immense, delicious kitchen to learn in. When I was only a teenager, I told my family that I wished to train professionally to become a great chef and travel all over the world. My uncle was a very powerful military man in Croatia, a general. In Europe, everything is so close, so small. He made it possible for me to attend the finest culinary arts schools—Zagreb, Vienna, Munich, Rome, Paris."

Then, as if one of Colorado's afternoon clouds blotted out the sun, a shadow covered her face. She glanced at him with a sad smile.

"Then another war came. My mother, father and younger brother were all killed. I don't know for sure about my brother, he disappeared. So my uncle sent me to New York."

The look of gloom passed and she smiled. "I fell in love with America. Everything about it. Its sophistication. Its movies. Its have-it-all culture. My uncle gave me funds. Some friends I met in New York were flying to Aspen for a ski vacation, so I joined them. I learned to ski in the mountains outside Sarajevo, and in the Alps. But they are nothing alongside your Rocky Mountains, I am correct?"

She flashed a world-class smile at him and went on.

"So I stayed in Aspen. First I worked as a chef at the Ritz, and now the Caribou Club. You have been there?"

"I have. Jean Martineau, the chef de cuisine, is a good friend of mine."

"So, you have, like they say, been checking me out, eh?"

You have no idea, Cutter thought. Quickly, he refocused.

"Let me tell you what I expect from my head chef at Double Dare."

Like everything else at the new ranch, Cutter explained, he expected that food would be created with passion and served to surprise. He intended dinners to be a time for guests to tell stories about their challenges and celebrate their lives. He wanted food and beverages as eclectic and adventurous as the guests. As an athlete himself, he also placed a premium on simple, little feasts as well—fruit, vegetable snacks, the perfect trail mix—for before and after workouts. The head chef would create and choose the entire daily menu. Most of the employees lived at the ranch and worked more than one job. It would also be the head chef's job to transform river guides and carpenters and bike techs into second-chefs and a first-class table staff as well.

Double Dare's fare might change from braised French lamb one night to marinated buffalo tenderloin the next and then to fiery, over-the-border Mexican specialties, so that no guest ever tasted even the same family of foods in any one visit.

"I am ready for this ranch," said Lexi, her eyes flashing with excitement. "I am young to be a head chef, I know. I am twenty-nine years old. But it has only taken me this long because I had to find someone like you who loves classic fine food, but also has a sense of adventure about cooking. About life."

"That's what Double Dare is all about."

"May I ask you one thing? Because I should know. Your first name is Blake, right, but you don't use it?"

"When I was a kid I was always either in trouble or playing sports. Mom, dad, coach, it didn't make much difference. It was 'Cutter, don't climb that tree,' 'Cutter, get off your uphill ski edge,' 'Cutter, that knot's not right.'

"My friends just kept it up," he shrugged, "because they could. They were my friends."

With a glance at her watch, Lexi declared the fish and pasta ready.

"Sometimes I think finely prepared food can be better than

foreplay," she said, never so much as glancing up from the dishes she garnished.

Cutter wasn't sure if she was unabashedly honest, terribly naïve or just trying to get the job.

Lexi left the head and tail on the trout. The meal was extraordinary. Her choice was a perfect Double Dare dish—refreshing, filling and something else Cutter didn't expect: after the simple yet elegant meal he found himself personally attracted to Lexi, too.

"So does this dish have a name?" he asked after cleaning his plate.

"Umm, no. How about Cutter's Trout?"

"Yeah." He squirmed. "That fits."

He phoned her that night and offered her the job, which she immediately accepted. The next day he canceled the Chef's Challenge for the two other prospects.

"Oh, thank God," one of them, a TV reality show cook-off star, said. "I haven't slept since I agreed to that damn Chef's Challenge."

Cutter knew he'd made the right choice.

Lexi reported to the ranch soon after, in time to suggest some smart improvements in the final design of the Double Dare kitchen and indoor dining area. She asked Cutter if she could help recruit and interview some of the kitchen and boarding staff. She was so organized and successful at it that he eventually turned over the final hiring to her as well—after he personally met each candidate she hand-picked.

They made love for the first time a couple months later, and Lexi moved upstairs into Cutter's suite the day after. By that time she was already acknowledged around the ranch as not only the boss's girlfriend but the firm, fair and capable ruler of the ranchhouse as well.

. . . .

As Cutter lay beneath Lexi's silky thighs and strong hands, relishing her massage, he realized they hadn't fought once in the time they'd been together.

So why is Lexi all over me about Serena?

Serena was imposing, and her looks and her competitive spirit had certainly been noted around the ranch. Obviously, Lexi saw them talking in the yard earlier in the evening. But Serena was only saying goodbye. Lexi had never acted jealously around him before, and with her exotic appeal, Cutter wondered how she could ever think she was second to any woman.

As if reading his mind, Lexi gave his shoulders one last long grinding squeeze and leaned down and kissed his neck. She rose to give him room to turn over beneath her, and then she eased down on him. He reached up with both hands and she entwined his fingers with hers.

"Thanks for the back rub," he said. "Three nights sleeping on the ground and swinging a Pulaski in between made my shoulders feel like someone had jumped up and down on them."

"You were tight as a braid," she said. Then, "Is she coming back next week?"

Uh-oh. "Who? Serena?" he said, feigning surprise that she had brought it up again.

"Everyone seems to like her," Lexi said matter of factly. Then she leaned down to deliver a deep, smothering kiss.

Cutter's last thought before surrendering entirely to Lexi was fleeting but unsettling: tread softly, buddy, the next time Serena is on the ranch.

Chapter 5

Double Dare's boss knew by the stew in his stomach that the mountain bike trail was unsafe.

At dawn, Cutter and Grateful Bobby had led a work crew along the escarpment above Dolores River Canyon to sculpt and direct drainage for what would be one of the most breathtaking rides in the West. Sunlight slanted over the Colorado Plateau. Standing near the rusty, sandstone rim of the canyon, Cutter swiveled his view southwest, where Sleeping Ute Mountain, still sacred ground to Native American tribes, was just waking. Then almost magnetically, whenever he stood above the canyon, his eyes sought the sparkling river, which served as the natural eastern boundary of Double Dare Ranch. From its source high in the San Juans, the Dolores tumbled more than two hundred miles, west and then north—one of the few rivers in the U.S. to flow north—into Utah, where it merged with the Colorado River.

El Rio de Nuestra Señora de Dolores, as its Spanish discoverers named it in 1776—River of Our Lady of Sorrows. To Cutter, the name resonated with the history and romance of this lesser-known corner of the world.

He insisted any trail improvements be observant of native plant species and especially skirt some petroglyphs in the area to ensure their protection. A veteran mountain biker with the calluses to prove it, his idea was to carve the route close enough to the canyon edge to deliver heart-pounding views of the Dolores, churning some four hundred feet below. But he didn't want to put riders into cardiac arrest in the process.

By mid-afternoon, the trail snaked around boulders and aspens that stubbornly clung to the shoulder of the gorge. Cutter's ever-present Australian shepherd, Maggie, herded them along, her nose brushing the back of his left calf from her usual station. Occasionally, the small crew of men and women working on safety tethers wrestled rocks, and rearranged them to prevent riders from turning too closely toward the rim.

"Bobby, this turn is just too tight, too difficult," Cutter said, a frustrated tone in his voice. He pointed to where the trail dipped into a swale and at the same time zigzagged around looming aspens that turned the path away from the cliff.

Taking in the red-tinged landscape, he added, "Between the aspens and the boulders, this trail looks like a slalom on Mars."

Next to him, the shirtless giant laughed. Shiny with sweat, his shoulders formed a wide, rippling surface. The lat muscles on either side of his back V'd down to his waist. A long ponytail of straight black hair held together by a leather knot barely swayed between chiseled shoulder blades.

The Colorado Plateau was sacred ground for both men.

. . . .

They stood on land shepherded by the U.S. Bureau of Land Management—public land. The trail project was only possible under the BLM's private-public partnership program. Double Dare Ranch lay well below them, out of view, spread out on a small mesa. The Dolores River ran along one side of the mesa. Great slabs of sandstone, stacked one atop another, climbed behind the ranch, steadily elevating above the river. This lofty rusted mantle hung over Cutter's property and roughly delineated its immensely valuable northern border. If Cutter's key to Double Dare was its access into thousands of miles of wild, untainted national forest and BLM lands, then this high border quite literally was the gateway.

Grateful Bobby's attachment to the land went even deeper. A member of the Arapaho tribe, up until a year ago the six-foot-eight, 275-pound specimen had played tight end for the Miami Dolphins, All-Pro for eight years running. With a sculpted body and a name like Grateful Bobby Long Water, he was an NFL marketing dream.

Cutter was especially proud of telling the story behind his friend's name:

"His mother named him after her favorite '60s rock band and the man she dreamed would be the next president of the United States—the Grateful Dead and Bobby Kennedy. They were both spiritual totems in her life at that time. Long Water is a tribal name. His father and grandfather and all the grandfathers before them were real tall, too. Native American names are very meaningful and usually they tell you something about a person's physical nature or a skill or special trait they have. With his strength and stamina, Bobby could swim amazing distances."

But the previous summer, the thirty-four-year-old player collided head-on with Delkirk Briand while blocking the linebacker during drills in Florida's steaming heat and humidity, and Bobby dropped unconscious on the field. Even Delkirk's infamously fetid breath couldn't rouse him as his best friend on the team and roommate bowed over Bobby, trying to revive him by flipping up one eyelid then the other.

It turned out to be the second best thing that happened in his life. The first was when Delkirk didn't attempt to give him mouth-to-mouth resuscitation. Later, the best medical experts the Dolphins' team health insurance could buy discovered that he had hypertrophic cardiomyopathy, an excessive thickening of the heart muscle. He was probably born with the condition, and while it was rare among superbly fit athletes, fatal cases leaped into the headlines all too often.

The doctors laid out the odds for Bobby. At his age, in the business he was in, it could kill him at any time, on any play. It took him about ten seconds to make his decision. He really only played football because he loved the physical release. He had invested his millions and was set for life. He thought it strange that a heart disease could sideline a body shape like his—always big, even as a kid, but lean and stretched out—while half the linemen in the NFL looked like rolling cardiac cases.

A week later Bobby retired and was home in Colorado when he ran into his old high school quarterback—Cutter.

. . . .

At seven thousand feet where the crew worked, they alternately felt the hot breath of the desert thermals and the cool alpine breezes of an early-fall day. Aspens around them rippled yellow, gold and russet. Adding to Cutter's unease over the bike trail, the deep-throated rumble of distant thunder announced the possibility of rain, and more likely, lightning.

"You've got to love this riding surface," Bobby said, leaning on a six-foot-long iron pry bar he'd been using to shift rocks. "It's low-grit sandpaper, so grippy the mountain bike gods must have designed it."

Cutter was becoming more uncomfortable, though, with the idea of sending bike riders, even experts, up on the exposed point of the rim.

"Yeah, but . . ." he floundered for a comparison. "It reminds me of the Portal Trail on Poison Spider Mesa outside Moab. For pure terror on a mountain bike, I'll never forget it. I knew a rider who fell four hundred feet there. This is just as high. I remember once sitting on my bike on the viewing deck at the Portal, trying to build up the guts to ride it. I felt like my feet were sliding toward the edge. I almost puked."

The unsettling memory came complete with the taste of bile, and it made up his mind.

"Let's not—"

The irregular engine revs of a large vehicle approaching from the nearby mining road interrupted him. The crack of downed timber and low-hanging branches raking metal ushered an invisible monster forward. The unmistakable square bulk of a black Hummer roared over a hump behind them.

Who the hell . . .?

Maggie was a small dog, slighter than a coyote. But as a watchdog she could be a raving bitch and she detested surprises. She barked uncontrollably, greeting the intruder as if it were a mailman in short pants. Everyone gaped at the truck as it braked to a stop and the doors flew open.

"Maggie—come!" Cutter commanded, calling the cinnamon-and-white Aussie back to him as a man jumped to the ground from the passenger seat.

Shit. Even after so many years, Cutter might have guessed who the intruder was by the destructive entrance.

"What do you want, Vuko?"

"It good to see you, too, Cutter."

The unexpected meeting instantly pushed unwanted memories into Cutter's mind.

The well-built man strolled in khaki cargo pants. Even in his fifties now, Cutter guessed, Radic Vuko moved with the cocky looseness of someone very sure of himself.

Cutter didn't think he looked much different than the last day he'd seen him. That is, before Cutter left him slumped and bleeding against the ropes course shed. *Guess they couldn't sew that ear back on.* Where the left one used to be, the skin was the color of a Southwest sunset. It looked like it had been stretched and smoothed with a clothes iron. A single pea-sized hole pitted the surface. *Can he hear? I suppose it doesn't matter; he never listened.*

Neither man considered a handshake.

Cutter stood silently. Waiting.

Vuko looked around like he was sightseeing. "Ranch look good, Cutter. You've done nice job. Although, what you're doing up here playing in rocks, I couldn't guess."

"You wouldn't get it, Vuko. You never did."

Then, the moment he had always anticipated occurred. Cutter asked: "Do you like the name—Double Dare?" Asking the long-awaited question made Cutter buzz more than if he'd had slammed a couple beers.

All the light went out of Vuko's eyes as he glared back.

"No," he said, struggling for words. "As matter of fact, I hate it. You think you're very clever, don't you, with your talk of dares." Vuko shrugged. "Well, enough talking."

Waving for the driver to come around the Hummer, he added, "I bring you surprise."

Cutter had never set eyes on Vuko's driver, but he knew the type. He was a piece of work from the same mold as most of Vuko's "associates." One of the ex-military types who used to hang around the ropes course. Much younger than Vuko. Oily, black, tight-cropped curly hair. Maybe Middle Eastern. Scary-wild black eyes. He closed the distance between them as smoothly as if he were on skates.

Shifting beside Cutter, the red dog rumbled like a rising storm.

"Maggie—stay!"

From a breast pocket Bug Eyes unfolded several sheets of paper and slapped them with purpose against Cutter's chest.

"I'm an attorney. You've just been served."

Cutter anticipated the shepherd's reaction and decided to save the stranger his shinbone—for now.

"Maggie—sit!" Whining, she obeyed.

Cutter looked down at the olive-skinned hand still pressing the papers to his chest. He made no effort to reach for them and slowly looked back into the stranger's face. "You know how to read these, right?" Cutter said, ready for whatever happened next.

He heard Bobby move next to him, noticing he still gripped the long iron bar, as the rest of the crew quietly ringed their boss and the two strangers. Neither Vuko nor Bug Eyes seemed concerned. The driver stepped back without a word, letting the papers flutter to the ground. Advance scouts of rain began to tap as rhythmically as a countdown. No one moved.

"That's a lawsuit shutting down this *place*"—Vuko hissed the word—"in thirty days. It charges you with theft of intellectual property, fraud and slander. I imagine by time we get past courts you will be poor man, Cutter. Maybe I give you job. Just like old times."

"Vuko, who would ever believe you possess any intellectual property. There's nothing up there to steal."

Vuko's face instantly bloomed crimson. He took a few steps toward Cutter, oblivious to the documents his boots trampled, and the dog about to emasculate him.

"This ranch—I take," he shouted like a madman. "Whole idea is mine. You think it's yours, you think you so smart, huh, college boy? But if it isn't for me, for what I taught you, for ideas I gave you . . . I have money and power to crush you."

"Maggie—stay!"

"I buy all this from you, Cutter," Vuko said, waving both arms expansively. "Pay you good money. You can even take profit. If you don't see smartness in that, if you don't take offer, then I swear I take it from you any way I need to."

The crack of thunder and flash of too-close lightning startled everyone. On cue, Vuko shoved his snarled face nose-to-nose with Cutter, like some demented jinn. Spit flying, he spoke only loud enough for him to hear: "I'd actually prefer to *take* it from you. Man-to-man. I owe you, Cutter, right? For this," he said, rubbing the ravaged side of his head, now slick with rain. "For what you do to me. And that's more than a dare this time."

The tirade caused Cutter to remember something else.

"Whatever happened to the girl you beat up?" he shot back. The men around them listened more intently. "Remember Nicole? Can you hear me, Vuko?"

Vuko stared mutely at him. He seemed to collect himself, as if he'd just come out of a drug-induced stupor, and backed away, one step at a time, not taking his eyes off Cutter.

The air crackled with lightning, and a rising zephyr carried the smell of ozone. Unable to control herself any longer, Maggie charged the stranger, lips curled, fangs flashing. Cutter didn't call her back this time, but the bitch stopped short and barked her warning.

"Get your ass off this land, Vuko."

"It's public land, remember. You can't kick me out. That's the secret of this place. I know this, too."

Then Vuko turned and headed to the Hummer, as Bug Eyes kicked the powerful engine to life. Vuko rolled down the passenger window, his glare pinned on Cutter.

"Oh, the girl . . ." he said, and shrugged. "Collateral damage."

The military euphemism for civilian casualties of war jolted Cutter like a fist in the face. He lunged for the Hummer, but the worn tread of his prosthetic foot skidded on red pebbles, and he went down on one knee.

Grateful Bobby reacted much quicker. Crew members scattered as the giant Arapaho raised the iron pry bar and hurled it at the vehicle in one fluid blur. He threw the thirty-pound rock mover as easily as if it were a lawn dart.

The point of the pry bar wasn't sharp, but it nosed to a tip like a ski pole, and Bobby's thrust punched it through the lower rear metal panel of the Hummer like a javelin through cardboard. Vuko jerked backward at the impact, gaping in disbelief, while Bug Eyes floored the accelerator. The huge tires spun in the powdery soil, spraying gouts of rock and debris behind them before finally grabbing the ground and bulldozing forward again into the forest, the firmly lodged pry bar waggling from the Hummer like a matador's sword from a dying bull.

Cutter stood flat-footed, shocked at the awesome, instant act of violence by his normally tranquil friend.

"Sorry," Bobby muttered.

"It's okay. It pissed me off, too," Cutter said, his pulse hammering.

"No, I mean, sorry I didn't stick *him*,'" the foreman grumbled. He walked to where the Hummer squatted minutes before and, kneeling down, began pawing the earth. "An old friend?"

"Actually, he used to be my boss," said Cutter, eyeing the vanished truck's path with a worried look. "Now he's just an angry asshole."

"Who was the girl?"

"A victim. He was right about that." Cutter didn't want to drag up that story now. "We had a run-in about eight years ago."

"Let me guess," Bobby grinned. "That's when he started shopping for hearing aids?"

Cutter didn't reply, his mind elsewhere. For a moment, he was back in the shadows of the Fort Collins gear shed where he and Vuko operated the ropes course together.

After what seemed like minutes later, Bobby called him. "Cutter, look at this."

Cutter took a knee next to his foreman and immediately recognized what he had been digging at, and how it might be significant.

"It's crypto, right?"

"Yeah, cryptobiotic soil," said Bobby. "It only grows about one millimeter per year, so a patch like this probably has a recovery rate of about ten *years*. It looks worthless. But to the environmental guys, the feds, it's like cutting down a rain forest, on a miniature scale."

For the next fifteen minutes the two men examined the area. Between the scattered rocks, a fine silty soil covered the ground with shreds of a crunchy gray lichen gouged out. Where the Hummer's knobby tires had dug in, only deep ruts remained. Bobby gingerly circled, pointing out the scar of a tread or grabbing Cutter's elbow as if to guide him around something holy. Twice he knelt in the dirt and ran his fingers over the ground like a detective searching for clues. After leaving little more than a few dark divots in the dirt, the rain quit. Thunder and lightning still stormed the canyon rim. Finally, Bobby stood and looked expectantly at Cutter.

"Have you got your camera?" Cutter asked. "Take some shots? This may help against Vuko, if this lawsuit is for real."

The ranch foreman trotted back with a small digital camera. Ignoring everyone, he began clicking off dozens of frames. Photograph after photograph of dirt.

Glancing up at the sky, Cutter was back in the present. "Bobby, let's get out of here. Don't open this trail yet. It's too dangerous. We'll wait and figure a way to move some more rocks to slow down the riders."

"Sure, Cutter," the Arapaho replied. "Too bad. I really like the trail name."

"What's that?" Double Dare's boss looked up, puzzled.

"You named it," said Bobby as the men began packing equipment. "Mars Slalom. It's gonna scare the crap outta someone some day."

Chapter 6

When the crew pulled into Double Dare's large yard, Cutter found Lexi pacing the deck even as an intermittent rain fell from the leaden sky. She was always there for him, he reflected. He needed to give her more time, take her to Denver or Santa Fe or San Francisco and do more of the showy things she enjoyed. Culture wasn't lost on him. He just didn't feel like he had to go shopping to find it all the time, like Lexi.

She looked worried—arms crossed, hugging herself against the chill, satellite phone clasped in one hand.

Something's spooked her.

"Patricia called," she said without preamble. "She said Two Havens had a lot of lightning. She was at the lower house, thought she smelled smoke, and she was worried High Haven might have been hit. She wanted to ask if you'd check it out with her. She tried to call you on the sat, but the storm probably made reception even flukier than usual."

Cell phones in this isolated country were nearly worthless because there weren't enough towers to pick up and relay the signals. Ranchers, farmers, the sheriff, even the soccer moms on the Plateau—anyone who counted on dependable mobile phone service—used satellite phones.

She dropped the blocky phone helplessly to her side. "She's seventy years old, after all, and all alone . . ."

"Keeps us mere mortals safe," Cutter muttered.

"What?"

"Nothin' . . . Just more bad news today," he said, reaching for her phone. "We had a visit up on the rim from my old boss, Radic Vuko. I told you about him. He—"

"Vuko? He's here?" She looked as stunned as if he'd just told her Yugoslavia had reunited. Her eyes flooded as her voice shook. "But why . . .? What . . .?"

The phone dialed and rang. He had a connection. He held up one finger, asking for her silence.

"It's okay, Lexi, it's okay," Cutter reassured her, surprised at the intensity of her reaction.

"But he's not supposed to be here . . ."

"No, he sure as hell isn't." Puzzled, Cutter stooped slightly, trying to meet her eyes, but couldn't catch up to them. *What's this all about?*

Holding the phone to his ear, Cutter's thoughts turned to Patricia Keeney. He wondered if he had half the grit to fight it out here that the matriarch of the valley had displayed her entire life. The widow, a descendant of Dolores Valley homesteaders, owned Two Havens, a much larger ranch that bordered the entire length of Double Dare and more across the Dolores River to the east. She had two houses: an older, conservative ranchhouse known as The Haven when it was built by her first husband, and High Haven, a classically painted Victorian that she built with her second husband. High Haven perched over the river, but much higher on the property.

She'd seen and survived more calamities than Cutter had birthdays. Fires. Droughts. Killer blizzards. Mean animals. Meaner moonshiners. Drug runners. And, worst by far, the game poachers that murdered her second husband when he stood up to them. That was ten years ago. Ever since, she kept house at High Haven during the summer, taking advantage of the cool wafts of air that meandered up the river canyon. When the first snow arrived, she simply drove her well-known green-and-white Willys jeep down the gullied road and parked herself at Low Haven until the spring. You could change your calendar by where Patricia lived.

Cutter shook his head, thinking of his closest neighbor in the valley, knowing that he and the rest of the community could count on Patricia doing her part. The thought made him stand a little straighter as her voice pushed the phone away from his ear.

. . . .

"I was afraid of this," Patricia blurted, recognizing it was Cutter calling by the phone ID. "High Haven's on fire. A lightning strike nearby. Ramworthy's got men here, we don't need help. I'll call you back."

Already the ashy, brackish air had snuck inside the house, pasting the inside of her mouth and tongue so she could barely speak.

She knew the assault on the west wall of the little house—the riverside wall—was the sound of the Ram Mountain hands slapping the yellow-plank and lavender-shingle siding with sopping burlap sacks and soaking the surface with garden hoses. Outside, smoke billowed white, obscuring her yard.

The gaunt, spare woman leaned to pull back the lace window curtain, ignoring the strand of gray-shot russet hair that escaped from her thin ponytail and fell across her strained face. The mutter of men laboring sifted through the walls. EFFers flailed at the gaily painted siding, chasing the char up the wall. Standing back, pointing here and there, a tall, leathery man with a mane of white hair shouted orders: Vernard Ramworthy.

Seeing her in the window, he rushed toward her.

"Patricia, you got five minutes to get out of there." His muffled voice butted the glass. "I don't know what this fire is gonna do. I know you don't want me in there. But five minutes . . . Then I'm gettin' you out even if I have to put you over my shoulder." Then he ran back.

She darted to the nearest table, intent on saving as many pieces of her life as she could carry. She filled one arm with the first few picture frames her bony fingers touched. Slowing, she caressed another, and another. In a worn doe skin-covered frame, three faces stared up at her from a sun-blanched photo: a handsome, bushy-haired young man dressed in a military uniform, hands held tightly with a teenage Hepburn lookalike, and a studious-looking, more finely built youth stood next to them. A river glistened behind the World War II-era trio.

Damn it! Half of my heart beats within these walls.

Her eyes welled with tears, but then something bumped the wall hard outside. Quickly, she set down the photo and blotted her eyes with her denim shirt sleeve. Satisfied no one was coming, she plucked the same frame again.

Patricia stood in her gingerbread house, at this moment, because of two men—one alive, one dead. And she loved them both, in different ways, to this day.

Neither one was abusive or guilty of any of the horrible maladies that afflicted lesser men. On the contrary, her first husband was a dogie-punching, bigger-than-life Colorado hero who in his mission to make money simply lost track of her. The couple simply fell out of love. They divorced amicably twenty years later. It was complicated for her, continuing to live in the valley.

Two years later, it got a lot more complicated when she wed for the second time. Patricia always liked men, and she had been with a few. She couldn't imagine how a woman could be so twice-blessed. Lloyd was every bit the man his predecessor had been. He built High Haven with his own hands as a wedding gift. An accomplished nature photographer,

Lloyd viewed things differently. On one of his legendary photography expeditions in the Rockies, he discovered a poaching ring and was killed for it. That was when Patricia first knew true sadness.

The scrape-scuff-scrape of gritty leather boots climbing wooden steps outside brought her back. Again she left the photo and went to the door.

"Please don't come in," she said, quickly stepping out and closing the door to them both.

"It's okay," Ramworthy replied, raising both hands defensively. Nevertheless, his eyes strained to see past her into the house. "The fire's out. That's what I came to tell you. Hell, I know you don't want me in your house. My boots—"

"You know that's not it," she snapped and brushed past him, down the steps and around the corner of the house. Blistered, sodden pancakes of paint hung and fluttered from the upper reaches of the wall. Closer to the ground, the structure was charred but still appeared solid.

"That was damned close," she said, speaking for both of them as she shook her head. "I tell you, Vern, the West is just burning up. You know how much I appreciate you coming over, fighting the fire and all."

"You should always call if you need help, you know that."

"It isn't that the house matters so much. But my things . . . silver pieces that my mother left me, Lloyd's photography, family pictures."

"I know, Patricia. I know."

They agreed she shouldn't stay at the house, and Ramworthy said he would leave a couple men at least overnight to make sure the fire didn't flare up again.

. . . .

"It's just that I was surprised about Vuko. And I was worried about that old woman," said Lexi, regaining her composure after Cutter guided her into the ranchhouse. "You never expected to see Vuko again, did you? You said he disappeared."

"No such luck." Waving the muddy documents as evidence, Cutter added, "He had a little terrorist with him, and he slapped me with a lawsuit to try and take away the ranch. He's going to try and tie it all up in court. I'll have to go to Denver tomorrow and meet with Michael Antonini."

"Can I come with you?"

"Sure, if you want," Cutter said, leafing through the papers, absentmindedly adding, "and I'll get my new foot fitted while I'm there."

I've got some business of my own to take care of, Lexi thought, knowing how simple it would be to convince Cutter she would be shopping while he met with his attorney.

Chapter 7

"So what do you want to do about it, Cutter?"

From the floor-to-ceiling windows of the fifteenth-floor office of Michael Antonini & Associates, downtown Denver looked larger than it was. Antonini had been Cutter's attorney for about four years, since the unknown entrepreneur had shaken up the prosthetics industry with its first bona fide athletic limb design. Cutter had bigger plans, but he needed legal and investment counsel to turn his vision into Double Dare Ranch.

Not waiting for an answer, the distinguished-looking man with gray-winged black hair and dressed in a V-neck sweater and plush corduroy continued, "For starters, we ought to give Grateful Bobby a bonus for nearly spearing Vuko. Of course, if he had hit him then you'd really need a lawyer."

Cutter kept Antonini informed of major developments at the ranch and tried to meet with his advisor at least twice a year in Denver. This was a hastily organized session since Cutter's regular business meetings always seemed to coincide with Colorado Rockies' homestands and involved reserving one of Coors Field's boxes and ordering-in brats and beers.

"You know everything I know about Vuko," said the ranch owner. "I'm guessing he's been tracking me ever since Fort Collins. He probably has a pretty good idea about my finances. He's got to be obsessed with Double Dare for his own warped reasons."

"I wonder if this lawsuit isn't just a bluff," said Antonini. "Vuko's macho maneuvering to scare you into believing the ranch isn't worth the aggravation and harassment?"

Cutter clicked a remote device and a screen slowly descended from the attorney's office ceiling. Another click and a laptop projector displayed stunning vistas from the red rock rim above the Dolores River.

"I think I know what Vuko really wants, and it's more than the ranch," Cutter said, perching his right leg comfortably over the arm of one of the lawyer's polished mahogany chairs. "I've got something I want you to see. And I have an idea."

The images on the screen changed dramatically. Cutter watched Antonini cock his head and squint in puzzlement as the laptop hummed and the screen filled, frame after frame, with nothing but close-up photos of dirt.

Chapter 8

Radic Vuko stared out the window of his Larimer Street penthouse only a few blocks away. The view was remarkable: the snow-capped majesty of Pikes Peak was visible, even though the mountain was sixty-five miles away. Any serenity the view might have brought Radic Vuko vanished when he heard what Lexi had to say.

"I forbid this!" he seethed, turning the full force of his glare on the young woman standing across the luxurious wool Berber carpet. "I sent you to this backward resort to advance your career and to give me progress about its weakling owner. Not—I say again, NOT—act like little girl and believe you have love for him. Not him!

"Love! There is no place for such a thing at this, this 'ranch.' Not for you. Not my niece. It cannot be. You will forget this idea. I forbid it!" he said, slashing his arm through the air as if he could physically erase the problem.

"Uncle Darko, I did not wish this—

"Hush! I am Radic Vuko. Uncle Radic, always."

"Uncle," Lexi Skupo continued, her black-olive eyes brimming pools. "I have told you about this ranch. I don't understand what it is you want with it. But I will not hurt Cutter. I am a woman. I will love as I please."

"Acchhh . . ." he growled, unable to find words to express his displeasure.

"You have no say. Why is this important?"

"I have no say? Me? Who brought you to this country, paid for education, gave you this extravagant life—"

"Then I will ask Cutter why—"

"No! You cannot! Not if you have regard for me. For your only remaining family . . . Lexi, Lexi." Vuko changed his tone, from outraged to placating. And then, arms extended, palms upturned, "Why we fight? To you, to me, we are both all that we have. It is our way. It must be this way."

"I will not leave him."

"I am not telling you to leave just now. But you cannot love this man. And," he said, taking her chin, softly yet firmly enough with his thumb and forefinger to enforce his will upon her, "you cannot betray me. Never. You bleed my blood."

He dropped his hand, and her chin followed, bowed on the elegant arc of her neck.

"I must go," she said, the words as soft and fine as dust.

He held her coat for her. She hugged him in a strong embrace, kissed him first on the right cheek, then the left, then again on the right, and turned to leave.

"Lexi," Vuko slowly released the words. "Not a whisper to him about me."

He closed the thick teak door behind the swirl of her full-length, blood-red cashmere coat.

She looks so much like her mother. She's still sad. That is why she's reaching for Cutter. Pity, that she has more sadness to see soon.

In the seconds it took him to walk across his walnut-paneled office and sit down in a cavernous studded-leather armchair, he thought of his past and his present. *Darko Magyar. Radic Vuko.* He believed his identities—both of them—were still safe.

Vuko picked up a copy of the morning's *Rocky Mountain News* in one hand. He stared out the window and followed the Front Range all the way to the purplish peak in the distance, but he was thinking about people and events much further away.

Cutter thinks he knows all there is about me. He thinks he knows why I want ranch. He thinks it's about personal. Or that I am greedy. He has no idea.

Vuko sneered.

All the years of planning, of watching—of hiding—are soon to give me what I want.

. . . .

Krajina, Croatia, 1995

It was to have been a joyous homecoming. The Croatian-born and American-trained military man was helping cleanse the Krajina, his bloodlands, of the Serbs. For longer than he had lived, the invaders persisted in encroaching on the loamy fertile land.

Instead, as General Darko Magyar rode in an armored troop carrier over the narrow cobbled streets of the city of Vukovar in the dawn chill, he found only bullet-pocked building walls and smoking, gutted houses.

The only countrymen who met him were those lying in bloody pools in the road, their rigored limbs crooked beneath them or splayed out, as if reaching for help.

When he came to the modest cluster of houses where he grew up, he signaled his driver to stop. The sky-blue door of his house, of the Magyar clan, hung ajar, and as he trotted around the front of the vehicle he saw one limp, bare arm hanging over the threshold. Blood dripped from her fingers. She lay naked, beaten, destroyed. His sister, his life. She had dreamed—he had promised her—she would join him in America one day.

By the early years of the Balkan wars, Darko had already made a reputation as a ruthless and efficient soldier and officer in the Croatian army. Eventually, American private military companies were hired to train the Croatians in wet work—insurgency, torture, executions—in the former Yugoslavia. They were mercenaries, and they identified him as one of the local up-and-comers. They taught him their tactics, their language and, not the least of their weapons, a brutal disregard for human life. He became one of their most valuable assets, an experienced, dependable Croatian warlord who could unleash or restrain merciless nationalists obsessed with annihilating the enemy Serbs. So on the day that he sat in Vukovar's streets and cradled the ravaged body of his sister, the rest of his relatives butchered inside the stone house, he was already one of them.

In the days and weeks that followed, Darko survived on hate.

Operation Storm was intended to free the Krajina once and for all. He fought relentlessly and freed his men from all limits of human decency in the brutal campaign to drive off the Serbs. The Serbs, who violated his sister and scattered his family.

In one terrible swoop, he commanded his soldiers to round up more than a hundred men from a nearby town. They drove them in trucks to a pig farm and a freshly dug pit. They marched the innocent into the putrid sties. Darko watched with the detached air of justification.

"Fire!" he commanded. "Kill them! All of them! Fire! Fire!"

His words and the victims were obliterated by gunfire. Then he waved forward bulldozers to bury the evidence.

In another town, he ordered the dead dumped down a well until it was so choked with bodies he had to order the idiots to throw the rest in the nearby forest. He didn't know how many they killed. He didn't count, and he didn't care.

In his occasional sane moments, he traced the faint trails of his kin. He lived in a cycle of monstrous violence. Some days he slaughtered his enemies' families; on others, he searched in blown-out buildings and makeshift graves for his own. His hope flickered: one by one, he learned of the deaths of his family members. Eventually, he believed the only surviving male in his family was a young nephew, Tito.

Even though he was an educated man, the tragic contradictions of his mission didn't register until the day his troops swept through an already ruined city. They had become inhumanly efficient. There was no one left alive to resist. In less than an hour, his armored vehicle led the army to the opposite edge of the town and he looked out onto a scorched plain. Fleeing before him, like rats in rags, ran scores of children. Only children.

"Tito! Tito!" he screamed, desperate to believe his nephew was among them. "Tito, wait!

He must find the boy. He had only a faint idea about where to begin.

That night Darko drove alone out of the encampment, blaming a hastily called operations meeting for his unusual departure. He used the same invented orders at checkpoint after checkpoint on his retreat away from the battle lines. Most other soldiers would have been arrested or shot as a deserter. But no one who stopped him to glance at his papers had the rank or courage to question a general. Finally, he was so far away that he could destroy all evidence of Darko Magyar—his general's uniform, his papers, his identity. With his new American military contacts, it was easy enough to create a new identity. His new name: Radic Vuko. Radic had been his father's name; Vuko would remind him every day of the town where his sister died.

The only thing he could not shed were the atrocities he'd committed. As he stepped across the Hungarian border, politicians in the West were already levying charges of genocide and planning trials for war crimes.

Before Darko could take his long-imagined journey to the States and use his training and connections to blend into the vast, anonymous American business landscape, he had one more place to go. A year before he found his sister dead, she and her husband had finally given in to their strong-willed oldest daughter, allowed her access to her inheritance, and with their reluctant blessings sent her off to study the culinary arts.

Darko thought he might find one of his last living relatives in Budapest. From what he remembered of photographs he had seen, she was beautiful. Maybe she would even know where to look for her brother Tito.

. . . .

The newspaper dropping from Vuko's limp hand to the rich carpet woke him. With a deep sigh he reached down to retrieve it. He walked around an immense, dark desk and dropped the paper there. It fell folded to an inside page carrying a *New York Times* byline below the three-column headline:

War crimes testimony at The Hague unveils U.S.-trained 'mystery general.'

Vuko was no master of personal introspection. He knew he had spent much of his life doing bad things. Unspeakable things. But when he ever gave such deeds second thought, he quickly categorized them—as if moving pieces over a military field map—as necessary actions he committed in the name of his country and his family. Above all, he loved his family. What was left of it.

He smiled at the irony. *I am like all American patriarchs. I am family man.*

. . . .

Cutter turned up the collar of his polar fleece pullover against the wind, which carried a taste of fall off the foothills to the west as he hurried to meet Lexi. As often occurred whenever they came to Denver, the two of them seemed to go separate ways—Cutter to a business meeting or the ballpark, and Lexi to dine and shop with her friends in the latest restaurant-of-the-week or indoor monument to bad architecture. Once they left the ranch, he reflected, the couple really didn't have much in common. Come to think of it, lately, even on the ranch they didn't have much in common either.

The meeting had gone well, he thought. He hadn't expected anything different from Antonini. He was a touchstone for Cutter, and it was always reassuring to listen to his counsel. Most importantly, his attorney and friend confirmed for him that he just might be able to beat Vuko once and for all. Antonini would start on the legal shenanigans immediately. Then he'd look into the federal land-use law.

Immersed in thought, Cutter unconsciously dodged pedestrians on the mall until one of them stopped in front of him.

"Cutter," said a blonde woman dressed in a wool business jacket and slacks, "how are you? What are you doing here? You almost ran me down."

"Serena," he replied, coming out of his reverie. "Hi. Sorry . . . I . . . uh, I was thinking. About things. I just had a business meeting. You look great. Where did you come from?"

She waved vaguely at a nearby office building just off the mall.

"So when are you coming back down to Double Dare?" he asked.

"I think this weekend," she said. "I get in the city and I either feel assaulted by all the work, or I don't exercise enough and I feel like I'm going to burst with craving for a physical challenge. I need diversions. I need a life. Maybe I need more sex."

They both laughed, although it startled Cutter as he secretly gave it a second thought.

"Well, I'll tell Mouse he better start thinking of something special for you on the Dolores. You almost got the best of him last time," Cutter said.

"No, please, don't give Mouse any encouragement. I'll see you this weekend," she said, grasping his arm with one leather-gloved hand and letting it linger a split-second before sliding it away.

Cutter turned his back to the wind again and hustled down 16th Street. He walked another block when he saw Lexi coming toward him, her jet-black hair blowing around her face and her arms crossed against her body to ward off the wind. As she saw him, she smiled and raised one hand.

The attractive woman waving would have stood out in any crowd, but her deep red coat immediately caught his attention.

Chapter 9

As he hiked Ram Mountain above the ranch in the cool night air, Cutter could think of only one thing that gave him more pleasure than the rugged beauty of Double Dare Ranch.

The Game.

Deep down, the core of Double Dare, its pure allure, all revolved around The Game. Creating and building physical challenges, and then turning loose the competitive spirit of fit, motivated people. Cutter had been in love with games all his life.

He and Nipsy, Double Dare's climbing master and an equally competitive soul, set out with overnight packs on what would be a four-mile, out-bound trek above and parallel to the Dolores River but deeper into the woods. Their destination, once they hiked above tree line: Moccasin Ridge.

"How do you want to do this, Nipsy?"

"The plan is to roughly pick the route for the new geocache challenge two nights from now," answered the slight, but tautly built man striding in the lead. "I figure the challengers will head out on Say Hey for about a mile, then bushwhack through the forest. It's tougher terrain and a little dark. But they'll sacrifice comfort for speed."

The Say Hey Trail was one of the main mountain bike paths that spidered out from the ranch. When a trail didn't already have a local name, Cutter named them in honor of baseball players, and this one honored the greatest player who ever lived—Willie Mays, the Say Hey Kid for the New York and, later, San Francisco Giants.

The moon rose three-quarters full and silvered the glades of aspen and ghostly meadows they came upon first. Each wearing headlamps strapped above their baseball caps, the two men climbed into denser patches of pine and spruce. Occasionally, Cutter hooked his prosthetic foot under a log, or stumbled on a tree root, but he hardly lost a step and pushed himself to make up any ground lost on Nipsy. The new prosthesis he fitted while in Denver rubbed and irritated his stump in a couple places, which wasn't unusual for a new leg. But the suction between stump and socket felt gel-tight.

The steady pace and hard work soon had both men puffing clouds of vapor, their chests working like bellows, lungs burning. Some people savored such moments, and Cutter was one of them.

Nipsy liked to talk. Or make others do it.

"So, dude," he wheezed. "I've never heard the real story—from you—about how you dreamed up this whole Double Dare thing?"

Cutter laughed. He couldn't help it. Nipsy, in his twenties, possessed about as much guile as a two-week-old puppy. He said what he thought in the instant he thought it. He also owned a reputation as one of the finest freestyle rock climbers in the West. Cutter liked him. Even more important for a climber, he trusted him.

"Ever hear of a card game called Canasta?

Nipsy's face scrunched in confusion. "Dude?"

"As a kid I used to spend hours, days, playing Canasta with Grandma Frances when there was nothing else to do. One day I realized, when the light was just right, I could read the cards in her hand reflecting off her bifocals. I couldn't tell the exact card, but I could pick out the black suits from the red suits."

"You cheated your Grandma?"

"No, that's my point. Cheating ruins the game. Any game. It makes winning too easy, and losing too hard. Too hard on you here," Cutter said, patting his rhythmically heaving gut for Nipsy's benefit. "But it taught me that by observing opponents, probing for openings and ploys within the rules, I could gain an advantage to bank and use when I really needed it."

Cutter gasped for breath. They had climbed non-stop, gaining about eight hundred feet to reach 7,500 feet in elevation. The exertion forced him to stop in the middle of the trail, hands on his knees. Immediately, though, he straightened and, hands now on his hips, he looked up into the blank night as he savored the sweet pain of pushing his body to its limits.

. . . .

As a kid, Cutter discovered that it didn't matter if the game was cards, Hide-and-Seek, Scrabble, dart throwing, deer hunting or playing strikeout in the street. They were all games. It didn't matter if he won or lost, although he liked winning considerably better. He could even make a game out of hitchhiking across the city.

The adrenaline rush of competition turned him into an athlete in high school. Then it got a little more serious on a college baseball field. The college game, with its structure and regimentation, took the fun out of it. He turned to the constant in his life, the dependable, unbeatable challenge of the outdoors.

Skiing. Hiking. Mountain biking. Whitewater kayaking and canoeing. Orienteering. Camping, no matter the season. Snowshoeing. Hunting and fishing. Zip-lining. And climbing. Always climbing. He started on gym walls and park overhangs. He graduated to the endless crags up and down the Colorado Front Range, the Flatirons outside Boulder and then nearby Eldorado Canyon. The tight-knit rockhound community eventually introduced him to ice climbing, and soon he was making weekend expeditions to ice-curtained hotspots around Ouray and Silverton—early forays to the charms of southwest Colorado.

. . . .

"Okay, but this place took some serious cash," Nipsy said. "How did you score that?"

"Climbing," Cutter answered. "You know that claw-foot prosthetic I use for ice climbing, the one with the articulating titanium blades that looks like the Terminator's toes?"

"Yeah, yeah," Nipsy urged.

"I sold my design for it to Össur Prosthetics, with my commitment to consult on a bunch of other sports-related limbs, for eleven million dollars."

The amount took Nipsy's breath away.

Cutter knew that it was a matter of public record. He didn't brag about it, but anyone with an Internet connection could trace the roots of Double Dare.

He pointed them once again toward Moccasin Ridge.

. . . .

Cutter didn't think he would ever be able to spend all of his money. At first, he was shocked, then embarrassed, at the balance of his bank account.

Even after he pushed away from his drafting table and design computer, it took him eight months before he could escape the endless parade of appearances on afternoon television talk shows, at prostheses trade shows and medical summits. As he crisscrossed the country talking about "Sasquatch," the only thing about him that people thought of as strange—well, not strange, but enviable—were all the gigs he turned down so he could experience his country. Not experience it from First Class at 40,000 feet, either. A duffel of exotic, spring-pinned prosthetic feet became regular pieces of his luggage.

A prosthetic foot to equip a transtibial amputation could cost twenty-five to thirty thousand dollars. Cutter could afford a state-of-the-art arsenal. Besides Sasquatch, for different trips he packed a split-bladed foot for hiking and bouldering or a shell-less model specifically designed to snap directly into a ski binding. He even helped design a foot with a stainless steel articulating ankle system for swimming that also fit a diving fin.

He had to field test the new gear, of course.

There was paddling through the Alaskan archipelago. Skiing—lots of it—in the bottomless powder of Telluride and Steamboat, Aspen and Winter Park. Mountain lion tracking around Pocatello. Circumnavigating Mount St. Helens. Volunteering on a fresh Ancestral Pueblo dig in Mesa Verde National Park. And, ultimately, after a couple aborted, fear-soaked hikes up trailheads, climbing big rocks again in Yosemite.

Along the way, the idea of a place like Double Dare—although the name hadn't occurred to him—began to take shape.

These were the spaces he dreamed of ever since he was a boy. Now, he wanted to build something in the wild. Add something to it. The Southwest kept pulling him back, like a sandhill crane being called to its wintering grounds.

Two months later, Michael Antonini called to tell him about the tiny jewel hidden in the folds and creases beneath the San Juan Mountains.

. . . .

As Cutter and Nipsy emerged from the forest, they could almost read a map beneath the moon's spotlight and the array of stars. Instead, they both looked down once more at the GPS units hanging from lanyards around their necks.

In two hours, twenty minutes, they had traveled 4.1 miles in first a northwest direction, then dead north, and climbed to over 8,000 feet. The time was 12:05 a.m. The temperature was an invigorating thirty-nine degrees. Humidity was twenty-two percent. According to their GPS, they were exactly 244 miles from Denver and 5,960 miles from Rio de Janeiro to the southeast—if either of them had cared.

"Welcome to Moccasin Ridge," Cutter said between short gulps of the crisp, thin air.

The nearly flat mesa appeared to be a barren, wind-scraped place. In fact, it was a ragged quilt of chipped rock and tough grass, lichen and ever-present purple aspen daisies. The occasional small boulder broke the pattern. It was perfect habitat for mountain goats and elk that remained on the ridges until the snow pushed them down. Any animals probably had fled ahead of their footfalls.

It was Nipsy's idea to build GPS into a challenge, and it was a quick jump from there to tie it in with the burgeoning sport of geocaching. Geocaching combined orienteering with an old-fashioned scavenger hunt. In geocaching, anyone can hike to the top of the world and place a logbook, a granola bar, a mini-Swiss Army knife or any cheap trinket and use GPS to document its location. Then, after revealing the GPS location on one of the scores of geocaching sites online, the hunt is on for anyone with the legs and skill. Many caches consist solely of a logbook for the finder to write his or her name, the date, maybe a hometown, and then leave it for the next geo-hunter.

Every member of the Double Dare staff shared Cutter's love of the outdoors and passion for competition. It was part of their job description. They constantly strove to out-do one another when proposing new challenges. For every challenge idea that made it into the field, Cutter paid a $1,000 bonus to the creator after the first twenty client requests or if it still remained in use after three months. That usually meant it was a success. Some challenges were retired if their popularity waned, or if it was necessary to cease in order not to permanently damage the environment.

Nipsy, like Mouse, nurtured a devilish obsession with challenges. In fact, the two guides had their own unofficial game going to determine who was more warped. Creativity ruled their competition. Very few challenges on the ranch could be safely undertaken at night, so Nipsy proposed the added twist of making geocaching accessible by day or on any full-moon night. As long as tonight's trial excursion didn't raise any unexpected hazards or concerns, the challenge offered the added attraction of taking place across a stunningly lit landscape.

"This is the best, Cutter," Nipsy said, pausing to admire the moonscape. "This is where I belong."

"How many Fourteeners are you up to now?" asked Cutter, referring to the fifty-four peaks in Colorado with more than 14,000 feet of elevation. Climbers, even hikers, across the Rockies considered it a rite of the sport to summit as many as possible. Many spent years in the pursuit.

"Forty-one." Moonlight bounced off Nipsy's proud smile. "I've got two years to climb the last thirteen if I'm going to bag them all by the time I'm thirty. I'm stoked for it, man."

"Did you ever think you wouldn't climb again?" Cutter asked, thinking back to the day he interviewed the engaging young man for the job at Double Dare.

Sean "Nipsy" Christian had told him the story behind his nickname. As a teenager learning the sport, he and his pack of adrenaline-laced buddies decided to do some bouldering in southern Utah's Castle Valley. It wasn't technical vertical climbing. They weren't roped together or anchored with protection. Midway scrambling up a 1,200-foot cone of scree—loose, jumbled sandstone—the steeply sloped rock slid out from under him. One panicked heartbeat later, Sean slid ninety feet down the jagged, rust-colored ramp, shredding the right side of his chest from his rib cage to nearly the top of his shoulder. Later, it took doctors with tweezers more than two hours to pick out the shards and chips and clothing fibers from the living stew that remained. The skin damage was so complete that it looked more like a burn scar than a climbing fall. They never found anything close to resembling his right nipple. His climbing friends, at that irreverent, indestructible age when no taboos existed and no quarter is given, were ruthless in bestowing a new nickname upon him—Nipsy—to memorialize the event.

"Climbing isn't a sport that automatically disqualifies you for accidents or close calls. If it did," Nipsy answered, spreading his arms as if he were the sport's official ambassador, "we'd all be eliminated."

. . . .

Standing near the top of Moccasin Ridge at midnight to pick the geocaching locations, Nipsy was in his element. Cutter came along, as he only half-jokingly said in the lodge before they left, "to chaperone." They all knew better. It was a ranch rule that no one went on the mountain alone after dark.

The San Juans were still very much a wild place. The remote mountains were a natural sanctuary for mountain lions and black bears, and even though the scientists in the city disputed it, some locals had been telling stories about the return of the Mexican wolf to the area for a couple years. There was no sense inviting a confrontation. Plus, Cutter's favorite days were those that included building a new challenge, and he promised to contribute some unique prizes for Double Dare's caches.

They planned two caches for their first public trial of the geocache challenge. With the rules that Nipsy first proposed and subsequently refined with Cutter during the hike, this would ensure strong competition for the inaugural group.

They could see by the topographic feature in the handheld GPS that the ridgeline stretched to their right a couple hundred yards and that it ramped into a steadily sharpening knife-edge until it reached a natural needle. First, they would angle up to intercept the ridgeline, where they planned to place their first cache. Then they would traverse the remaining mile or so and climb the last two hundred feet to the needle to leave the last prize.

The climbing was neither technical nor even dangerous, but the altitude stole their oxygen and they were breathing hard when they reached the ridgeline. In the stillness, as they calculated the final pitch, the distinct, hollow scrape-clop of horses' hooves on rock rose with the breeze. Looking down, Cutter and Nipsy saw two riders emerge from the tree line and slowly pick and wind their way toward them.

When the riders drew close enough for everyone to identify each other, all were surprised.

"Cutter, you don't have the sense of a rock rolling downhill to be out here at night," said the lead rider, who sat straight and tall in his saddle despite the white hair beneath his felt Stetson.

"Hello Mr. Ramworthy," Cutter replied. "Shouldn't you have drunk your glass of milk and tucked yourself into bed by this time of night?"

"Yeah-up," he said as he swung out of his saddle. "And I'd probably had two wet dreams by now if Manny hadn't seen your lights weavin' and dancin' all over the mountain. We figured some yuppie campers had gotten themselves lost, and I damn well didn't want them going beddy-bye in the trees and lighting a bonfire, as dry as things are. I'd forgotten that you boys like to play cowboys and Indians in the woods. What the hell are you doin'?"

Cutter couldn't help but smile at Ramworthy's aw-shucks delivery. Like Patricia Keeney, he was well into his silver years and had lived in the valley most of his life. His Ram Mountain Ranch sat on the opposite shoulder from Two Havens above Double Dare and was even larger than Patricia's spread. The property lines of all three ranches abutted the huge expanse of BLM land behind and above them. But Double Dare was like a gold nugget caught between two boulders. Even though the ranch served as a tiny gateway, it offered visitors the same access to thousands upon thousands of acres of BLM land as the two much larger ranches.

The two proud men had botched their first meetings and still didn't exchange much more than waves out their pickup windows or brittle greetings on the street.

Ramworthy disliked the whole idea of Double Dare. But unlike Vuko, Cutter knew, his opposition was based on Old West ideals and concern for the land, not hate and greed.

When the little ranch came on the market, Ramworthy thought it was perfect for a wildlife refuge and encouraged the state to buy it and turn it over to the Colorado Division of Wildlife. From the first hearings about the notion of Double Dare, the old man fought it and tried to unite the valley against Cutter. He railed that the "re-zort" would only attract rich city brats in SUVs who had no respect for the land and who would dangerously increase the chance for fire. Oh, and they'd get lost a lot. Under his breath he huffed that the increase of "tourists" would also instantly be followed by "bo-teek shops" in town and demands that the market start stocking something called "toe-fu." Cutter respected the man, even liked him a little.

He turned to Ramworthy's foreman.

"Manny, I want to tell you again how sorry I am about what happened to your brother in the Little Cahone Fire."

"*Gracias*," the man said. "I appreciate the donation you made to our family for his funeral."

Ramworthy broke in. "So what's goin' on here?"

Cutter took a deep breath and explained that they were on the mountain to set up and test the logistics of a challenge based on the sport of geocaching and its use of GPS.

"This is a GPS . . ." he said, offering the device to the older man.

"I know what a GPS is." Ramworthy waved it away. "I may be old, but I'm not senile. I've got TV—color, mind you—and even a computer," he added with a twinkle in his eyes. "I tell you, though, Cutter, I still think this whole Double Dare scheme is a crazy idea. And prancin' around up here in the middle of the night with . . ." He looked over at the younger man with Cutter as if just noticing him.

"Who's he?" he asked.

"This is Nipsy," replied Cutter.

"Of course he is," said Ramworthy, looking at him doubtfully.

"Hey, dude." The climber waved. His reward was Ramworthy's scowl.

"Look, why don't you tag along with us and we'll show you how we're going to do this," said Cutter. "It won't take long."

His policy had always been one of openness about the ranch and the challenges. The best thing he could do is include his nervous neighbor in building the challenge and at least demonstrate this was a responsible operation, that they were taking advantage of the same glorious resources Ramworthy enjoyed all of his life and, maybe, start breaking down his objections to Double Dare.

Ramworthy grumbled something about them being here anyway. So with Cutter and Nipsy leading, the group hiked to the ridge. Once there the Double Dare men collected a few small boulders to cover the prize, which Cutter pulled from his pack.

"You gonna just leave it there?" asked an incredulous Ramworthy. "Hell, why don't you set a picnic and leave them some Yanni music, too. You call that a *challenge*?" he said with a snort.

Cutter and Nipsy looked at each other and smiled. This was good. Ramworthy did understand The Game.

Together they decided to place the cache on the north-facing side of the ridge. At this juncture the drop-off on the opposite side was dangerous but not fatal. The face sloped slightly and one could climb down without ropes using natural hand- and footholds. The light glowed even brighter than on top of the mesa because the three-quarter moon shone directly on the ridge face. This was Nipsy's deal and so Cutter pulled a quart-size, bright orange Nalgene water bottle from the pack and handed it to his foreman. Inside the bottle some additional transparent material, with a flat object inside it, silently bumped the sides.

"So . . ." Ramworthy said. "What's so damned important?"

"We're calling this cache Cooperstown," Cutter said. The rancher tilted his stubbled face toward the stars and squinted his eyes, slowly shaking his head. Cutter smiled even wider.

Nipsy scooted over the edge and back up, having left the watertight bottle in a neat crevice about thirty feet down the face, before Ramworthy recovered. With his head lamp, he noted the coordinates with the GPS and Cutter wrote them in a notebook to be given to the geo-challengers—at N 37.8067199, W -108.7931577.

They all hiked up the ridgeline to spot the second cache. As they climbed the rocky ridge, they knew that the opposite face also grew steeper and higher until at the end of the mesa it dropped nearly vertical, requiring at least moderate technical climbing skills and gear to negotiate it. The mild breeze that never ceased on the exposed ridge, and the placid munching of the horses as they tore off bits of sparse, dry grass, were the only sounds as they reached the end of the plateau. Miles to the east, under the moonlight, Lone Cone Peak, at 12,600 feet and wearing its first coat of snow from the previous chill night, glowed soft and ethereal.

From his pack, Nipsy produced a climbing rope and equipment. Cutter pulled out another clear orange water bottle. An object rattled inside.

The veteran mountaineer studied the rock shelf about ten feet from the edge until he found two fissures about five feet apart that satisfied him. Then he chose a combination of different size "nuts," climbing anchors, wedged them into the granite cracks, rigged a nylon sling between them and pulled them together with a figure-8 follow-through knot and a single carabiner. Clipping the nylon rope into his harness, Nipsy then backed to the edge of the cliff, and after clearing the rope dangling beneath him and checking his footing, he expertly dropped over the ledge. Moonlight pooled on his helmet. Those above listened to the sizzle of the rope as he slowly rappelled downward, searching the cliff face for another hiding spot.

"Got it," Nipsy yelled. Only minutes later, picking out handholds and footholds like they were numbered, he glided back up the face.

Cutter recorded the second set of coordinates—at N 37.8076655, W -108.7918455.

"How about if we name this one Nipsy's Drop?" he said, not expecting any argument.

"How about if we all go home and go to bed," Ramworthy grumbled. "Are you done playing games up here?"

Making it clear that he wasn't inviting discussion, the rancher hoisted himself onto his horse and without another word turned the animal back down through the rock field. Manny gave Cutter and Nipsy a tiny wave and followed his boss.

After deciding to leave the climbing sling and carabiner in place for the real geo-hunt, the two men walked back in the direction they had come. Once off the ridge, they planned to find a protected spot in the trees and sleep in bags overnight on the mountain. They had traversed only a short distance when their softly spoken words about a good night's work and the dramatic new challenge to be tested in a few days were carried away by the night wind.

. . . .

Fifty feet from where the four men had worked at the top of the ridge, one of the small boulders stirred, then shifted. The ground around it—tufts of grass, patches of lichen, fist-sized rocks and the dirt itself—rose with the boulder like a science-fiction creature from an old black-and-white movie. Hands in mossy, crusted gloves peeled away two strips of camouflaged cellophane, revealing two wildly white eyes that blazed in the night like lamps.

The small man wore an ingeniously made ghillie suit. Hunters and soldiers had used countless variations for centuries. This one was a wide, raggedly cut circle of thick netting painted in random grays and greens, browns and blacks, with rocks and grass affixed to it. When he was wearing it, the man was difficult to locate even when standing. The "boulder" was his head beneath a black knitted wool sock, topped off with a similarly camouflaged mesh hood.

The only moment when he came close to being discovered occurred when the two horsemen broke out of the trees onto the rock field. They surprised him. Having already crawled on kneepads and padded gloves to keep close to the two men on foot, he had to freeze directly between the riders and the hikers. One of the horses stepped on a corner of the tightly woven netting as they passed him. Later, as the four men bent intently over their gear, it was easy for him to creep behind them, close enough to see and hear what they were doing.

When they left, he walked to the ledge. The twinkle of moonlight on the stainless steel carabiner at his feet caught his eye. It took only seconds for him to replace the carabiner with one from a camo-dappled pouch.

Chapter 10

Radic Vuko sat at the restaurant's granite bar and savored the slivovitz as the Balkan plum brandy burned its way down his throat. He was satisfied with himself and with how things were going.

His lawyers were building his case to take control of the ranch—not that he'd ever walk into a courtroom. But it kept the pressure on Cutter. That was his real strategy. Then, he received the phone call he was expecting this morning from his associate, who reported the steps he had taken on the ridge in the San Juans. *Military technology was so interesting. So . . . useful.*

It was time to take a moment for Rad. He knew how to take care of himself. He lived well. And with luck and the right touch, he expected things to get even better in the next few hours.

. . . .

When a select few women enter a room, everyone notices. Serena didn't know how it worked, but it worked. The tasteful little black dress certainly had something to do with it as she maneuvered through the room. Vuko pulled a bar stool out for her.

"You look exquisite tonight," he said. He leaned in to kiss her mouth, but his lips grazed her cheek as she turned away from him at the last second. Whenever she was around Rad she felt uneasy. She didn't know what this meeting was all about yet. She sensed it was about more than just sex.

He ordered her a martini and they exchanged the latest gossip around Denver. He seemed willing to talk about his public business interests, the fitness and self-defense training and a personal security firm he owned. She had heard rumors through her own business network that Vuko tightly managed a portfolio of real estate and development investments, but he didn't hint at it. A waiter came to lead them to their dining table, and any further discussion of his background was abandoned at the bar.

"So," Vuko said later as he forked the last of grilled duck breasts in juniper butter sauce, "you are going to ranch this weekend?"

She had made a reservation at Double Dare. *How did he know?*

After a flush of surprise, she nodded. "I need to get out of the city and I want to try the kayak challenge again. That damn river beat me the last time and I'm better than that."

He loved competitiveness in women. Very sexy.

"I want you try a new challenge that I learn they unveil—like painting, yes?—for first time this weekend. It's about geocaching. You know of this challenge?"

She did, and it sounded like a good workout, and fun. Her former installation techs used GPS in the field and they had shown her how it worked.

"No, I want to get back in the kayak. I—"

"No, you not hear me, Serena," he said with an edge. "This is assignment. I want you to do Geochallenge. The moon will be full in two nights, so they are making it a special night event. A big deal. Call tonight and make it your reservation, because there will only be three people in race. You can tell them you saw it all on website."

"Alright, Rad," she said through gritted teeth. "Anything else?"

"Yes, as matter of fact there is. There will be two caches offered to challengers. Make sure you choose Cooperstown." He annunciated the word carefully.

"How do you know I'll be given a choice?"

He sniffed bitterly. "You kidding me? Trust me, Mr. Chivalry will offer lady the first choice."

She glared at him.

"I need to stay briefed on everything going on at that place, you know that," Vuko said, trying his best to slough off the directness of his orders. Shrugging, he added, "Is business, Serena."

She slowly nodded. "Okay." She began to gather her purse and get up.

"What are you doing?" he asked, all concern.

"I better get some rest. I have to travel tomorrow. I have to bone up on this challenge if I'm going to be worth a damn, and then I'll be up all the next night, it sounds like."

"I thought you come back to penthouse tonight," he said, stroking her arm. His manicured fingers curved beneath her upper arm at her armpit and brushed the skin peeking beneath it. She couldn't help but glance at the taut, shiny slab of flesh where his left ear used to be.

Standing, she leaned over as if to kiss him good night. Instead, she whispered into his right ear. His good one. "It's business, Rad, I know you understand. I really loved the duck. I'll report in when I get back."

. . . .

Vuko didn't turn to watch her strut out. He sat deathly still and stared at a modern oil painting on the wall. It allowed him time to get over his shock and realize he'd be sleeping alone that night.

Serena was a valuable asset to him, someone to confirm intel about the ranch and to throw into the field. But he knew she was putting him off. It might be she played this game too freely, too coyly. It might not be long before he decided she played the game too well.

Chapter 11

"Awright, awright," Cutter called over the boisterous crowd. "This is Geochallenge. Listen up and we'll get tonight's event started."

Gathered in the ranchhouse great room, Double Dare's guests buzzed from a full day of exercise and accomplishment. Some had topped it off with another gourmet feast prepared by Lexi and her staff. Those slower to recover munched on fruit, veggies and hoards of energy bars. Contented, about forty adventurers lounged on brass-studded leather couches and overstuffed chairs that seemed built for giants. Fall splashed all over Colorado, and no mountain aspens dripped with more color than in the San Juans, attracting a full house for the weekend. Guests lined the aspen-stave staircase and leaned over a balcony draped with Native American rugs and local hides and pelts taken in regulated harvest hunts. Soft light from the Spanish-accented sconces and candelabras treated two John Nieto wolves in kaleidoscopic colors well on the walls.

Every board and nail of the ranch came together based on the premise that everything in life is a challenge. After all, the ranch was conceived in a dare. The large room had heard a lot of trash talk. Some boastful. Some idle. A lot of it good-natured. A little downright wicked. Most of it backed up by skill and experience. So when Double Dare officially unveiled a new challenge, life was good.

Cutter raised his voice again.

"You all should know Nipsy and Petra," he said, gesturing first to Double Dare's climbing master next to him, and then to another popular ranch guide with climbing experience. "The three of us will act as 'buddies' for tonight's competitors. We'll accompany each one every step of the challenge, but without participating or interfering unless the safety of the guest requires it."

Since the new challenge previewed on the Double Dare website two days ago, traffic on the site had set a record, and guests had lobbied the owner and staff all weekend to add more spots in the challenge premiere. But Cutter and Nipsy agreed on a small field for the first Geochallenge, especially because of the night setting, in order to test the concept and guarantee a quality experience.

"Okay," Cutter yelled, "here are Double Dare's inaugural Geochallengers . . . First, Serena, come on up and stand with us."

Well-known as a ranch regular by now, the tall blonde, sculpted in skintight Spandex running gear, drew a chorus of hoots, wolf whistles and catcalls as she climbed from the crowd. Feigning embarrassment, she bowed theatrically.

"Another guy many of you know—and that could be good or bad—" said Cutter, smiling, "let's hear it for Deputy Tim Riordan."

Months earlier, a meet-and-greet trip up the Double Dare road qualified the Dolores County Sheriff's deputy as the first resident in the valley to go out of his way to welcome Cutter. Since then, he'd become a real friend. At six-foot-two, he was the beneficiary of nearly constant rigorous law enforcement training, plus all the physical exercise the San Juans could throw at him.

"Tim usually attempts a Double Dare challenge every few weeks," Cutter went on. "In dreaming up new challenges, the staff began to think of them in terms of: Can Tim beat this? I had to remind them that challenges need to be designed for every ability level, or else the ranch will go broke."

The anecdote drew a round of laughs, and raised some eyebrows as well.

"Our third competitor may come as somewhat of a surprise. He's a newcomer to Double Dare, but I've known about Willy Wiltz for a long time. He's one of the best windsurfers in the world. Willy, come on up."

Wiltz lived in the San Francisco Bay Area. Now in his fifties, he still braved the fifty-degree swells slamming outside Crissy Field and the world-class winds that blew through the Golden Gate. When Double Dare announced the Geochallenge, he beat out the crush of takers who raced to register online, and hopped a plane immediately to arrive in time. Stocky, with powerful shoulders and Popeye calves, Wiltz looked to be in excellent physical condition as he joined the group. But he also had just climbed off a plane from sea level, and Cutter made a mental note to keep an eye on him when he started feeling the altitude; to him, it wasn't a question of "if." But he also knew Wiltz to be a gamer.

"Okay," Cutter yelled over the party, "Nipsy, give them the rules one more time."

"Geochallenge," the mountaineer began, "is intended to honor the spirit of geocaching and, in the best traditions of Double Dare Ranch, to test your mental agility and physical stamina. You don't have to be a navigational wizard, or a great climber, or an Ironman—or Ironwoman," he hastily added with a nod to Serena as a crescendo of boos came down from the rafters. "But you need to be a little of all three.

"There are two caches out there. The first, Cooperstown, is rated a 4 on the geocache scale. This scale represents the amount of brainpower it takes to find the cache, as well as the outdoor skills required. The second cache, which Cutter named Nipsy's Drop . . ."

More good-natured jeers pelted the climber.

" . . . is a 5. Now, you say, 'Well, you have three challengers. What's with that?' The backbone of Double Dare is competition. All three challengers will designate here which cache they will go after. Once they are close enough, the first two challengers to lock in the coordinates of their cache on their GPS will then have fifteen minutes each to find it. If they both fail, the third challenger can choose either cache and take the place of that person. If the third challenger doesn't find a cache in fifteen minutes, the challenger on the sidelines can choose to replace either one, and then it's his—or her—turn again. Et cetera, et cetera. In the end, one challenger goes home empty-handed.

"That's why we keep score, folks," he shouted, as the raucousness rained down again.

Cutter stepped up. "I promised Nipsy I'd put up some prizes that would be worth something. Inside the Cooperstown cache is an autographed 1998 Todd Helton Topps rookie baseball card. The person who finds Cooperstown keeps it."

The news drew derisive groans from half the crowd who knew Cutter for the baseball nut he was. Helton was the Colorado Rockies' all-star first baseman, and a Colorado sports hero, but it was just a baseball card. They didn't even come with bubble gum any more. The other half of the group looked at their neighbors with is-that-all-there-is stares.

"And," Cutter continued, undeterred, "with Helton's card also comes a weekend in Denver that includes two seats in my club box at two Rockies games, two nights at the Hotel Teatro and all you can eat and drink." That got the room roaring again.

"Inside the Nipsy's Drop cache is a climber's carabiner. The challenger who finds it can cash it in with me for an all-expense-paid, guided climb by Nipsy of any Fourteener in Colorado they choose.

"That's on Double Dare time, Nipsy," Cutter added, nodding at the man.

"Bitchin', dude." The climber grinned. Nipsy had seen the carabiner when he stashed the bottle in the cliff face. But he knew nothing of its meaning and he shook his boss's hand in thanks for the honor. And in anticipation of a few paid days off.

The crowd grew more restless, eager to start the challenge.

"Remember," Cutter shouted, "as Nipsy explained, each geochallenger will tell us here which cache they plan to go after. But that doesn't mean they're entitled to it; it's first to find, first to keep."

With a look at Tim and Willy, he said, "That said, if you gentlemen don't mind, I'll give the lady the first choice of caches.

"Serena?" Cutter asked, and waited expectantly for her choice.

Chapter 12

The moon rose over Ram Mountain and lit Moccasin Ridge above tree line like an athletic stadium.

The group of six started out from the ranch at about the same hour Cutter and Nipsy had when they set up the Geochallenge. But the adrenaline pumping through the lean bodies of the three challengers, who mostly jogged the course, contributed to a much faster pace. Tim, with Nipsy as his spotter, led most of the way. Not far behind came Serena with her partner, Petra. Willy was sucking air and straggling. As his spotter, Cutter could see after the first mile that the thin air was kicking his ass. He seemed to be enjoying the workout, though, and self-assurance coated him as completely as his sweat.

The Californian's steady, slower pace allowed Cutter plenty of quiet time to turn the night's puzzle over and over in his mind.

He was startled enough when Serena arrived at the ranch that afternoon and he couldn't goad her into another try at the kayak challenge. She said she wanted to try something new that might help rebuild her confidence. It seemed like an excuse.

But then later, when Cutter offered her first choice of geocaches, he was shocked when she chose the obviously easier Cooperstown. That wasn't the aggressive, sassy Serena he thought he knew. First of all, she could walk a few blocks any day of the baseball season and see the Rockies. And, second, he would have bet the ranch she would leap at the challenge to try and beat the two guys to the more difficult and rewarding cache. Cutter didn't get it, and for what must have been the tenth time since they started the Geochallenge, he shook his head in bewilderment.

He and Willy emerged from the forest tree line to a scene that looked positively lunar. A barren world of strewn rock and shadows stretched above them.

Like the others, the pair stopped momentarily to get a quick GPS fix, then began picking their way upward. The light was so bright they could make out the shapes of Serena and Petra, about halfway up the granite scree. Tim and Nipsy were too far ahead to see.

. . . .

The cop and the climber reached the ridgeline as Tim homed in to Nipsy's Drop with his GPS. It took him to the cliff edge, where he realized he had some climbing to do. Tim had thought as much. He noticed at the outset that all three guides carried light climbing gear in their packs, which could have just been for safety reasons. But, he told himself, this was a challenge, right? He peeked over the brink. The moon shone on the cliff face like art lighting on canvas. Nothing that looked like a cache in obvious view, though.

Tim easily found the anchor setup Nipsy had left behind. The climbing master clipped Tim's nylon line into the attached carabiner and gave the rope a few strong tugs to make sure the anchor was set. The sheriff's deputy, who had considerable experience in climbing harnesses from all his police training and mountain rescue, was buckled in and ready to go.

. . . .

For both communication and safety, Nipsy, Petra and Cutter all carried two-way radios. Nothing bugged Cutter more in the wild than to hear his staff or guests talking loudly or blindly shouting each other's names when it wasn't necessary. For him, it broke the natural spell of the outdoors: the wind sighing through the pines and aspens below, like it was now. The babble of a creek. Fall leaves crunching underfoot. There was another reason he preached trail etiquette to his guests, too; they saw a lot more wildlife when they kept conversation to a minimum.

The radio on his lapel clicked and squawked as the other Double Dare spotters checked in.

"Cutter, Petra—we're ready to climb here," Nipsy said.

"Serena's just about ready, too," Petra said. "She's just sweeping for Cooperstown's coordinates. Even though it looks like pretty simple bouldering at this level, I'm going to rope her up to be safe."

"Good move, Pet," Cutter said, his voice clear and strong over the distance. "Willy's got his second wind. We'll keep moving towards the ridgeline so he's in position if either Tim or Serena can't find their caches within the fifteen-minute window. He says he'll go after Cooperstown, if he has the chance, since we come to it first. Squawk me, both of you, when you start climbing."

Only a couple minutes of dead air passed before Cutter's radio squealed again.

"On belay!" Nipsy said. "Climbing!"

Seconds later Petra sang out. "On belay! Climbing!"

. . . .

Tim backed over the edge of Moccasin Ridge. His feet shoulder-width apart and legs tensed, he took another step back and then bounced beyond. He stopped his descent after fifteen feet or so to check his GPS again. He needed to move to his right slightly, and he crabbed his way across the face. On the ridge above, Nipsy kept an eye on the rope to make sure the cliff edge didn't bite too hard into it.

Tim was rappelling again. Nipsy knew he was getting close to the Nalgene bottle and thought to himself that the moonlight should make the orange plastic glow like a buoy against the gray granite.

"Got it!" Tim's triumphant cry rose from below.

Weird, Nipsy thought. He could swear he smelled the faintest whiff of truck brakes burning. As he lifted his head, he heard the snap and ping of metal shearing. Like shrapnel, a piece of the carabiner shot through the night air and sliced the right side of his face.

"Ah-ah-ah," Tim yelled. A split-second of silence, and then his voice below screamed in terror and pain.

Blood spurted from Nipsy's face. He scrambled to look over the cliff.

"Tim! Tim!" Nipsy yelled into the bright night.

The wind whispered back, and it wasn't what the frightened mountaineer strained to hear.

"Aaaaaaaaaaaaahhh," the deputy screamed again. "Hurt . . . bad."

"Tim! Hold on. We'll get you. Hold on!"

Nipsy focused now. He pulled a bandanna from around his neck and began dabbing at the blood that seemed to be coming from a cut on his cheekbone while at the same time he fumbled for the radio. His mind raced. *What the hell happened?* He had checked the anchors. He'd checked them twice. "Cutter! Cutter!" he shouted into the mic. "Tim fell. We've had an accident. Get up here."

Petra's voice broke in. "We're closer. We're on our way, too."

"Nipsy, we'll be right there," Cutter said.

Petra and Serena reached the higher end of the ridge first and Petra immediately started working with Nipsy to clip her ropes into a new harness that could lift Tim when they reached him. They could clearly see him in the glow of the moon, lying crumpled on a ledge maybe sixty to seventy feet below. But they heard nothing. Despite all of their cries and encouragements, the young sheriff's officer hadn't uttered a sound since Nipsy heard him cry out.

"Nipsy, is Tim okay?" Cutter gasped as he clambered over the rocks. "What happened? What happened to you?"

"He had just picked up the bottle, I think," Nipsy said, as he continued working on the ropes. "You know, it was about thirty feet down. And I looked back and all of a sudden a piece of metal tore loose from the anchor sling, just came flying at me. The 'beener or the sling—I don't know which—failed. I'll show you later."

Cutter could see that Nipsy and Petra nearly had the web of ropes ready that would form a harness, and he pulled his rope out to use to lower Nipsy down. There was no arguing that it would be Nipsy, who already had his harness and his pack on, including medical first aid materials. Nipsy rigged a new two-point anchor, tested it firmly, clipped in and disappeared over the cliff edge.

He zipped down the line to Tim in seconds, but he didn't like what he saw when he reached him on the narrow, sharp ledge. Tim lay unconscious. Dark, sticky blood glistened on the rock beneath his right leg, which was twisted at an impossible angle. Nipsy didn't want to move him, didn't want him to hurt. But he had to stop any serious bleeding fast. He moved Tim's left leg to take some weight off the right, but what it revealed turned Nipsy's face white. Tim's femur had shattered and jutted through the skin of Tim's thigh below his athletic shorts.

"Cutter," Nipsy yelled up at the cliff ledge, "it's bad. He's unconscious. Probably in deep shock already. The bone . . . his femur is broken and it's jabbed through the skin. We gotta work fast."

Petra had emergency medical training and after Nipsy relayed up Tim's rope, she and Cutter both joined him on the ledge. On top, Willy used Cutter's satellite phone to begin contacting rescue officials and call in a Flight For Life helicopter. Serena had been silent since she reached the cliff and now sat forlornly on a flat rock. She pulled a long-sleeve fleece around her shoulders, which were shaking beyond control.

Tim's injury was unnerving, as bad as Cutter had ever seen. Petra immediately set about stabilizing him and stopping the bleeding. As she worked, Nipsy pulled his own long-sleeved T-shirt over his head to use as a bandage. She had only heard of Nipsy's terrible namesake scar on his chest. She shuddered when she saw it.

The fit young man beneath her hand moaned softly but didn't regain consciousness.

Within half an hour a muffled *whump-whump-whump* grew steadily louder, and the distinctive orange and yellow chopper swooped over the next ridge like a giant dragonfly. Relying on their GPS coordinates and an emergency beacon from Cutter's pack, the twin-engine Eurocopter 145 picked them out easily.

Infamously brutal high winds and blizzards often held the mountains in their grip and made many rescues difficult. But the calm night, exposed ridge, haunting moonlight and the skills of the three guides on the ledge made this one easy. With the sheriff's deputy strapped inside, the French-built copter peeled away and headed back down the valley. ETA on the emergency helipad at Mercy Medical Center, thirty-four miles away in Cortez, was twenty minutes.

The five remaining adventurers from Double Dare Ranch quietly reassembled on top of the ridge. A couple felt nagging guilt and second-guessed what they could have done. All felt a deep sadness and terrible hurt for their injured friend. Petra said that if Tim had been higher when he had fallen, or had not landed on the ledge, he would likely be dead.

When Nipsy climbed back on top of the ridge, without stopping to remove his harness, he went to Cutter and held before him a shiny but deformed carabiner. The distorted piece of equipment had a hairline crack and the metal actually looked *torn* where a jagged piece was missing. It appeared as if the carabiner clipped into the anchor sling had blown apart.

Nipsy rubbed the cut on his face, which began to bleed again. He tried to visualize again how the accident could have happened. Tim's weight on the rope must have pulled the device apart—something he'd never heard of—just enough for it to snap out of the anchor sling. Then the sudden release of heat and pressure must have allowed it to nearly close again so that it remained on the rope, where Nipsy had found it.

"This is not the 'beener I anchored here, dude," Nipsy said, his voice shaking and elevated only enough for Cutter to hear.

Chapter 13

Four satellite phone calls went out from Moccasin Ridge before the dawn, but none of the callers were aware of the others. Two calls went to the same person.

Minutes after the quiet group of five packed up their gear and dejectedly started down toward the tree line, the rocks and grass close by Nipsy's Drop began to stir unnaturally again. The earth rose into a disheveled lump, from the top of which an eerie turquoise light suddenly glowed.

"Mission accomplished, sir," were the only words murmured, then the phone blinked out.

The person on the other end of the call put his phone down but kept it close by.

. . . .

Like everyone else, Serena walked down the ridge in a state of disbelief. But none of the others imagined how shocked and guilt-wracked she was. She suspected all along that Vuko was something less than a saint. A rough character like him didn't acquire his power and his money without getting his hands dirty, and from the personal contact she'd already had with Radic Vuko she believed he'd been rooting around in the human swamps for some time. But this . . . this was something else. Tim could have been killed, and Vuko had something to do with it. *She* had something to do with it, she quickly reminded herself. It was the chilling, inescapable truth. And she didn't even know how. Or why.

Once into the trees the five hikers spread out their sleeping bags in the spot they chose earlier, and in half-hearted tones bid each other a good, if short, sleep. Serena mumbled to Petra next to her that she needed to pee and walked off into the woods. Once she was a safe distance away she speed-dialed the number on her sat phone.

"Yes," the voice answered, snapping as if he were expecting the call.

"You fucking asshole," she hissed. "You used me. You almost killed a man tonight. He's a cop, you know, you dumbshit. What are you doing,

Rad, what's this whole game you're playing? Hell, that could have been me. How did you know I wouldn't be my stubborn self and pick the other cache? You fuck! You bastard! I don't ever want to speak to you again. I don't ever want to see you cross my path because you're worse than bad luck. You're evil! You used me!" And she threw the phone as hard as she could at the trunk of a thick spruce.

God, she thought, and I almost slept with that *thing*.

. . . .

God, Vuko thought, putting the phone down again, I bet she's a maniac in bed. He thought he might still find out from personal experience.

. . . .

When Serena left her bedroll, Cutter rose and walked away in the opposite direction. He broke out of the thick gambel oak again, fishing out his own phone, and sat down on a boulder. He wasn't surprised to find Sheriff Jeffrey Morningstar, Tim Riordan's boss, awake and already alerted about the accident. Cutter filled him in with details. He didn't mention the doubts that nagged him about the piece of climbing equipment Nipsy had shown him. The sheriff reassured him that Tim was already being prepped for surgery, and gave Cutter the phone number that he asked for.

Cutter clicked his GPS and saw that it was almost three o'clock in the morning. Still, he knew he had to make the call.

He was exhausted, physically and emotionally, after a full day of work at the ranch, the nighttime climb and then the adrenaline-sapping reaction to the accident and rescue. Yet it wasn't the kind of weariness that he usually welcomed at the end of a good day. Anything but. The stump of his leg throbbed dully in its silicone-lined socket. He felt desperate and alone. How could this have happened? He knew the precautions he and Nipsy had taken in setting up the challenge and knew his climbing master didn't make mistakes. Not on such a simple climb. Not ever when it came to safety. And yet his friend lay in the hospital busted up and ready to go under the knife.

And what about Double Dare? Could this close the ranch? Was this the extra ammunition Vuko needed to grab it once and for all? Some bad publicity. Another legal challenge. The thought of that bastard rolling up in the yard, his shit-eating grin leering out the window of the Hummer, made his stomach twist. The thought crushed him. And there was Vernard Ramworthy. Was this all he needed to completely turn the town against him and ruin his dream? Morbidly, Cutter found himself picking the rancher to win over his former boss. If someone was going to beat him, at least Ramworthy's intentions seemed honorable.

Shit. He rubbed his face in both hands, bowed his neck and tried to stretch away the worry that bunched the muscles. Then he powered up the phone and punched in the number.

The man answered.

"Mr. Riordan," he started to tell the father, "my name is Cutter and I run the Double Dare Ranch . . ."

Chapter 14

In the Old West, Cutter thought to himself, they would have called this a lynch mob. He opened the door of Dolores' ritual lunch spot and watering hole, making the familiar little bell tinkle. In modern parlance, he was walking into a town meeting about "issues."

The day after the Moccasin Ridge accident the town buzzed with the news and wonder over what it meant for business in general and Double Dare Ranch in particular. Mort Watson, the mayor of Dolores, presided over an impromptu gathering of mostly the local business community that had been tipped off to hang around after lunch at Watson's restaurant, the Disappointment Café. Despite the name, the food was actually pretty good. The place wryly took its name from an important part of the Plateau's history, the nearby Disappointment Valley. Legend claims that one hot summer day in the late 1800s, when pioneers and settlers looking for a new life pressed westward, a party of surveyors that had run out of water trekked into the mountains in search of a creek they expected to find. Instead, they found a dry creek bed, hence the name—Disappointment Creek.

A century later, it apparently never occurred to Mort that a restaurant by the same name might not exactly instill culinary confidence, no matter how hungry people were.

Cutter knew Vernard Ramworthy probably instigated the gathering. He immediately picked out the old rancher from the crowd, sitting in his usual booth facing the room with Manny, his foreman, Sam Reilly, his lawyer, and Thad Hedges, one of the major land developers in the county.

"It's going to make it even tougher on this valley, I'm telling you," Cutter heard Ramworthy preaching to the coffee crowd as he walked in.

Cutter had been tipped off about the meeting by the sheriff. Both agreed it was better for Cutter to face the town's unease over the accident and be sure at least that they all had the facts and not just Ramworthy's account of what happened.

Cutter knew nearly everyone in the café. He liked most of them and made it a point to try and do business with them all since coming to the valley. It was good for Double Dare, and besides, he believed in keeping his dollars in the community if possible.

The ranch and his business plan behind it had received a mixed greeting from the tight-knit, isolated community when he arrived. The southwest corner of the state, one of the poorest parts of Colorado, was already numbed by the five-year drought. Then the national economy started to slide, the number of tourists began to dwindle, and soon crops and old businesses alike began to dry up and blow away.

Double Dare Ranch not only brought a new enterprise into the valley, but it also helped begin replacing one generation of visitors to the valley with another. These new guests, as they passed through town, needed gas and food and motel rooms when Double Dare was full. But it also became pretty clear in a short time that this new wave of mostly affluent adventurers and young families in SUVs craved the accoutrements of their lifestyle. The past spring a new mountain bike shop, Rim Riders, opened in Dolores. The local grocery market extended its hours and hired more locals to fill them. A new Southwest art gallery survived a decent first season, and a Mexican family that had lived in the valley for three generations opened a restaurant featuring the fiery recipes of their matriarch. The latter created some much-needed alternatives to "The Disappointment," as the locals wryly referred to Watson's café.

Personally, Cutter's favorite hangout was the new Dolores River Brewery. Mark Youngquist, the thirty-something owner, had remodeled what at various times in the building's history had been a post office, liquor store, jail and grocery into a friendly room with a twelve-foot-high copperplate ceiling and the best Extra Special Bitter brew Cutter had tasted.

Still, when Double Dare opened its doors, the mayor was the first in line to slap Cutter on the back and shake his hand. At the opposite end of the reception line stood Ramworthy and a handful of ranchers and business owners who liked the town and pristine valley much the way it had always been. It wasn't so much that they wanted to control it. They just didn't want to see it change. Most of them had lived their entire lives in the area. Their blood and sweat were mixed in the hard, red clay soil, and Cutter understood why they felt so strongly about protecting this precious place. When Double Dare opened, Ramworthy was convinced it would not only change the valley, he seemed to believe Cutter was on some sinister mission to ruin it. More regular-thinking folks saw that didn't make sense. The success of Double Dare depended on protecting everything in the valley that its longtime guardians held dear.

"Well, I guess I'm not surprised to see you here," the white-haired man said across the room to Cutter as he closed the wooden door. "One thing I'll say for you is you don't duck and run."

"Mr. Ramworthy, I'll take that as a compliment coming from you," Cutter replied, deciding to take the respectful route to start. He smiled and added, "I just happened to be in the neighborhood."

"Rii-iight," the other man said, drawing out the word.

"Actually, since so many of you are here," Cutter went on, still standing, "I thought I'd tell you how Tim is doing. I just came from the hospital. As most of you probably know, he underwent surgery early this morning and the doctors said it went really well. His leg is badly broken. But he will walk again, that's the most important thing. They said they could see the steel in him so they expect he's the kind who will do the hard work necessary to eventually lead a normal, active life. You all know Tim, so you know that's probably an understatement."

Ramworthy stood up. The two men faced each other across the room, with friends of both seated in between. Some scrubbed the remains of lunch from their plates with chunks of Mort's Texas toast while others held up thick white coffee cups, signaling for refills.

Ramworthy got right to it.

"Cutter, this valley can't stand another black eye. It can't stand another setback that costs us jobs and our livelihoods and forces families to split and give up and quit this place. It's bad enough with the fires keeping folks away. When you came here you told us your outfit was safe. What the hell happened up there that got that boy so busted up? Because if word gets out that your place is putting people in danger, it's not just your business that's gonna be hurt. Bad news is like cow shit; it doesn't worry much about whose boots it sticks to."

"All we know is that a piece of climbing equipment failed," Cutter explained. "It looks like an accident, but we don't know for sure."

From behind his lunch counter Watson shouted, "What do you mean you don't know if it was an accident? Are you accusing someone of something, Cutter? We don't need that."

"Are you gonna shut that place down until you find out?" someone else yelled.

"Look, Double Dare Ranch has been a damned good neighbor to us all," said a man who also stood. Bryan Boonstra and his wife moved from Iowa to open the Rim Riders Bike Shop. "It has brought business into this valley. It brought me into this valley. Cutter has helped fight fires on nearly every ranch in the county, including yours, Ramworthy. I'm a newcomer, but I trust Cutter enough to know he isn't going to intentionally put anyone in danger."

"I'm not so sure about that," said Sam Reilly, never one to shrink from an opportunity to impress the world—or his largest client—with his skills as an orator. Now he stood alongside Ramworthy. "The entire notion of this Double Dare Ranch is provocative and teeters on the edge of what normal society would deem to be safe or insane. We would all likely describe Tim Riordan as the finest, fittest young man in the Four Corners, and yet look at his fate.

"And I must wonder," said the lawyer, pausing for effect, "what the recent lawsuit against your company portends?"

The café erupted with shouts and chairs being pushed back as half the room seemed to jump up. Cutter couldn't have answered if he wanted to, which he didn't. He had hoped Vuko's legal play wouldn't get dragged into this. It figured Reilly would know.

"Mr. Ramworthy," Cutter finally shouted above the din, "you were there the night we picked the climbs and set up the equipment. You watched us. Was there anything careless or dangerous how we went about it?"

"I didn't see anything wrong or I would have said so. But I can't be watching over every one of your silly games to make sure you don't do something irresponsible."

That did it for Cutter. The two sides blathered back and forth. Nothing was going to be solved here. He knew that when he walked in the door. He hoped to at least head off Ramworthy's accusations and the bad feelings that would likely spring up after, like bindweed, among his neighbors. He had turned over the suspect climbing hardware that Nipsy brought up from the ledge to Michael Antonini to have it analyzed, but he wasn't prepared to lean on that thin straw in this room. Not yet, anyway.

"What's wrong with you people?"

The sharp voice of a woman who had been quietly listening opened a hole in the clamor like a branding iron. Patricia Keeney stood and the rest of the café wisely took it as a hint to shut up.

"Listen to you all. You sound like a bunch of spoiled children. Cutter is a neighbor. A damned fine one, I happen to believe. He's fought fires with me. He helped me deliver calves last spring when he should have been working on his own place.

"Vern Ramworthy," she said, her eyes landing on the rancher across the room like a laser gunsight. "I've known you for an eon, and I've always thought you were a fair and decent man. What you're doing here now is neither fair nor decent. This man has fought fires next to you, on your land.

"Manny," she said, swinging her glare to the rancher's foreman. "Cutter not only fought fire with you, he honored you and your brother by helping to bury him.

"Mort." The woman turned and the restaurant owner seemed to shrink. "Cutter's donated time and money to every cause in this town, and he's put butts in these café seats."

Clearly in a seek-and-destroy mood, Patricia looked around the room for more targets. As she did, Stetsons dipped and eyes suddenly found the crumbs on tables before them extremely interesting.

"We're all a little edgy these days with the fires popping up everywhere and business being so shaky and all. But it's just these times when we need every friend and hand we can trust, and I decided a long time ago I can trust Cutter. He's having some hard times now just like some of you, only different. But I'll tell you: if he goes away, if the Double Dare goes belly up, we'll all be worse off. Not just because we'll miss the money his people bring to town, or the magazine stories that bring the people. We'll miss him. Because he's one of us now. He proved himself to me a long time ago."

She shouldered a tooled-leather bag, plopped a bill on the table, and walked across the silent room to the door. Cutter opened it for her and followed her out.

"Will you marry me?" Cutter said as Patricia paused on the old-fashioned, warped plank sidewalk. It was the first time he had smiled in nearly twenty-four hours.

"Too late," the woman replied, the stern look on her face softening into satisfied creases. "You might have had a chance some years ago."

"I can't tell you how much I appreciate what you did in there, Patricia."

"I meant it."

"I know you did. That's why it means so much to me. Besides that, you bought me some time with them," he said, nodding toward the café.

"Before the peasants storm up the road with torches and pitchforks in the middle of the night, you mean?" It was her turn to smile now. Just as quickly, the mirth in her eyes winked out. "What did you mean in there when you said you 'think' it was an accident? Something more to it than that?"

"Maybe. I should know in a few days."

"Hmm." The woman nodded, head bowed in thought. She adjusted the bag strap on her shoulder. "You know, Cutter, either way it doesn't look good for your outfit."

Chapter 15

"The strategic prerequisites we have initiated are proceeding as plan," Vuko said. With a self-indulgent smirk, he added, "Even better than plan."

He was the only one seated in the fifty or so richly upholstered captain's swivel chairs inside his corporate theater. He spoke at the giant screen—or rather at sixteen different windows projected on the giant screen, each inhabited by the face of one of his private security clients. It was like a Hollywood Squares of Bad and Anti-Social People. Vuko imagined each one with a price tag attached to their face.

A colonel representing the white-supremacist group Defenders of Patriotic Extreme States based in Montana: $3 million.

The head of one of Los Angeles' most violent Hispanic gangs: $1 million.

The owner of a legitimate personal bodyguard service based in New York: $400,000.

A prince in charge of the military of a small emerging nation in central Africa—he might have to make that a house call, Vuko thought: $5 million.

The overly enthusiastic leader of a sheriff's SWAT unit from a small, rich and unsuspecting town in Florida: $50,000.

The rogue's gallery of unsavory characters went on.

Vuko had rounded them all up in a special video conference call to update them on his planned training facility, its logistics and when it would be available for on-site occupation. His audio/video technology enabled him to view all of their faces, but they were not allowed to see him or each other. It was a natural security precaution and rather than anyone feeling slighted or mistrusted by it, they appreciated his company's professionalism.

Instead, on their monitors at home, each of them saw a map of Dolores County, Colorado, USA, a tighter topographic map of the Dolores Valley, color-keyed to designate federal, state and private land, and an array of high-quality photographs displaying all the charms and natural challenges of what he had told his clients would soon be the new headquarters of American Security Training, Inc. Not coincidentally, it looked exactly like Double Dare Ranch.

Once the ranch was his, Vuko rehearsed to himself again, he planned to use it as a base for his new business, which would utilize his skills as a mercenary genius. His own force of handpicked ex-military staff would be free to teach combat and survival training under wilderness conditions. The remote location effectively eliminated any local or federal surveillance, allowing him to engage in the lucrative weapons trafficking market. Able to thoroughly control access into the ranch and at the same time use the rugged trails and forests to reach thousands of miles of empty BLM land, he could even hide and train a small army for a couple days, which is where the big money could be expected. He thought it would only be a matter of time before he put some of the other clandestine private military companies out of business.

"As you see," Vuko explained with an electronic pointer, "the camp is small compared to large private properties surrounding it. That is to our advantage because its size doesn't attract attention from federal authorities or media, and the expanses around it provide natural security and screening from trespassers.

"The beauty of Camp AST," he proudly prattled on, "is its location. It is gateway to one of the largest public wild places in America, which holds some of the toughest training terrain on any continent. At right time of year and with advance site preparedness, we can be same as . . . uh, duplicate, yes? . . . summer desert or high-altitude winter conditions.

"Trust me, gentlemen—and ladies," he added sarcastically, as a bone to the chairwoman of the National Women's Self-Defense League, which was considering holding its annual national convention at the facility, "you can be assured of complete, total privacy, and AST will tailor our training to your individual requirements. Large scale, or small. Live weapons instruction or hand-to-hand tactics. Survival training, instruction in private interrogation techniques—"

"Vuko," the bearded man from Montana interrupted. "This ranch offers the ideal environment to train for the kind of conflict our organization is anticipating. But most of us know that you don't own this place yet. Why should we think you ever will? I need more assurance than your flimsy lawsuit."

Vuko anticipated this question. It was an obvious one. Privately, he knew the intellectual property lawsuit that he threatened against the ranch was a blind. But he relished being able to personally throw it in Cutter's face, all the same.

"It has come to attention that the present business recently experienced a personal injury accident that could result in considerable damages, and that the owner is facing a public relations revolt in town," he replied. "There are too many challenges he faces that I believe will force him to close business and sell property before end of year. To me."

That should have ended the question-and-answer segment of the conference, but the Montana man had other ideas.

"My sources tell me that your background is military. But when I tried to check that out, I hit a wall. Now why would that be, Mr. Vuko?"

"Much work I did in military was classified," he replied smoothly, "so it is not surprising you could not access my *bona fides*."

"Did you work in the Balkans?"

Vuko was shocked. He wasn't going to let this line of questioning go any further.

"I'm afraid our time is expired. I will keep you all briefed of progress here and inform you when project is fully operational. In meantime, I suggest that you arrange your funding so that as soon as we launch, you are in strategic position to schedule immediately. I will be in contact."

He disconnected the call.

What was that redneck doing, Vuko asked himself? What did he know? The guy was ex-Army, too, and the food chain between the military and the mercenary world was direct and active. And potentially dangerous.

It didn't happen often, but Vuko was shaken. He was too much of an egotist to believe that he could be threatened. But there was one dark area in his past that could leave him utterly vulnerable. Prosecutable. Maybe even executable. He would never let himself be taken to face that.

Chapter 16

Cutter listened to what he was being told in utter astonishment.

It was awful news, stomach-turning, and yet it carried some solace for him and certainly would relieve Nipsy's conscience.

Michael Antonini was calling with results of the metallurgy tests on the suspect carabiner.

"Cutter, this isn't our climbing carabiner. Someone must have switched Nipsy's original one out."

It took some extra time because his experts said they had never encountered anything like it before.

"Held in the hand or beaten with another solid object, the stainless steel clip seems indestructible, as it was made to be," the lawyer explained. "But when placed under heavy, sustained stress the metal turns as soft as aluminum. It actually begins to warm and 'sweat' because its molecules decompose. Then it catastrophically fails. Blows apart. The truly ingenious thing is once the pressure is released, the metal recovers. It seems to knit back almost to its original shape and strength. The only explanation, the lab guys say, is that it's special ops—classified military hardware."

The two friends agreed that except for telling Nipsy, Cutter wouldn't share the results with anyone else for now. It wouldn't gain them anything, and news that the ranch suspected someone of tampering with climbing equipment wouldn't exactly instill confidence in the guests.

Nipsy had already personally re-inspected and load-tested every carabiner and every other piece of climbing gear on the property with no failures, and Cutter would instruct him to continue periodic, random checks. *Well, at least Nipsy might start sleeping again at night.*

"Cutter, this can only mean one person did this, almost killed Tim. No one else connected in any way to the ranch has that kind of background. Or motivation."

"Yeah, I know," said Cutter, seething inside. "Vuko."

Chapter 17

The two weeks following the dustup in the Disappointment Café flew by for Cutter. Even though Double Dare hit its first lull in business since it opened, the shoulder season between summer and winter, he and his staff were as busy as ever tending to die-hard guests and conducting final planning for their first season of winter challenges.

The weather gods continued to smile on them and delivered a classic Indian summer. Bluebird-bright sunny days, with cool nights, permitted the last few weeks of sleeping with the windows open. Unfortunately, the West's forests and vast grasslands remained dangerously dry.

In Double Dare's short history, Sunday afternoon marked the ranch's traditional time to kick back. He remembered the Sunday ritual beginning one weekend when Mouse and Grateful Bobby organized an impromptu softball game between staff and guests. When the guests heartily endorsed it, and Cutter had seen the teamwork it built among the staff, he made the game an official weekly Double Dare event. The next Sunday he surprised both teams with a new horse trough full of iced-down beer behind the backstop. After that some of the mountain bikers began cutting their Sunday rides a little short, coming off the Say Hey Trail behind the ranch to watch the game and razz the players. Then the kids who were staying with their parents at the ranch started infiltrating the staff lineup, eager to play alongside their new role models, and some of the town people started driving out at Cutter's invitation.

"Awright, everybody over here," Cutter yelled, trying to organize the crowd. "Especially you folks new to the ranch. Listen up, 'cuz like everything else here, we play this game by Double Dare rules."

The softball field was built on a bluff slightly above and just east of the ranchhouse. As it was only the ranch's first year of operation, they'd only had enough time to till and groom the infield and build a backstop and outfield fence. The fence, as every weekend player worth his or her batting average knew, was a target. Something to take aim at and hopefully pound home runs past. Because of the unusual environment in which Cutter laid out the field, though, it served an added purpose at

Double Dare. Cutter pushed the ten-foot fence back as far as the bluff would allow—a safety barrier preventing a vertical drop more than twenty feet to the Dolores River, as it burbled along the ranch's eastern property edge.

"The first player to hit a ball *out* of this ballpark was Grateful Bobby, in the first game. He hit three home runs and for that he is banned for life," he said with dramatic seriousness. "We can't afford to fill the Dolores with softballs. A shot *over* the fence is an automatic out."

Groans from the crowd. And a few boos.

"So how do you hit a home run here?" asked a guest who had just run up from the ropes course.

"Line drives, or outfield errors," said Cutter. "If you look close you can see the fence is *raised* two feet off the ground. It puts a premium on cutting off the gaps and good defense. It's a home run here if the ball goes *under* the fence."

Every week or two, a staff member drew the duty of walking the river and retrieving the softballs washed up on the rocks below the bluff.

"I know," Cutter said with a satisfied grin, relishing the teams' grudging compliments. "It's the perfect softball field."

As the players took some outfield flies to warm up, he couldn't help notice the puffs of dust they kicked up in the outfield buffalo grass, a somber reminder of how dry it remained. Cutter shook his head, his smile fleeting, trying to remember the last time it had rained more than a few pitiful drops. This year the usual afternoon fall squalls seemed to bring more lightning than moisture.

He grabbed a growler of Dolores River Brewery RyePA—Rye Pale Ale—poured a glass, and with the ever-present Maggie at his heels, started looking for their special guest. He stopped to help write the kids into the lineup. It was Petra's turn to be official scorer, and the final box score would be posted after in the ranchhouse and on Double Dare's website for the regulars who weren't here this weekend.

He chatted with some of the gear-heads about new mountain bike technology. Frequently, the ranch and all of the Four Corners area were test grounds for many of the high-end bike manufacturers. A visiting sales rep for one company had heard tales of Double Dare's collection of bikes kept for guests and asked Cutter if he could see the stable. Cutter walked him to an enormous two-story, gambrel-roofed barn, fitted with twelve-foot-high double sliding doors. He shoved back one of the doors mounted on overhead rails and flipped a switch that lit up the interior like a new car showroom. Only this was bigger.

"It isn't quite as big as REI, but when those boys and girls want to have some fun, some of them come here."

The bike man gaped in awe. Inside the cavernous barn there appeared to be every brand of mountain bike, downhill and cross-country ski, snowmobile, all-terrain-vehicle, kayak, canoe and piece of gleaming climbing gear that could possibly exist. And, in most cases, there were a dozen of each.

Moving on, Cutter saw Serena and Mouse each gathering river information from kayakers who had undertaken the challenge of the Dolores earlier in the day. No one had picked up all three coups yet this summer, and Cutter made a mental note to ask Mouse if it was time to ease up just a little on his coup positions. Serena caught his glance and gave him a wave and a look that promised she'd find him soon. He realized it was the first time he'd seen her since the geocache disaster.

The party hum grew and took on a happy glow. Horseshoes clinked in the background. A group of young boys and girls laughed as they retold stories about the paintball challenge they played earlier in the forest.

Ahead a ring of people gathered around what Cutter guessed would be Grateful Bobby and Nipsy demonstrating the fine points of Hunker Down, another much-loved ranch game. Inside the ring the two contestants each balanced precariously on his own four-inch wide metal ammo can, approximately forty feet apart. Each held one end of an even longer piece of one-inch climbing rope between them. Basically, the game was a two-man tug-o-war. Had they been standing on the ground, Nipsy would have no chance against the brawny foreman. But the balance required to stay atop the ammo can—the object of the game—instantly neutralized any advantage in size. In fact, both men teetered uncertainly just waiting for the signal to start the match.

Someone in the crowd counted down and then the war was on. Bobby started with a wicked jerk of the line, thinking he might catch Nipsy off-guard. But the smaller man anticipated the move and let the line slide through his leathery hands. Surprised by the slack line, Bobby flailed backward and struggled to maintain his perch. Seeing his opportunity, Nipsy reeled the cord back, adding to Bobby's troubles. But the big man bent his knees, lowering his center of gravity, and with one rippled arm outstretched for added balance, he tightened his grip on the line with the other hand like a clamp. Now Nipsy had to recover, shifting his weight back as the rope suddenly stopped. The two took turns with false pulls and feints, hoping their adversary would overreact and throw off his own balance. But as they did so Nipsy slyly took in the line a few inches with each pull and parry until soon Bobby found himself literally at the end of his rope. Desperate, he tried to yank Nipsy off in one game-saving tug. But again the canny climber anticipated Bobby's tactic and let the cord simply slide through his palms. Bobby completely lost it and tumbled backward, landing with a grunt as the crowd yelled its appreciation for Nipsy's sleight of hand.

Cutter laughed out loud, even after having watched this rivalry played over and over each Sunday. He searched the circle of faces standing or sprawled around the combatants. Not finding the one he looked for, he moved along, knowing his two foremen and their challengers would go on like this for hours.

One of the ranch hands passed by with a platter of breaded Rocky Mountain oysters, the West's original hors d'oeuvre, and Cutter snagged one succulent mouthful. He realized then he was starving and all the cooking smells seemed to bloom around him at once. Sizzling elk steaks and buffalo burgers. Tangy chicken and morning-caught trout. Fresh corn on the grill and artichokes in the pot, and Western Slope peach pie waiting at the finish line.

Folks tried to look casual as they headed for Lexi's grill and buffet line.

He should have expected to find Tim Riordan camped out close to the food. The sheriff's deputy reclined on a long Adirondack lounge with his full-length leg cast elevated on top of a little Everest of pillows. Cutter might have also located his friend by looking for all the pretty girls at the party since they were all waiting hand and foot on him. Lexi had just delivered a plate stacked with enough red meat to feed a wolf litter, and Serena arrived with a frosty RyePA.

"Where are the native girls that are supposed to be dropping grapes one by one into your mouth?" Cutter kidded him. "I swear I'll have them switched when I find them."

"Well, they were just here, but they had to go adjust their coconuts," Tim laughed.

"How's the leg?" said Cutter, extending his hand. He had visited Tim several times in the hospital but knew this was one of his first days getting around in the world again.

"I'm doing good, Cutter. The doc is proud of his handiwork in surgery. He told me to get my appetite back and we'd start serious rehab in a few weeks. That's going to be tough, I know, but it beats lying around. The sheriff came by and said he was going to move this lounge into the jail and make me answer phones."

Cutter filled his own plate with chow and rejoined Tim. Cutter caught him up on news at the ranch, and the deputy explained that when he got back on his feet the department planned to send him to some special evidence-recovery training until he could return to more active duty.

As the people around them migrated toward the food, Cutter finally brought up the subject he ached to speak with his friend about.

"Tim, I've told you how sorry I am about the fall, and you have no idea how badly I feel that Double Dare had anything to do with it."

"Cutter, you know I don't blame you or Nipsy or anyone. I put myself in that position. No one held a gun at my head. I've never heard of a carabiner failing like that, but with the law of averages, I guess it had to happen sometime."

"I want to tell you something that only Nipsy and one other person know about," Cutter said, lowering his voice. "But if anyone knows, it should be you. I've got proof that that carabiner didn't fail by accident. I had it sent away for analysis, and the results proved that our carabiner was switched out. The metal is an alloy that was specially . . ." he paused, grasping for the right word. " . . . *designed*, I guess. Designed to fail when placed under a certain load or pressure. The lab had never seen anything like it before. The only place it could have come from, they believe, is the military." The two men wore the same puzzled, concerned looks.

"But who . . .?" Tim started.

"I've got my ideas about the 'who.' But I don't have any way yet to trace the carabiner to him. I'm working on that. I will definitely keep you informed. Unless you feel differently, or unless as a law enforcement officer you think there's a better way to handle it, I'd like to keep this between us until my legal people can come up with something. Of course, I'll take care of all the medical bills and expenses . . ."

"Cutter, I know you well enough, that's the last thing I have to worry about. But if anyone intentionally did this, I want to see them caught. They should face charges for attempted murder," Tim said, his tone certain and intense. "I could have been killed. Someone else could have been killed. Is someone after you, or the ranch?"

Cutter didn't want to name names yet, or throw around suspicions, even with Tim. Not until he had more to go on.

With perfect timing, Serena strolled back and sat with them. Cutter and Tim exchanged glances, and Cutter shook his head slightly to indicate he had not shared the information with her.

"Tim, since it's just the three of us, I want to tell you how terrible I felt that night you fell," Serena said. "I'd do anything to have that night back to do over again."

"Serena, you have no reason to blame yourself," Tim replied. "You couldn't have changed anything. It's okay."

"I know. But I just feel so bad," she said as moisture started to well in her ultra-blue eyes. "Tim, I . . . I wish . . . I didn't . . ." She bowed her head and two tears plopped into the paper plate in her lap.

Cutter understood how she felt, but once again to him the young woman seemed to be overreacting. She acted as if she held herself personally responsible. She looked deeply upset.

"Serena," Cutter said, "I need a beer. Walk over with me?"

Turning to him, she sniffed and smiled self-consciously, nodding her head, not trusting herself to speak more.

"Tim, don't run off," Cutter kidded his buddy, who waved him away.

He and Serena headed back toward the softball field. They didn't notice Lexi pause in mid-serving in the food line, tracking the pair as they walked away together.

"He's good, huh," Cutter said, reassuring Serena. "Tim's tough. He's going to be fine."

"I know," she said. "I just feel so responsible."

"Serena," he said, turning to her and grasping both her shoulders in his hands as he looked directly into her anguished eyes. "You had nothing to do with it. Let it go."

"Oh, what do you know?!" her voice lashed out at him, taking him aback. Now her eyes blazed at him. "You have no idea how I feel."

But she never finished. Instead, she turned and marched away through the milling crowd of ballplayers, staff and partiers.

She did it again, Cutter thought, baffling him with her actions and her words. He shook his head. *She really did blame herself. What the hell . . .?*

"Cutter."

Chapter 18

He turned to find Lexi standing behind him brandishing a serving spoon dripping with barbecue sauce.

"What's going on between you two?" she demanded, her eyes flashing with suspicion.

"What?"

"Every time I look, you and Serena have your heads together. What's going on? What are you doing?"

"What am I *doing?*" he repeated, lowering his voice and closing the distance between them. "Right now I'm looking at you like you're a madwoman. What's wrong with you? I was talking to a guest, a guest who happens to still be very upset from witnessing Tim's accident. And you're walking around yelling at me like some jealous fishwife. What is it?"

"Maybe I have reason to be jealous," she snapped back. "Maybe I'm tired of watching the two of you dance around each other like dogs in heat, and the two of you getting pretty emotional out here. I'm tired of it, Cutter."

And then it was her turn to stalk off.

I really want that beer now.

"Cutter."

What now? This can't be happening to me.

"Hi, Patricia," he said, turning to find his Two Havens neighbor studying him. "Tell me, is there a sign on my back that says 'Line forms here to kick Cutter's butt?'"

She played along, smiling, looking around at his backside.

"No sign. I'm thinking you're just some kind of masochist, because every time I meet you, someone is telling you what a dumbshit you are."

He grinned. "Would you like a beer? Before Lexi comes back with my deer rifle and an instruction manual on how to shoot it."

The days were growing shorter and this one was waning. They walked to the beer trough, arriving at the softball diamond just in time to see the sun slip over the horizon and a line drive to right-center skip under the fence and over the bluff.

"Staff 11, Guests 10," Petra yelled.

Behind them lights covered by multi-colored parchment bowls and hung from the eaves of the ranchhouse glowed and bobbed softly in the evening breeze. The crickets and frogs warmed up their duet down by the river, and the first few bats came out to test people's night vision and imagination. Some folks packed up food and gear, and the mellow sounds of twilight goodbyes and truck doors thunking shut signaled the evening's end.

Suddenly, he saw people everywhere running back toward the picnic area. The sandy circle where laughing combatants had squared off all afternoon in Hunker Down clearly became the epicenter. As Cutter looked down from the softball field, the bodies jostling for a vantage point around the day's final pair swelled from a single ring of people to two-deep. Then four-deep. Then Cutter started running, too, the screeches and grunts from the two opponents growing louder with every stride.

. . . .

Lexi walked away from Cutter at the picnic angry and dissatisfied. She hadn't gone looking for Serena. But as she weaved through the throng of plate- and drink-carrying neighbors and guests, the tawny sway of hair and straight-backed carriage of the other woman suddenly loomed ahead of her.

Without hesitation, she tapped one of the broad shoulders with the serving spoon she still carried. Brownish-orange barbecue sauce smeared Serena's skin and the white strap of her tank top.

"What do you think you're doing?" Lexi said. She was surprised when Serena turned to find her palming tears from her face.

"Huh? Lexi . . . What do you mean? Look, let's not do this now."

"What's your interest in Cutter? He says there's nothing going on between you two. That's not what it looks like to me."

"Okay. Okay. If you want this. First of all, I happen to like Cutter. I could like him a lot. But to him, I'm just a guest, a customer. Secondly, who the hell do you think you are challenging me?" She eyed the stainless spoon Lexi still held poised. "Are you going to do something with that?"

Unaware she still held the spoon, Lexi tossed it aside. The simple act snapped her out of her rage, and she registered the stunned looks she and Serena were drawing from people forced to walk around them. Over Serena's shoulder, she saw the Hunker Down circle. Empty. Inviting.

"From what I hear, you're bad luck when it comes to challenges," she said, still staring past Serena. "You panicked in your kayak at Snaggletooth, and you almost got someone killed in Geocache."

Serena's eyes bore into Lexi, and she closed the space between them. When Lexi didn't flinch, or shift her view from something behind her, Serena turned to see what she was looking at.

"Now?" Serena asked.

"Now."

. . . .

Head bowed so that her thick, black mane draped over all of her face except one eye, Lexi glared down the rope at Serena. The blonde woman flexed her tall, lithe frame slightly up, then down, on the metal can, seeking her balance point.

Casting quick, furtive peeks out the corners of her eyes, to both sides, Lexi suddenly realized what a scene they were creating. People she knew from all over the valley, people she worked with, cheered and jeered for action. *Oh, my Lord, this has turned into one of those Wild West catfights. Not what Cutter would like.*

Lexi jerked the rope, thinking she might catch Serena off guard and end the contest quickly. Then she relaxed her hands, anticipating the less experienced woman to take the bait and pull back.

Serena didn't disappoint, yanking hard, and yelping out loud when she nearly tumbled backward with no resistance.

"Cute," Serena said when she had recovered.

"Maybe smart," Lexi answered at the other end of the rope. "How many times do you think I've watched these oafs play Hunker Down, and how many times have you tried it?"

The answer: hundreds, and never.

The two women exchanged false yanks and tugs as they unconsciously slipped into another Hunker Down tradition: talking smack. The crowd around them howled with delight. A hole opened in the packed perimeter and Cutter popped into the front row. He wasn't smiling.

"So is that supposed to be a Double Dare trick? Act like you know what you're doing so I'll start doubting myself?" With that, Serena followed up a false tug with a powerful pull that nearly caught Lexi with her weight wrong.

"Not bad," she said when she regained balance, still wobbling precariously on the four-inch wide can. "I think you doubted yourself when you drove up the road, sweetheart."

Lexi tried to shake the hair out of her face, and sweat flew. Serena leaned downward to mop her forehead on her bicep, afraid to take either hand off the rope for an instant.

"You don't know me. What's this supposed to prove anyway?"

"It won't prove anything. Maybe just put you in your place. In the dirt."

The circle of friends and strangers oooh-ed like a knockout punch had landed.

Serena reacted as Lexi hoped she would. Serena repeated the strategy that almost toppled her a few minutes before—faked a hard pull, exaggerating the motion, and then used both arms and shoulders to try and drag her off her perch. Lexi waited for it. This time when Serena put her weight into the second pull, Lexi let her have the rope—all of it—and she sprawled backward into the sand with an angry shriek.

Lexi and Cutter reached Serena, slouched in defeat, at the same time. They each extended a hand to help the woman up. She ignored them both and scrambled to her feet. The crowd, most of them unaware of the personal stakes that were in play, melted away.

"I guess you win," Serena said, her eyes flashing from Lexi to Cutter. The tears were gone and replaced by a flinty defiance.

She brushed sand from her sweaty skin. Where it had caked to the barbecue smear on one shoulder, it formed a greasy, gritty poultice. She scraped it off with her hand, then wiped her hand on Lexi's Double Dare shirt front. Her lips curled into a bitter, damn-you-anyway smile.

"It really doesn't matter. It doesn't change anything." She brushed past them. "It's okay, Cutter. I'll still be around."

Chapter 19

The wolves were returning to Colorado. Many people in the southern reaches of the Dolores Valley had seen sign of the ghostly hunters, or heard their mournful howl fests at night.

Cutter rehearsed his plan, as the pickup rumbled toward the ranch at the end of the dusty road, and as Grateful Bobby explained once again what was at stake.

"The Division of Wildlife is considering catching and releasing at least one wolf," his friend explained. "The DOW is opposed to reintroduction. But it figures if it can implant a tracking chip under one wolf's hide, it can begin to plot where they're hanging out and how many there are."

Bobby had talked of little else for the past few weeks. Cutter knew the issues.

Lobo, as the Spanish first called the desert wolf, was reintroduced to the Apache National Forest in southern New Mexico in 1998. The notion that some could have crept north into the edges of Colorado in the years since was not only possible, but likely. It was just a matter of time, the wildlife experts said. Local ranchers grudgingly agreed. The state began working on a plan to make the homecoming manageable to all parties.

Wolves and ranchers didn't get along. They never had and never would, the herders swore. Too many lost calves and lambs to the predators, and that became even more of an issue now with such expensive genetics bred into their herds and flocks. Losing a calf in the early 1900s meant a family went without a meal or two. Losing one today could cost a ranch thousands of dollars in research and kill a breeding line that went back generations.

Cutter thought he knew one rancher old enough to have heard the wolves' mournful cries outside his window at night as a boy, and who might believe the West was less of a place without them. It gave Cutter the idea for a very special Double Dare challenge with numerous possible benefits.

That rancher lived tucked back in the valley ahead.

"Do you think he'll go for it?" Grateful Bobby asked for the tenth time that morning.

"I visited Ram Mountain Ranch once nearly two years ago after I bought what was to become Double Dare," Cutter replied. "I went to pay my respects to a longtime valley resident, who opposed the sale, and tried to patch up the hard feelings. He seemed to appreciate the gesture of acknowledging him as an important neighbor. Let's just say he stopped short of sending me off with any fresh-baked goods. He still believes the land could be put to better use than to entertain pests from the city."

Cutter restlessly shifted his hands on the wheel. "We're about to find out if Vernard Ramworthy is as crusty as he seems or if he's what's left of the real American West."

The ranch buildings, like Ramworthy, were showing their age a bit, Cutter thought as they drove through the gate with a massive bighorn skull and rack mounted on the log crossbeam. The big house with gable windows, which had to be nearly a century old, needed a good scraping and several coats of white paint. But the yard and grounds were neat and the stock pens sturdily built and recently repaired with rough-cut boards that would take another year for the weather to turn from blonde to gray.

As they turned into the yard in front of the house, Cutter caught sight of something behind the barn he hadn't seen on his first visit—the unmistakable tips of the rotor fans of a helicopter. *I wonder who flies that pretty little bird?*

He had phoned ahead and Ramworthy and his foreman, Manny, stood leaning on the posts of the wide covered porch. They all knew each other and after some stiff greetings they moved to some intricately woven willow chairs, and Cutter got right to the point.

"Mr. Ramworthy, how would you like to trap a wolf?" he asked.

The old man looked slowly from Cutter to Bobby to Manny, and then back to Cutter. He gave a sharp snort that signaled to Cutter he considered him either crazy or unqualified. Still without saying a word, the rancher pushed himself out of his chair, opened the wooden screen front door and let it bang behind him as he entered the house. Two of the three men left on the porch stared dumbly at each other. Manny smiled. Only a minute or two passed and Ramworthy returned carrying something in one gnarled brown-spotted hand.

The framed photograph, aged in sepia tones, showed a man standing with a grimly satisfied smile beside a barn. On the wall was nailed the hide of what Cutter took to be a big coyote or a smallish wolf. At the top of the photo, printed in neat, black-inked letters onto the white sky, read: **Cecil Ramworthy, Conejos County, 1945.**

"There are no wolves in Colorado," the rancher said in a raspy voice. "That was the last one, and my father shot it through the head sixty years ago."

Cutter marveled at the rough, sad piece of western Americana. It was a time before environmentalists, a time when ranchers took action against nature's threats to their home and property. It was life.

"It was different back then, wasn't it?" Cutter said, looking thoughtfully at the photograph, not really asking a question or expecting an answer.

"It was better, some would say," Ramworthy replied. "I'm not one of them, really. Life was hard. Like you say, it was different. Oh, I miss the great herds of elk and deer, and the isolation we had. Here, it was as if no one else but you and people you knew lived on the planet. But life does change, and you have to go forward. We don't have children dying of tuberculosis or scarlet fever in town, and a young man like Tim Riordan won't have to be a cripple the rest of his life. A lot of old people say they miss the good old days. But it's usually because they just don't remember the bad old days that went with them."

In Cutter's experience, that represented a state of the union address for Ramworthy, and it startled him. He couldn't decide what impressed him more—his wisdom, or his willingness to share it. He never thought of Ramworthy as an enemy. He seemed more like someone who didn't know him and what he was about, and so he hadn't been given the opportunity yet to offer or withhold his trust.

"So, do you believe the wolves are coming back? That people around here have seen them?"

Ramworthy looked at Cutter as if his steely gaze could bore through him.

"Yep," he said, finally.

Beside him, the Mexican foreman silently nodded his agreement.

"We want to find out for sure," Cutter said, turning quickly to Grateful Bobby and back again. "If we can talk the DOW into the idea that it's in everyone's best interests to at least know if the wolf has returned to Colorado, can we tell them that you'll allow us to try to trap one on your land? It's the biggest spread in this area and the southern border fits the wolf habitat. For my part, I'll pay all the expenses, take care of the insurance, daily checks, that stuff.

"My only request of you and the DOW is to allow me to include a small number of Double Dare guests in the experience—learning how a wolf might be captured, helping with the set up, and if we're successful, letting them observe the implanting and release by the DOW and help with the monitoring. Heck, it's free labor. We both know how monotonous such tracking can be."

"More games, Cutter?"

"Look, Mr. Ramworthy, whatever you think of my outfit, this is a chance to expose people who care, people whom I think you will approve of, to an important part of the wildlife history and natural environment of this country. It could change the lives of some city dwellers, if you want to look at it that way. I'm not doing this for money, or ego, or even thrills. Is it personal? Yeah—as personal as it is for you. I think we both have personal feelings about this land or we wouldn't be here. It's too hard a life for someone who doesn't care about it."

From under the brim of his sweat-stained straw cowboy hat, Ramworthy matched Cutter's hard stare. Then looked to each of the others in the small circle.

"Okay," he finally said. "Make your call to the DOW. Tell 'em we'll look for the wolf in Alkali Canyon."

Chapter 20

Lexi took the phone call and instantly wanted to throw up.

"Lexi, hi, it's Serena. I wanted to make a reservation for this weekend. I want to try the kayak challenge again, too, please."

She made small talk that nearly killed her. She didn't even consider telling Cutter that Serena called.

She and Cutter had hardly spoken with each other since their argument at the picnic. Neither did anything dramatic. They slept in the same bed, but clutched opposite edges of it, warily jerking away from each other if they happened to touch. During the day they walked around each other as if they were avoiding a crime scene, each hoping—and dreading—that the other would break the stony silence. If misery loves company, they were the perfect couple.

. . . .

He found the reservation written in Lexi's elaborate script. He felt as if he'd just stepped on a land mine and couldn't move for fear of it exploding. He decided to tread softly into the subject—the subject being *them*—by a safer route.

"Lexi," he said, speaking her name for the first time in days, "have you heard the weather forecast for this weekend?"

The look he got back said stormy.

"Look," he said, throwing up his hands, shedding all pretense, "Are we ever going to talk? Are you going to tell me what's going on?"

"You still haven't told me what's going on," she said, black eyes darting, "with her."

"Lexi, you're seeing things that aren't there. Serena is a client. Period. What ever gave you reason to believe anything else? We've never betrayed each other."

His words made her flinch. She dropped her eyes to the bed sheets she was folding.

"You're always talking to her. She's always around you whenever she's here. She seems to be something you want."

. . . .

Truthfully, Lexi admitted to herself, Cutter's naïve American notion of what might constitute a betrayal erased all worry in her about the other woman. He had no idea of the true darkness of betrayal. A sexual tryst would be a small thing compared to the guilt she dragged around these days, ever since Darko sent her to this place. She had fallen in love with Cutter. Deeply, undeniably, foolishly in love. It should never have been this way.

Lexi didn't plan to come to America with her uncle so many years ago. When he found her in Budapest, she realized now, he was the desperate one. He shocked her with the news of the massacre of her parents in Vukovar, and when he explained that her younger brother—her beloved Tito—was likely dead as well, she collapsed as waves of grief broke over her. No, she couldn't imagine where to start looking for little Tito. He convinced her that because they were probably the only ones remaining of the Magyar clan, that they needed each other. Like many of her Croatian friends, she dreamed of one day traveling to the United States, of gazing up at the mythic Statue of Liberty, walking the fabled streets of New York and, fantasy of fantasies, somehow finding a way to live and remain there. She knew she was smart and she discovered her life's passion in the cooking schools. Could it ever be possible—a chef? In America? Darko promised it for her. They were the family now, he said.

Once in America, he made sure she continued her training at the best culinary institutes that the most food-obsessed nation in the world could offer. Bright, young, attractive, talented—she had the whole package, as they said here. Her career took off: New York. Chicago. San Francisco. And then Aspen. But after a year or two she grew weary of the fly-in friends and all-night parties. When Darko called to say he knew of a job in southern Colorado and that it included the chance to run her first kitchen at an exclusive resort, she asked jokingly whom she had to sleep with. She laughed; he didn't.

"The one thing you will promise me, on your mother's grave," he told her sternly, "is never to speak of me to anyone at this ranch. They are never to hear of me. You may never tell of any Darko. Never."

He made such a big thing out of it. It would bind the two of them to the lives they left behind in their homeland, he said, because everything there now was dead.

Once Cutter offered her the job, her uncle said it would be easy for them to remain in touch, but only by satellite phone. When they talked, he always asked about the ranch, how bookings were going, if the business was succeeding. When Cutter asked her to accompany him to Denver the first time and she told Darko, he suggested they meet—but only privately, and she could not tell Cutter.

Who am I to make this good man think of betrayals? I doubt Cutter has ever even cheated at cards, never mind at love.

She didn't know why Darko was so obsessed by Double Dare Ranch, but she hated the secrets she hid and how it made her feel. How could someone be so happy with someone they lived with, and yet so unhappy in life? But this wasn't really her life, or her dream. It was the life Darko pointed her toward, and it was Cutter's dream. What did *she* really want?

It wasn't this rough, leathery, ranch life. She longed for finer things. The silver settings of Denver. The shops of New York. The kitchens of Paris. Each day that she lived in this wild country, she only dreamed of being farther from it. Cutter was wed to this land of red dirt and sage, sudden blizzards and surprise blazes, stubborn men and strong women. When she answered his ad and cooked for him that day, she thought that she could lure him away to a different life. Her kind of life. Darko encouraged her to do it. But she couldn't wait any longer. She could see no *dobar dan*—no good day—ahead for her in this charade.

. . . .

"Lexi, I don't want Serena. I have you and everything I want right here," she heard him say, breaking her reverie. He wrapped her in his arms. "You have to believe me. You also have to understand that I have a business to run, and treating the people who come here as friends and not just customers is something I will always do. I want it to be part of the feel of this place. It's another thing that sets it apart. When Serena comes this weekend, I will welcome her. I will encourage her when she gets in her kayak. I won't be sleeping with her. That's not on the ranch menu," he said, his eyes brightening.

Looking up, Lexi smiled back at him. He kissed her, softly at first, then with a deeper fervor. She kissed him in return. As she did, she began thinking about how she would leave him.

Chapter 21

They agreed to an early start, heading into what they all hoped would prove to be reborn wolf country, and it was still dark when Cutter drove a nearly full Double Dare van through the Ram Mountain gate to pick up the owner. He had saved the shotgun seat for Ramworthy, and as the rancher climbed in, the interior dome threw weak light on the rear passengers, his special guests from Double Dare.

"Well, well," the rancher said in surprise, looking into the sleepy-eyed faces of eight children. A few he recognized as local kids, especially one, a blind boy he knew was named Peter. "This wasn't what I expected when you said you were inviting guests."

"This isn't about money or privilege," Cutter answered. "For me, it's about saving something important. For them," he said, with a nod toward the back.

"Mornin'," Ramworthy said to them all.

They mimicked his greeting, with a few sleepy-eyed "sirs" thrown in for good measure.

Cutter had never seen Ramworthy look so pleased.

"Well, come on, Cutter," said the rancher, "let's go find us some wolves."

The silver van, followed by the flatbed pickup carrying Grateful Bobby, Manny and a large aluminum crate strapped in back, pulled onto the county road and headed south.

. . . .

Ramworthy chose some broken-up rocky netherland—between forest and desert—that spilled out of Alkali Canyon at the remote edges of his ranch as the place to bait the wolf trap. Geology and erosion had heaved and eaten away the rough country so that it looked as if a giant tan blanket had been carelessly tossed over the land and it had fallen in fold after rugged fold. Pinyon-juniper and sage, yucca and low cactus, thistle and blacktip senecio fought for survival with dry wild grasses. The rancher believed the maze of arroyos and choked ravines to be the ideal hideout for new dens.

"Scrubby country," Grateful Bobby observed as he got out of the pickup.

"Does anything live here?" asked one of the Double Dare kids visiting from the city, the breeze blowing his hair around his face.

"Deer. Antelope. Coyotes. Javelina. Pikas. Rabbits. Rattlers. Some wild horses," Ramworthy answered. "And, at least a long time ago, wolves."

"What happened to them all?" asked a young Hispanic girl from Dolores, keeping up the barrage of questions the kids peppered the rancher with. After they got past the gruff exterior, they found someone just like their grandpa.

"They were killed off," he said, looking far away. "The ranchers didn't like them eating their cows and sheep. They thought the wolves were all bad. There used to be different species of wolves throughout Colorado. But about one hundred years ago the territorial government placed a bounty—"

"What's a bounty?" the girl piped up.

"It's like a reward." Ramworthy smiled, not holding back. "For every wolf scalp and set of ears someone brought in, they paid fifty cents. Then it went up to two dollars. Within about forty years, the wolves were all gone. Shot or poisoned. But a few smart men caught the last five known Mexican wolves and put them in zoos so they could reproduce." The rancher seemed to think twice.

"Reproduce means, uh . . ." he started.

"We know what it means," Peter said, saving him, as the pack of kids broke out in giggles and howls.

"Well then," he said with a flustered frown, "from these five wolves, the pack was re-stocked until it was healthy enough that some Mexican grays could be released into New Mexico and Arizona about seven years ago. That's where we think our wolves are going to come from."

"When will they be here?" another boy asked.

"We hope . . ." Ramworthy caught himself. "We think they are in parts of Colorado now. That's what you're going to help us find out. But it could take time."

Ramworthy listened as Grateful Bobby proposed setting the trap in a small cluster of PJ but within view of the jeep road so it could be easily checked. The trap would have to be monitored daily, and he had worked out a schedule for himself, the Division of Wildlife and hands from the Double Dare and Ram Mountain ranches to divide the trips. The kids were assigned days as well—locals during the week after school, the city kids on weekends when they were visiting Double Dare. He showed everyone the implant and tracking equipment and explained what would be done once they caught the wolf. He reminded everyone that could be tomorrow, or the next day, or the next week.

With a man on each corner of the crate and the little people crowding in between, they shuffled it into position. A Mexican gray was smaller than its northern cousin, the timber wolf, and typically weighed fifty to ninety pounds. The spring-loaded wire mesh gate on the aluminum box was about four-feet square; the box's length was about six feet. A haunch of deer meat would be hung at the far end of the ventilated box, which allowed the breezes to carry the gamey scent outside.

Ramworthy spent much of the day observing the group—children and adults. Peter, the redheaded teenager, impressed him. Born blind, he was friends with all the kids, and their unofficial leader, despite his blindness. Bright, inquisitive and brave, he refused to use his disability as an excuse. His pals admired him for his surprising deeds, like his mastery of Double Dare's ropes course, a feat Ramworthy promised himself he had to see. Adults were drawn by the boy's surprising insights.

As the rest of the group moved away from the trap, Peter remained. "I want to feel the inside," he said.

"What?" Grateful Bobby asked. "Why?"

"I want to feel what it's like inside," the teenager said again as if it was as natural a request as any of the others.

Immediately, every other kid wanted to do the same.

"Absolutely," said Ramworthy, eyeing the boy.

With Bobby manning the open gate as a precaution, Peter climbed into the box and began to explore the sides and corners with his hands. Ramworthy tried to put himself in the boy's place, imagining what his eyes could not see. Peter crawled all the way to the back, discovering the hanging clamp that would eventually hold the bait. He clambered back out, and without comment seated himself on the parched grass next to the old rancher while the rest of the mob each took their turn.

"Peter, what did you find?"

"I just wanted to feel what a wolf would feel like in there. I know we're trying to catch one for good reasons, but he won't know that. He won't *see* that. I should know what that feels like. It's like when I first tried the ropes course at Double Dare Ranch. Cutter asked me if I wanted to feel what it's like to climb in a high place. He gave me the chance I might never have had."

Ramworthy knew about the ropes course and understood the lessons it held. He also knew a little about Peter from stories in the local newspaper reporting the awards and school recognition he'd earned, but he'd never talked at length with the boy before. An idea came to him.

"Peter, what does Double Dare Ranch mean to you?"

"That's a good question, Mr. Ramworthy. At first I thought it was going to be just a bunch of games for little kids, or kind of a dude ranch for city people. But its real purpose is to challenge yourself. Cutter . . . Mr. Cutter . . . didn't have to bring us kids along today. I bet he could have really impressed some of the city people by taking them on a wolf hunt, even though it's not really a hunt. He asked me what I thought about the idea a bunch of weeks ago and I said that I'd like to go because it might help save the wolves. He said that's why he wanted to do it, too.

"Excuse me. I'm going to go help them put the bait in now," Peter said, and then he was gone, following the voices over to the trap.

The rancher felt like he had just been taught a serious lesson. A blind teenager, of all people, forced him to consider that he might not be seeing things as clearly as he believed.

Chapter 22

The river felt different to Serena.

She was in a mood, all right. She was determined to successfully complete the challenge, but at the same time she was dangerously detached. She drove the kayak through the whitewater like a dagger one moment, then coasted along like a tourist the next.

She had been reading more about the river valley. She didn't often enjoy poetry, but she discovered one passage from a faded, cloth-bound book in Double Dare's library. The poem was called "Dolores," written by Alfred Castner King, a lover of the Southwest, more than a hundred years ago. The poem's ending haunted her like a song that she couldn't get out of her head.

But the river still mourns for its people
With weird and disconsolate flow,
Dolores, The River of Sorrow,
Dolores, The River of Woe.

A sad poem, to be sure. Serena couldn't decide what it described better—the river country and the strange disappearance of its native ancestors centuries ago, or the portent she felt in the waters today.

The Dolores ran lower and colder than on her previous visits. It had been a long time since it had taken Serena more than one attempt to accomplish anything. Besides her golden hair and long legs, she had been born smart and stubborn, and the combination proved a blessing and a curse. As she had driven west on I-70 out of Denver, she was stunned when she realized that she was about to make her *second* attempt at mastering the Dolores and Mouse's wicked course. She *never* needed a second chance. Seven hours later, as she hummed down Colo. 145 outside Telluride heading south to Dolores, she still hadn't shaken the surprise of it.

What the hell is wrong with me? Her mind pinballed back and forth, as it had for the past weeks, between Vuko, Tim, Cutter and life's great mysteries. She hadn't spoken with any of them. Vuko phoned her nearly every day, but she screened her calls and didn't return his. She was still shocked she'd been his pawn.

And then she came home one night after a walk to find a single piece of cream-colored stationery lying on her granite kitchen counter. She had no idea where it came from.

The initials **R.V.** in the letterhead instantly chilled and warned her.

My dear Serena,

Did you think this would be so easy? Do you still wish to command your own business, or are you content to go on slaving so that others may have what they desire? We had a deal. Live up to it. And we can both still have what we want.

Your friend,

Radic

His words made her skin crawl, just as his voice did when she'd heard it over the sat phone on the ridge. She twisted the paper into a ball and jammed it into the breast pocket of her periwinkle-blue fleece vest, banishing it from her sight.

She would have liked to talk with Tim again and check on his recuperation. But every time she thought of calling him, her stomach fluttered as if she had swallowed a live trout.

As for Cutter, he carefully greeted her when she arrived the night before, which came as no surprise considering the last impression she'd made at the ranch—the embarrassing Hunker Down debacle. *How could I let Lexi humiliate me like that?*

Cutter told her that he wanted to watch her kayak run today, but he was nowhere in sight at the put-in. Ninety minutes of river later, she had to think hard just to recall the last bend of rapids she'd passed through. She was out of it.

With each paddle stroke, two red-flagged carabiners clinked together on her float jacket. That much at least gave her some satisfaction. Mouse hinted a couple times the night before that he was thinking of changing the kayak course for this last run of the season, citing lower flow and new rocks that were showing. She knew immediately he was testing the water with her, gauging if she would welcome or detest an easier course.

Thank God, it didn't look like the river master had made anything easier so far. That would have been the ultimate humiliation.

Serena began to feel better, as if she'd rediscovered some of her old swagger. The Grandfathers, the bedroom-sized boulders that hid the third coup and guarded the final stretch of the river before

Snaggletooth, lay just ahead. The water would be different now, she told herself one more time.

. . . .

"Lexi, I'm headed to the river to check out Serena's kayak run," Cutter said, as he headed for the ranchhouse door.

The look she gave him confirmed that winter was truly on the way. Despite their shaky truce, the relationship remained strained, and his plans seemed only to tighten the day.

Damn it, Cutter swore to himself as he hurried across the porch to his pickup, this was business. Even if at one point he had momentarily considered exploring the signals Serena was sending him—he'd thought about it, he confessed—he never acted upon it. *I want a personal relationship at a certain level with my best clients. It's how I build trust and confidence, the way I run this business, and damn it—I'm not going to apologize for that.* He stomped on the gas pedal, leaving a rooster tail of road dust behind.

Once the Dolores River rushed past the shoulder of Double Dare Ranch, it continued its run northwest between Ram Mountain and Two Havens. The gravel county road crossed Bradfield Bridge, named after one of the valley's most respected original ranchers, and Cutter followed it up from the river bottom into the town of Cahone on U.S. 491 to the town of Dove Creek. There he turned back east again to reach the river and access to the put-ins and pull-outs that Double Dare and commercial rafters used. The road zigged and zagged around harvested fields of hay, alfalfa and beans. Cutter's mind slipped into cruise control and he used the spare minutes to think over a dozen ranch details. He didn't register the plume of dust coming toward him until both vehicles reached the "T" that funneled toward the river.

Cutter swung the silver pickup hard into the turn at the same time the other driver did, and both vehicles raised a cloud of dust so soupy that neither could see. Both drivers slammed to a stop. Before the beige grit in the air could even settle, Cutter gave Maggie the "Stay!" command and tore out of the cab on a mission to explain in vivid language the rules of driving backcountry roads.

He couldn't believe his eyes.

Out of the swirling dust he saw a black Hummer and man in camouflaged fatigues.

"Vuko. Ahhh, shit." He spit grit.

"Cutter, where you going so fast?" the other man said with a jackal's smirk.

As the two old adversaries glared at each other, the words seemed to hang in the air with the dust.

"Get out of here, Vuko, I'm working," Cutter snapped and turned to get back in the truck.

"You know, you have nasty habit of telling me what I do. It goes back a long way. Like on canyon rim, this isn't even your land. And you don't have your Chief and his tribe with you this time."

Cutter looked at the ragged hole left in the Hummer's rear panel and felt a tickle of satisfaction. He heard the scuff of dirt as Vuko took a couple steps toward him, a clear message that a roadside confrontation was what the man had come for. Cutter's stomach dropped.

Vuko's steps brought the Australian shepherd to the open window of the truck. Cutter saw her ears pull back as she glared at the stranger.

Vuko wants this, what the hell. We might as well spill all the poison, years of it, in the middle of the road. We're alone. Whatever happens, no one loses or gains anything. We both get the satisfaction of spitting in each other's face, grinding home how much we despise each other. Who will know? It will just be one more ugly episode. Because there's no way in hell either of us will ever give in.

He turned back to face Vuko and waited. The dust settled. The only sounds were the shrill *peee-eeep* of a red-tail hawk overhead, the wind threading through the range grass and the random ticking of the two truck engines as they cooled.

Vuko's face cracked with a wide, malevolent smile, as if the moment could not be sweeter.

"What are you doing here?" Cutter asked.

"It is free country, remember? I am here to support a friend, a woman who's playing one of your silly games on the river. You know, I've always thought this *ranch* is bullshit. A bunch of spoiled sissies leaping around in woods, then hugging each other after about how rugged it was, how tough, over their gourmet dinner and wine. These people could not survive in wild, save themselves, any more than they could live through war. They make child's play. But, I make business associate of one of them. Actually, I'm just trying to get in her pants."

"Serena?" Cutter asked, incredulous, ignoring the rest of Vuko's diatribe but unable to resist the personal bait.

"Yes, Serena, sure. You so surprised, Cutter. You think she's too refined for old soldier like me, eh? Or maybe you had ideas about getting your own piece of her? We are business acquaintances, she and I. She couldn't resist my charms, you see."

Cutter wasn't quite sure what the revelation really meant, but he knew it couldn't be a coincidence. He'd sort that out later. But it likely meant Vuko's appearance here wasn't by chance. Cutter turned again to leave.

"Why you hurry, Cutter? We could probably settle this whole ranch thing right here. That's what it's always been about, right? Look, I even make you offer again to buy you out, we can avoid the whole court thing. Five million, what do you say?"

"Vuko, are you crazy? Let me re-phrase that, since the answer to that has always been obvious. Do you really think this is about money? Did you ever think that? If so, you've got an even smaller mind than I thought."

. . . .

Vuko stilled himself. *Not yet. This is too good. I would like so much to beat this simpering cur. That may still happen. But I dream for too long to make this too quick.*

"It's about my idea, that's what it's all about," he said. "I took you into business. I taught you everything you know about outdoor survival, ropes business, and even about being a man. You were a gifted outdoors trainer. You had physical endurance of camel—even for a man on one leg." He motioned toward Cutter's prosthesis. "We could have made lots of money together. I told you how. The only thing keeping you back—still today, right now—is it is just a big game to you.

"Remember those talks we used to have, Cutter, after we worked our asses off all day and night? We'd close the gate after the last corporate baby pissed himself up on the high line, and we'd turn out the lights, and we'd go back in the shed and crack beers, and we'd talk about dreams. About building a most excellent, private complex that really tested men and prepared them for—"

"No!" Cutter snapped. "That's your interpretation of it. You had . . . you have, I guess, this warped vision of preparing an army for . . . for I don't know what. Of holding this power over people. I don't know what you're afraid of, who you think is chasing you, or threatening those of us who live normal lives in this country—"

"Normal? You call your life normal, Cutter? You're not even forty.

Big millionaire. You have everything world can offer. You're out here playing in woods with your friends like nothing is bad in world. Well, Rad is here to remind you there is bunch of bad out there. I want what you have, it's as simple as that."

"You could have had it," Cutter said. "But you never listened to my part of the dream. You never accepted it. I want to challenge human capabilities and have some fun, not train a bunch of thugs to line your pockets. You were never satisfied with the idea of running a legitimate business. One that built up people, all kinds of people—young ones, old ones, weak ones, broken ones . . . women."

. . . .

Cutter stopped himself as the night in the equipment shed years ago came hurtling back. The girl, Nicole, was an attractive Colorado State co-ed who Vuko had hired part-time to schedule customers and fetch and store the huge amount of climbing gear used by the business—the Rocky Mountain Tactical Ropes Course. Earlier that afternoon, he and Vuko had yet another argument over how something should be done.

"We talked of this. Many times. I'm not running schoolhouse," Cutter remembered Vuko instructing him.

"And I'm not interested in joining your little army," he replied, shoving a coiled rope into Vuko's chest. "I quit."

Cutter waited until later that same night to return to the ropes course to clear out his personal equipment. As soon as he killed the lights of his battered Chevy pickup, he was concerned. The ropes course arena sat on the outskirts of Fort Collins, where there were no streetlights. Yet a dull glow from the lone window of the gear shed marred the moonless night.

As he approached the shed, Cutter saw that the door had been left slightly ajar, and he could hear what sounded like an injured animal. Whimpering. A gasp. A dull *thwack* as if someone had thrown raw hamburger against a wall. Unable to imagine what he'd find inside, he stooped to pick up a four-inch thick fence pole that was lying next to the shed. Its wood was cracked and splintered from exposure.

He pushed the door inward and stepped through.

Vuko stood over Nicole, his back to Cutter. Both the attacker and his prey were clothed. Even though clipped short, the hair at the base of Vuko's neck was dark and matted with sweat. The bullish man's shoulders bunched and heaved beneath his muscle shirt as he gulped air. Powerful arms bowed out from his body. His fists clenched—open, closed, open, closed.

The young woman's nose was smeared and bloody and the left side of her face looked scraped and already starting to bruise. She held both arms crossed over her chest. Cutter didn't know if the man had snapped and beat her over some slight, or if he was walking in on a rape attempt.

Nicole's eyes darted to Cutter, and Vuko turned. Cutter braced himself as he cocked the fence pole over his shoulder like a Louisville Slugger.

Vuko started toward him and, his voice quaking with rage and contempt, muttered, "I dare you. You don't have the . . ."

The treated greenwood pole struck the left forearm Vuko threw up to defend himself with a hollow thunk, snapping the bone before plowing on. Cutter's downward, hacking swing raked the side of his former boss's head, cleaving away most of his left ear, leaving it hanging by its gristly lobe. Vuko collapsed in a heap as blood pulsed down his neck.

"Never dare someone who runs on one leg."

"I'll get you," Vuko moaned as he tried to sit up. He couldn't, slumping to the floor again. "I'll get . . . you."

Cutter ignored him as he helped Nicole up. She lurched on rubbery legs and he curled his arm around her shoulders for support and steered her outside. Her arms were all that held her torn, bloodstained blouse around her.

Behind them, Vuko staggered into the shed doorway, bracing himself with his one functioning arm. "I'll make you not forget this, Cutter," he said. He coughed and spit blood. "You'll need more than wood club the next time I see you. That ranch you're always talking about that's so important to you: if you ever get it, I swear I will take it. I'll . . ."

Cutter watched as the man's knees buckled and he slid down the doorway, painting it black with blood in the night gloom.

"I'll beat you like girl for this." Then Vuko pitched forward and lay still.

Cutter didn't doubt Vuko's threats for one moment.

. . . .

Cutter snapped back to the present. He remembered something else. Feeling ashamed that he ever had anything to do with Vuko. He felt the warm flush of regret and anger flood his face again. And he remembered the day, only weeks ago, up on the canyon rim when Vuko confirmed his cruelty once again.

Now they faced each other less than six feet apart.

. . . .

Suddenly, Vuko rocked back and then forward, convulsing in strange, hacking laughter. He rested both hands on his knees and glared at Cutter. His head tilted down, but his eyes were locked on Cutter. Sunlight glared white off the slabby skin missing an ear.

Confused, Cutter took a step forward, both arms bent slightly, balling his hands into hard fists.

Then Vuko, reining his crazed cackle into a taunting, self-assured grin, spoke the three words he had saved for this one exquisite moment of payback.

"I dare you," he said slowly, letting the words do all the damage that he could. Finally, after all the years, he reveled in the satisfaction of replaying the scene in the ropes course shed. *It will be different this time. I'll get what I want. I'll beat you to a pulp, and take your bloody ranch.*

. . . .

Cutter understood. Vuko's words made him tense every muscle. They felt tighter than piano wire. Then he relaxed.

"You did it again," he said. He leaned forward slightly, and chose his next words. "You dared me. That didn't work out so well for you the last time. Or . . . maybe you didn't hear me."

It sounded hollow. But it was all he could think to say that he thought might inflict real pain in the other man.

The words seemed to burn Vuko like an acid bath. His face bloomed red, and his eyes sharpened.

Cutter expected to be attacked and Vuko didn't disappoint. Cutter knew his only chance was to try and end this quickly. He feinted with his right fist and tried to catch Vuko with a left. As Cutter swung through air, two words Vuko had just spoke echoed like an alarm: *child's play.*

The ex-military man let Cutter's momentum carry him past, leaving him off-balance, and then he drove both hands, fingers interlocked, into Cutter's exposed back and kidneys. The force of the blow splayed out Cutter in the middle of the dirt road, helpless to protect himself. Groaning in agony, he rolled over slightly and struggled to get up. Vuko took a step next to him, pulled back one leg and drove his black field boot into Cutter's abdomen. The woosh of air pushed out of Cutter's lungs brought a maniacal smile to Vuko's face. He cocked his leg for another kick when the dog launched out of the truck window like a rust-colored rocket.

Maggie's leap from the cab caused her to drop to her stomach when she hit the ground, but that was just part of the blur. Vuko heard her coming and instinctively his right hand went to his hip, reaching for the service gun that wasn't there. To the already very pissed-off shepherd, it was like holding out a T-bone. She weighed only 40 pounds, but her breed was all hips and jaws. She clamped onto his hand and began a vicious tug-o-war, bracing her powerful rear legs in the dirt as her neck jerked and her teeth gnawed. Vuko screamed as blood stained the dog's snout crimson. He tried to kick the bitch off, but his first attempt was a panicked, ill-timed swipe that missed. He knew if he was to have anything more than a claw left he must get her off fast. He pulled his hand and the dog in front of him and this time his heavy leather boot caught her squarely in the ribs, sending her flying with a yelp of pain as she let loose. She cried out again when she landed, and then lay whimpering, breathing hard.

Cutter struggled to get to his elbows and knees, fighting just to breathe. He began to panic, collapsing, and Vuko moved in to do more damage. But a low, threatening growl from the dog behind him and the blazing pain in his shredded hand discouraged him. He had done his work well enough. Those who saw Cutter later wouldn't find a mark on his face, but he'd be pissing blood for a week.

Cutter slumped back into the warm brown earth like roadkill, afraid to move, afraid the electricity would arc through his back again. Vuko knelt down on all fours, bringing his face down to Cutter's.

"I want you gone," Vuko said.

Through a mist of vivid pain, Cutter tried to summon words. "You'll have to take it from me in court," he gasped.

Vuko shook his head, a storm building on his face again. He knew many stubborn men. He was one of them.

"Believe me," he said, "it won't get to court. That's your second warning in the last five minutes."

Cutter's eyes closed. He barely heard the boots shift and stir the dirt, the metallic thunk of a door and the throaty rush of the truck engine coming to life. Vuko left the same way he arrived, the rear treads of the Hummer spraying Cutter's body in the road with dirt. Cutter wasn't conscious enough to care.

. . . .

Serena's red kayak sliced between the first two Grandfathers, stained black by river spray but only half as high as on her last trip. *The water is different.*

She timed her visit with a second and final release of water this year from McPhee Dam. Even though the flow ran lower, Mouse's course was true so far. She knew now that she'd find the third coup exactly where it was before when it eluded her. She also knew she would have Snaggletooth to deal with again.

On her first failed run, the Dolores had spilled up onto both banks like an over-filled sluice. Now she saw some stretches along the river's edges where smaller rocks sat bald and dry, so she kept the kayak in the main channel. What used to be Class V rapids were reduced to III and even II. With less maneuvering to do, she found herself cutting quickly through the labyrinth. It wouldn't be long now. One more hard-right bend to the river . . . Serena could hear Snaggletooth's roar now . . . with a few aggressive slices of her paddle, she cut off the corner and the kayak shot through the aqua-green water. Her eyes went directly to the spot where the prize should be, strung on invisible fishing line. *Where was it?*

No red, no sparkling metal. Her pulse quickened, and she muscled brace strokes with her paddle to slow down the racing craft and buy her some time.

Where was it?

Something glinted at the edge of her peripheral vision and she looked right. As she studied the river above the channel leading into the waterfall, she swore. The now haunting refrain echoed again: *the water is different.*

In the middle of the river a rock island some fifty yards long, with shocks of willow stranded on it waving in the breeze, had emerged with the Dolores forking in two strong flows around it. Probably Class III on either side. At the far tip of the island was a boulder about the size of a Volkswagen. This must have been the boulder, hidden beneath the much higher flow, which sabotaged her attempt to reach the third coup weeks ago. Now it sat, beached, a monument to her failure and her rising panic now. She should have pulled over to the bank upriver and scouted Snaggletooth, Serena told herself, but she thought she knew what to expect of the river.

The sparkle that first caught her eye twinkled again as the carabiner danced in the light breeze, reflecting a sliver of sun. She tracked it to its source—on the opposite side of the rock island. In her eagerness to make the last turn, the kayak's speed had taken her more than halfway down the left side of the unexpected island. The flow was still too fast to paddle back the way she had come, which would have made access to the coup and entry into Snaggletooth easier and safer. The carabiner hung across the river and was parallel with the big rock marking the tip of the island. Thinking more tactically now, she allowed for additional, smaller rocks below it. Her only option was to continue down the left side of the island, turn right below the boulder and then stroke like a maniac against the river's current to reach the right bank before the Dolores blasted her over Snaggletooth. She couldn't shake the sickening image of sliding over the waterfall backwards in the kayak.

This wasn't a game anymore, Serena told herself. This was one of those honest-to-shit, real-life gambles she'd read about other stupid experts taking on a rock climb or an out-of-bounds snowboard run. She damned well better get it right.

"Screw it," she said aloud. *It's not worth a broken neck.*

She tread water easily for a few more strokes. Now it felt like a no-brainer: she'd slip over to the nearby bank, pull her kayak out and call it quits for this season. She could walk up to the road and follow it a quarter mile to the pretty grotto beneath Snaggletooth where her friends were waiting.

It took her only a moment to process this idea, then discard it. Then she turned downriver.

Oh my God, Serena thought as the current grabbed the kayak.

The red boat instantly drew even with the big rock. Snaggletooth was as loud and greedy as a giant drain immediately below, and she dug the blade into the current in deep, desperate strokes. She paddled as fast and hard as she ever had. She felt her heart pounding in her chest. The kayak's nose peeked past the boulder. The red neckerchief and carabiner were dead ahead, but a deep sadness struck Serena when she realized that she would never make it.

Suddenly she couldn't move her leaden arms. Her neck ached from strain. Another outdoors commandment came to her*: never ski the toughest black-diamond trail on the last run of the day.*

She'd been on the river too long. Her strokes became sloppy, shallow and, finally, weak. In a final, heart-pounding attempt to reach shore, any shore, she pivoted the kayak and pointed it downriver but diagonally toward the right bank between the coup—a forgotten trifle—

and Snaggletooth's gaping slot. She prayed for the bucking current to work for her and save her life. It worked. The frenzied flow and her feeble strokes drove her to the river's edge. But the kayak's nose bounced off the slick, rocky bank and Serena lacked the strength to brace the boat closer. She threw the paddle towards the bank in panic and lunged half into the water as she tried to grab and hold onto one of the rocks. But her spray-skirt, the rubber gasket that sealed watertight the shell hole she sat in, still snuggly held her in the boat. The Dolores swung the kayak back into its icy grasp. Serena flailed in the water as she slipped backwards toward the twenty-foot-tall waterfall.

It was pure luck, or the beneficence of the Blessed Mother for whom the river was named, that caused the kayak to shoot across the maw of Snaggletooth at a right angle and, instead of going over, wedge in the narrow slot like a springtime log. Serena now hung nearly upside down over the frothy white abyss, still trapped in the boat by the tough rubber spray-skirt. She dangled there, shocked and helpless, as the river cascaded over, under and around the boat.

Below, Mouse, Double Dare's river master, and a score of staff and guests who jumped up excitedly at the first glimpse of the red-hulled kayak, just as quickly bit off their yips and cheers as they watched in horror as the river pummeled Serena and the boat. It was like watching video of a tsunami wave rolling toward a busy beach, the former Olympic kayaker said after, and knowing you could do nothing to help.

Serena was in an even more dangerous position than if she had gone over Snaggletooth. She could drown where she was, or at any second the kayak could break free and cartwheel off the rock shaft below. Neither her plastic helmet nor her spine was built for that sort of punishment. She was beyond terror. She felt a fleeting, crazy rush of hope, like waking to find the doctor pulling the electric-shock paddles away from her heart, and she didn't wait an instant longer.

Serena tore at the taut black rubber gasket holding her in the kayak, pulling loose one corner, then another. Her body weight and the pounding water did the rest: She tumbled awkwardly out of the kayak amid screams and cries of friends. Amazingly, she didn't so much as graze the moss-streaked sandstone walls before she slammed into the pool.

Mouse had already steered the yellow paddleboat halfway across when Serena burst to the surface only feet away. Mouth agape, Grateful Bobby watched with the other spectators in the grotto, as she fought the river. When she was close enough, he grabbed her flotation vest at the shoulders and yanked her out of the water like a sodden rag doll. Above the pool the red kayak shifted in the notch for a few expectant seconds before the torrent spit it out like a watermelon seed. It spindled into the water beneath the falls with a puny anticlimactic splash.

"Are you alright?" Mouse shouted in her face. "What hurts?"

"My hands," Serena said. Peeling off her gloves, she held up bloody fingers, the nails ripped by the river rocks.

Mouse peered into the pale face that looked out from an insulated blanket. They both were still shaking.

The usually glib river master had been uncharacteristically somber since pulling her out of the river. Silently, he held up three fingers and tilted his head with raised, questioning eyebrows.

Serena began to cry, and held up two fingers.

. . . .

The silver Double Dare flatbed pulled away from the river. The yellow raft and a fleet of wildly colored kayaks, including Serena's, lay stacked like fat crayons on a trailer behind it. As the truck crested the knoll at the top of the river pull-out, the three faces in the front seat—Mouse, Grateful Bobby and Serena—registered surprise to find Double Dare's boss stretched out in the sage and lamb's tongue at the side of the road, gently stroking his little red dog. Mouse slowly steered the flatbed over even with Cutter and casually leaned out the window. Maggie stirred as if to get up, whined, and seemed to think better of it.

"Hey, Cutter," the river master greeted him. "Goofing off again? Where have you been, we missed you. Man, you would not believe what Serena just did. You would not believe what just happened. You missed all the excitement."

Squinting up into the sun from what to Mouse looked like a stiff, twisted position, Cutter replied rather weakly.

"Well, I was having a little excitement of my own."

He struggled to push himself up on one arm, scattering weed dust on sunbeams, and Mouse heard him bite down on a sharp gasp. Cutter looked up again, as pale as a corpse, and then fell backwards. The people inside the truck scrambled out of the cab as quickly as if they'd found a rattlesnake under the floormats.

Chapter 23

"It only hurts," Cutter smiled, for what seemed like the one-hundredth time that a staff member stopped by the porch to check on him, "when I move anything."

By the next day everyone at Double Dare knew that the Boss and Maggie had both fallen somewhere near the river and were busted up. They'd live, but neither would be laughing or barking out loud for a while.

The town doc checked out Cutter and diagnosed him as having a severely bruised kidney, bruised lower back muscles and a cracked rib. The purple-red contusions and surface abrasions were so extensive, though, he wondered aloud how they could result from a simple fall.

"It's a mystery," Cutter agreed, tight-lipped.

As in many small rural towns, the local MD was a practitioner of true general medicine, and he examined Maggie on the same visit to the ranch, on the same table. Vuko's kick had cracked two of the Aussie's ribs, but she didn't seem to have suffered any internal injuries. Cutter knew that if the dog hadn't treated Vuko's hand as if it were a chew-toy, he would have suffered much more damage.

Three days later, Cutter was tired of retelling the story he had hastily made up. Something about getting tangled up with each other climbing out of the truck cab at the river, Cutter skipping his back off the door jam and then falling on the dog. There was no point in telling anyone about the fight. It would only launch Grateful Bobby on a seek-and-destroy mission from which no one could call him back.

Cutter may have looked incapacitated, sitting in one of the willow rockers as the last hummingbirds of the season whirred from one feeder to another on the porch. But for the first time since Vuko reappeared, Cutter felt like he held some of the cards. He knew secrets now he didn't know a few weeks ago. For the first time, he possessed the beginnings of a strategy. For the first time, he felt like he was in The Game.

Cutter's satellite phone buzzed at his side.

"Cutter," said Michael Antonini, "I found Nicole."

"Where? How?"

"She's a stripper at the Diamond Cabaret in Denver. And the reason she disappeared eight years ago? Vuko sent his goons to the hospital with an offer of twenty thousand dollars if she didn't press charges. She just went away."

The news stunned Cutter. But it fell in place with what Vuko had let slip during the fight.

"I ran into Vuko a couple days ago. Literally."

"I heard you had an 'accident.' Who looks worse?"

"It's got to be me," Cutter said, grimacing. "Michael, I'm convinced Vuko never intended to take us to court as a way to get Double Dare. He's a psychopath. But he's also educated and intelligent, and so obsessed with taking the ranch that he would never back off if he thought his lawsuit would do it. But yesterday, while he was busy kicking my ass, he said 'Believe me: it won't get to court.' Just like that." Cutter could still feel the rank spittle on his face.

"He's bluffing us," the attorney said. "The thing is, with the right judge, this intellectual property claim might work. So why isn't Vuko pushing it?"

"I think it's because a courtroom is the *last place* he wants to have to walk into. Somebody's got some serious dirt on him somewhere. Have we really, really looked hard into his record? What else has he got in his past, Michael? What is he afraid of? You've got to look harder."

The two friends were also convinced that Vuko was somehow responsible for the defective carabiner that nearly killed Tim Riordan. It was the only explanation. The metallurgy tests proved conclusively that the equipment had been intentionally *manufactured* to fail.

All these nightmares didn't start occurring around the ranch until Vuko dragged his knuckles onto the property, Cutter thought.

"Vuko is behind it all," Cutter said. "I don't know how. He must have pulled it out of his military bag of tricks. We may not be able to prove that, but it's time to deliver the little surprise to Vuko that we know we *can* prove. You know what I'm talking about. Let's drop a lawsuit on his desk and see how he likes it."

They finalized plans and hung up.

After a few minutes speaking with Antonini, Cutter's back muscles were screaming. By the end of the call, he was nearly doubled over in pain. His severed leg was one of his few body parts that didn't ache. Tentatively, he leaned forward in the rocker, trying to stretch and lengthen out the pain, and got back a sharper stab than he asked for. It was okay. A couple days—at the most—on the porch, he told himself. And he was getting things done. Unraveling secrets. There was one more remaining.

Just then, he spotted a telltale plume of dust in the valley below that signaled a vehicle heading to Double Dare.

Serena would have to wait.

. . . .

Minutes later a dualie pickup appropriately adorned with the ram brand passed under the gate and pulled up in the yard. Vernard Ramworthy, with Manny riding shotgun, eased his way out of the cab and stepped onto the deck.

"Morning, Mr. Ramworthy. Manny," Cutter nodded. "Sorry if I don't get up, but I did a stupid thing yesterday and fell and—"

"Yeah, sure, whatever you say, Cutter," the white-haired rancher said, clearly dismissing his story. "I heard you fell out of your truck and I just wanted to come over and see if that was humanly possible for a semi-coordinated, grown man." He smiled, and Cutter matched him, giving up.

"Really, I didn't come over here to nursemaid you. But I figured while you were settin' still it might be a good time for us to settle this water thing between us. I've been thinking about it. I've been watching what you've done with this place. I watched you with those kids the other day, getting them involved with the wolves. Especially the blind boy, Peter. I see now what you're doing, and I understand it. I think it's alright. The river season's about over this year," he said, looking up like an arthritic hound sniffing the weather, "but next spring, you can count on using the Dolores across my place."

Cutter couldn't have been more dumbstruck if the rancher had used a cattle prod on him.

. . . .

The "water thing," as Ramworthy called it, had been his contention that he owned the riverbed and course that the Dolores River traveled through his property. Many longtime landowners in the West with rivers and streams passing through their property agreed with him. It had been the subject of lawsuits, fistfights and worse for years. The current-day boom in recreational water sports had only complicated matters. Some particularly prickly landowners had taken to stringing fence and barbed wire across streams and under bridges. Ramworthy had been more civil, but every bit as determined, about defending what he saw as his right when Cutter moved into the neighborhood. On a day just like this one more than a year before, as carpenters and fence builders and painters scrambled to build Double Dare, the rancher drove up and told him how it was going to be.

"Cutter, I won't allow your rafters or your fishermen or anyone just looking for a place to piss to come through my property on the Dolores," he said straight-out. It was the first time they had met or spoken directly to one another.

Cutter had spent enough time on public and private wildlands and waters to understand the issue, and also to know that Ramworthy was probably pushing his case beyond normal practices. As long as recreational boaters stayed in their canoes and kayaks on the river, it wasn't trespassing; as soon as they stepped onto private property on the riverbank, though, an unfriendly landowner could send his dogs out first and ask questions later. Cutter expected to have this discussion, but with Ramworthy it hadn't lasted long enough to be called a real discussion.

A small ranch, Double Dare was only one hundred and sixty acres, the size of an original homestead. Compared to the neighboring ranches, Double Dare bordered a relatively short portion of the river. After passing by Double Dare, the river continued on to divide the Ram Mountain and Two Haven spreads, and then below them splash across public land once again. Double Dare's access usually satisfied most of the guests who fly-fished, and the kayakers and rafters found it challenging enough to practice on. For long river trips, though, Cutter trucked his guests and their gear down to the put-in and avoided altogether any confrontations with his new neighbors, until they had a chance to size up each other.

"Mr. Ramworthy," he said that day, "I understand your concerns and we won't cross your land on the river. We're going to use the public put-in."

"Hmmmph. Okay," he said and turned to leave. But Cutter stuck his hand out to shake, feeling pretty sure it wasn't in the old man's code to ignore the gesture as long as he saw it as a genuine one. Surprised, Ramworthy looked down at the outstretched hand, and then took it. Without another word, he climbed back into his truck.

. . . .

Now it was Cutter who looked down, surprised to find the other man's leathery, knotted hand stretched out to him. He gripped it firmly and the two men of the land, young and older, held each other's eyes. They understood one another.

"I would have been over earlier," Ramworthy finally said, "but, damn it, we had to put out another fire. Small one. Must have been smolderin' overnight from last night's lightnin'. Manny spotted it over in Narragu-innep Canyon and we got over there quick before it could do anything. Sonofabitch, Cutter, we shouldn't still be fightin' fires this late."

"Have you ever seen it this dry here, this long?"

"Yeah, I have," the rancher said, pulling the straw Stetson off his head and raking fingers through his snow-white mane of fine hair. "It didn't turn out too good. We've been lucky to get through this summer without a big one."

He got up to leave.

"Well, I'll let you get back to your knittin'." He chuckled and winked. "Take care."

Cutter watched the man hobble over to his truck, stiff after sitting. He thanked his stars again, or whatever it was that guided him to make the right choices sometimes, for treating the man with respect from the start, even when it didn't seem to be welcome.

"Keep your garden hose handy, Vern," he said to the retreating figure, who waved in acknowledgment without glancing back.

Amazing how things play out, Cutter thought.

He saw Double Dare's hulking foreman stalking across the yard, intent on some mission.

"Bobby," he called out, "have you seen Serena?"

The big man nodded. "Yeah, saw her about an hour ago headed up Say Hey alone on a bike, said she needed to stretch, think about stuff."

Cutter waved his thanks.

Serena. The other loose end.

Lexi would have come unglued if she knew how much Cutter had been thinking about Serena since they came off the river, but this was different. Vuko's revelation about Serena haunted him. And Vuko had acted like he knew her well enough to . . . well, there was that. But to travel from Denver to support her through her kayak challenge, even if he didn't stick around? *So evidently neither of them planned to run into each other at the river.*

Cutter shook his head and reached down to stroke Maggie behind her ears. The dog groaned in pleasure. For a day when he'd never left the front porch, Cutter thought, it had sure proved interesting.

The sat phone buzzed again, and Cutter cooperated. It was Antonini again.

"Our surprise should be on Vuko's desk by tomorrow."

"Do you think he'll take it seriously?

"I learned one more thing: we were right about his lawsuit, it's a bluff. No lawsuit has been filed against you or Double Dare Ranch with the Colorado Attorney General's office."

"Then this should rattle him," Cutter said with some relief. "The scary thing about that is, Vuko is unstable enough without being rattled. Who knows how he'll react when he feels someone reach out and poke him in the chest."

Chapter 24

Serena thought that the harder she worked, the farther she pushed the yellow mountain bike away from Double Dare Ranch, the better she would feel. *I just need a good, heart-strangling workout, time to think everything through, and I'll be better.*

She clicked her cycling shoes into the pedal traps and chose the Say Hey Trail that curved above the ranchhouse and served as the main access for bikers and horseback riders into the backcountry. It was the same trail, wide enough at the start for two bikes to ride abreast, that they used to reach Moccasin Ridge the night of the climbing accident. Once beyond the softball field, it disappeared into the ponderosa and aspen and gambel oak forest, climbing alongside the Dolores River. The trail's switchbacks teased her with intermittent views of the river. But the comforting shoosh of water—like an invisible window sliding on an endless silicone sash—was always with her.

At first the 18-gear Specialized Stumpjumper's knobby tires hummed over the trail shaded and kept moist by the trees, the red, rich dirt padded with dead needles and leaves. But as Say Hey tilted upward and narrowed to a singletrack about two feet wide, the trail demanded Serena's full attention. Head down, she plowed ahead.

There were fewer ponderosa and aspen as an endless sea of gnarly pinyon-juniper and gambel oak stretched to the western horizon. The trail surface changed into crunchy granite and shale chips the size of ball-bearings. Rib after rib of exposed juniper roots burst through the ground perpendicular to the trail, making it even more of a test. Even the $2,200 fully suspended alloy frame she rode couldn't diminish the shaking her arms took. She knew she had to cross the roots almost exactly perpendicular or they would throw her front wheel—and her—sideways. Not a fatal fall, but one that usually left the rider with bruises and black-and-bloody chain tracks zippered across your shins.

At about eight thousand feet elevation, almost to the edge of the forest, the climb leveled out and Serena approached a fork in the trail. Taking a water break and straddling the bike, she knew she faced a similar juncture in her life. She had two options—Cutter or Vuko—but they were mutually exclusive.

A magpie screeched, bringing her back, and for a moment she was lost in the Colorado sky, which was as blue as a mountain lake.

She knew that either direction on the trail would lead to BLM land. To the right, Say Hey pointed toward Moccasin Ridge, standing guard over Double Dare Ranch, and she'd been there, done that. She chose the left, which looked like it might traverse above Ram Mountain land, eventually winding toward the Canyons of the Ancients Monument.

The Canyons of the Ancients was a 176,000-acre pinyon-juniper -choked maze dotted with half-buried ruins and kivas left by Ancestral Puebloans. On Serena's trail map the monument looked like half of an octopus, and she planned to cross over only a few of the tentacles that reached up to Ram Mountain and federal land.

Climbing off the bike, she peeked at the odometer on her handlebars. Five miles of hard work. Her body felt fine. Mechanically, she flexed her curled fingers and rubbed the life back into her tingling forearms from wrist to bicep. Her head and her heart, though, still ached with fear and failure. She gulped more water, then she dumped the bike in its track—against the ground its yellow paint job stood out like a taxi cab—and struck off on foot.

After another hour of pulse-pounding vertical, she stopped in half PJ forest, half sage meadow. Behind her, the tall timber gave up. The trail she was on, faint remains of a thoroughfare scraped into the rock for eons by elk and mountain goat hooves, wandered away and then disappeared. Above her, the empty ridge climbed to the north. She looked south and east, gazed at the Dolores Valley stretched out below, and plopped down where she stood in a soft hummock of lichen and grass. The panorama should have offered peace and beauty, but she wanted to cry. It all just made her feel so small.

The past weeks and events had been a downward spiral.

I lost my job. I allowed Lexi to publicly embarrass me. I failed the kayak challenge—twice!—and almost killed myself. For what? A piece of silver jewelry and some bragging rights?.

Absentmindedly, her slim fingers sought out another silver charm pinned to the collar of her periwinkle-blue fleece vest, the one that matched her eyes. The pin design copied an old-fashioned compass rose, the four corners honed to knife points. She won the pin in the Geo-challenge, and Cutter awarded it to her in a reserved ceremony after . . .

After Tim's fall. She gulped, her throat aching with the effort of holding back tears.

It wasn't the Double Dare challenges. It's knowing that I put my life at risk and endangered the lives of others, Mouse and Nipsy, that's unforgivable. At the very least, I threatened their jobs and the ranch.

The thought shocked her. *Am I like that? Is that me?*

A late-afternoon breeze suddenly made the wooded, protected copse around her shudder. It chilled the sweat that still clung to her skin, and she realized her stomach was growling. She unzipped the breast pocket of the fleece. Her fingers felt the crinkle of paper inside, but it wasn't the fat brick of granola she thought she stashed there when she left the ranch. Instead, she withdrew two objects that she had utterly forgotten: the Todd Helton rookie baseball card, and a cream-colored ball of richly textured paper. Even as she uncurled the paper's folds and smoothed its creases on her knee, she remembered what it was. Her eyes sought out the blocky **R.V.** initials as if for confirmation just before her first tear splattered the page.

. . . .

Patricia Keeney felt like a carefree teenager. It was her first horseback ride in weeks. At age seventy, she usually heeded the pleading of friends and neighbors about riding alone. But it had been too long since she'd walked Frisco, her roan and white paint mare, up through the aspen and pines into the San Juan Range. Riding reminded her of her childhood and her parents. Besides, she'd left an obligatory message, as if she were a five-year-old, with Manny about where she was going. Poor Manny.

"Aaaii-ee, Miss Patricia," Ramworthy's foreman reacted, when she called him. She intentionally avoided having to explain to Vern. "Mr. Ramworthy, he's not going to like this. It's dangerous for you to ride alone. Please . . . please, wait. I will be right over and come with you."

"No, you won't. I'll be long gone. If anybody wants to know, just tell 'em I went up to check on High Haven."

The ride up to the storybook house was glorious. It wasn't until she and Frisco reached within a couple hundred feet of the house that the light breeze in her face carried the unmistakable musk of wood smoke. She felt an instant rush of panic, even as she kicked Frisco forward. But quickly she realized there was no new wildfire, only the stubborn stink of charred siding and surrounding brush that would linger until the first snow, at least. Approaching the house from the opposite side of the lightning strike, she couldn't see any sign of fire damage yet. The big front door swung open easily and another wave of cooped-up smoky air rolled over her. She left the door open.

Patricia just wanted to touch a few things, then she and Frisco would be on their way. Her mother's huge teak bed frame and dresser with the oval mirror that Papa brought back from his mariner days in the Far East. Two antique floor lamps, one with a stained-glass shade featuring snow-capped mountains and heavily antlered elk, the other with a marbled shade shot through with veins of gold and iron. Boxes of books and framed paintings and photographs. Papa's leather-and-brass steamer trunk in which she carefully packed pieces of table silver given to her by her mother and grandmother. And there was the leather-framed photo of the inseparable trio by the river. She picked it up and packed it in the steamer trunk, not fooling herself that it added much more protection.

She closed the front door, and since the day still felt fresh and mild, she led Frisco by the reins around the house. Patricia glared at the blackened wall before she and the mare clopped past, heading north and west toward the nearby river. The home site had been chosen years ago for its close proximity to a series of pools that temporarily slowed the Dolores River from a torrent to a tranquil interlude, and was a familiar horse crossing.

As she led the horse across the river, she felt as if she were walking in her own footsteps. On top of Frisco again, Patricia decided to make her way along the edges of the forest and explore ridges she hadn't been to in some time. But she quickly discovered that bushwhacking through the forest was too slow, and dangerous for Frisco. The amount of downed timber shocked her. Bleached gray and dry by the wind and sun, sheared-off limbs poked jaggedly at the sky. If Frisco made one mis-step and went down, either one of them ran the risk of being impaled.

Fire was even more of a concern. There had been fire warnings nearly daily, and if a blaze were sparked, almost nothing could stop it. Too much fuel lay strewn everywhere. She knew of other areas like this—the Zirkel Wilderness—where fires had started and had simply been allowed to burn themselves out. That sometimes took weeks, even months.

The thought of a blaze in this forest terrified her, but she knew the day would come.

Patricia looked for a way out of the labyrinth, a place where the trees thinned and she could see through the forest screen to either rock or sky. A spidery patch of unnatural blue caught her eye through the denseness. *Wildflowers, maybe, although it was late in the season, and this was more intense than even lupine.* The downed timber appeared a little thinner to their left and she turned Frisco in that direction. They clopped methodically, doing their best not to set a hoof on a tree limb that could roll beneath their step or snap and jab the horse.

. . . .

Two prizes, Serena thought. One reminded her of a once-thriving career and the rush of achievement. The other represented something inside her that had become warped, misshapen and unlike her. She slid the baseball card back into her pocket even as her other hand worried the rough ridges of Vuko's reminder.

She couldn't get the note's message out of her head.

"*. . . We had a deal. Live up to it. And we can both still have what we want.*"

Could she?

If the ranch's value was somehow weakened, but not destroyed, maybe no one would want it. But I would.

If the business staggered, and Cutter didn't have the army of friends and customers standing by to be part of Double Dare, maybe I could help him rebuild it. Maybe.

If Grateful Bobby and Mouse and Lexi all went away, then I wouldn't feel pressured by them. I wouldn't look up to see their disappointment and pity before they hastily looked away. I'd be the real Serena again, the one with all the right answers and all the right friends. I would.

She clutched the piece of paper in one hand and with the other turned and fumbled with the zipper on the tiny daypack she had unclipped from the bike's handlebars and taken with her. Without looking —her red-rimmed eyes were locked on . . . nothing—it took her a few seconds before her hand clamped on the object she sought and pulled it out. Through the cloudy plastic canister, she desperately studied the matches.

. . . .

The paint horse stepped into the little clearing with Patricia bent over its neck as she tried to avoid the last tree branches that raked and scraped her head and shoulders. Readjusting her men's felt Snowy River hat, she looked up to find someone—a woman—sitting in the grass, her back turned toward Patricia and the sputtering breezes. She wore a deep indigo vest; that's what she had glimpsed through the trees. The woman hunched over something. Reading a map? Fixing a snack?

Patricia started to call to her—she knew no matter how she made an entrance she would likely startle her—when the woman straightened as if finished with what she worked over.

She looked like one of the guests from the Double Dare Ranch. The ridge here was above and west of Cutter's place, maybe five miles or so away. She'd seen her at the barbecue. She was the woman who got in that awful mess with Lexi. The sad one.

Patricia couldn't believe what she saw next. The stupid girl flicked a match, she was smoking!

No, oh God, she was . . .

"Noooooooooo!" Patricia screamed.

Serena jumped, startled, and the piece of paper that was just beginning to flicker to life in her hand fell into the parched grass at her feet.

Chapter 25

Vuko dropped the thick legal file that had just been delivered by courier on his office desk. It landed with the thud of something to be taken seriously, and he sat down behind it with a sigh. He started to open it with his bandaged right hand before a searing flash of pain shot through it. He reminded himself to watch out for the damned dog next time. And, he thought bitterly, he'd make sure there would be a "next time."

With his left hand, he turned back the cover on the folder.

Damn it! The Bureau of Land Management, with Cutter as the witness, was trotting out a lawsuit against *him*?

Over . . . *What the hell was cryptobiotic soil, and who cared anyway?*

A notice in bold black type at the bottom of the title page, though, began to twist his contemptuous sneer into something else.

THE SUBJECT OF THE AFOREMENTIONED LEGAL ACTION, MR. RADIC VUKO, IS HEREBY REQUIRED TO APPEAR IN U.S. FEDERAL COURT IN DENVER, COLORADO, FOR PRELIMINARY HEARING ON OCTOBER 25 AT 1 P.M. FAILURE TO APPEAR WILL RESULT IN CHARGES OF CONTEMPT OF COURT AND THE ISSUE OF A WARRANT FOR FEDERAL ARREST . . .

Today's date was October 18.

It took him only a few pages more to realize that the game he had tried to play with Cutter had backfired.

Cryptobiotic soil, according to the environmental experts quoted in the file, is a fragile combination of moss, lichen and algae that in arid areas of the American Southwest basically bonds the desert's topsoil and keeps it from blowing away. The stuff was a protected organism under something called the 1976 Federal Lands Policy and Management Act, Vuko read with disgust. According to the BLM's lawsuit and Cutter's complaint, it didn't respond well to his seven-thousand-pound Hummer's seventeen-inch Goodyears pulverizing it on the day he confronted Cutter with the phony lawsuit to try and take the ranch.

. . . SUBJECT TO A FINE AND INCARCERATION . . .

Hell, the last place I want to end up in is a courtroom, where some ambitious law clerk with an Internet connection might discover Darko Magyar and his dark secrets.

A single word rocketed through his brain: *extradition.*

"It's just fuckin' dirt!" he shouted out loud in frustration. The legal packet included photographs showing where the tire treads blasted through the crap. One photo even captured the torn ground with the Hummer's blocky black frame just disappearing behind a boulder in the background.

His ego was taking a massive shelling lately, Vuko thought. The strutting strategist in him could not believe that all of his plans—the spies, his legal tricks, the intimidation, the operation on the ridge, leaving Cutter for roadkill in the dirt—all of it failed. He could not allow that to happen. Failure was not an option.

He stopped and thought about that. If anything, Vuko was a realist. He admitted that failure looked like a real possibility. The weight of disappointment, the years of planning and shaking hands and taking risks, crushed him. How could it have happened? He was so close to having what he wanted. And then, taking another mental leap, he thought, how can I get away?

There were loose ends, the tatters of his plans, which he would have to tend to. The crypto-whatever thing—"Psshhh," he hissed, waving his uninjured hand in the air—he could walk away from that. He could disappear—again—in a lot less time than a week. He would have to notify his business associates and clients. He had time to gather up all his records and contacts to take with him. He still believed his idea of establishing a private paramilitary training facility on a small-army scale was possible. Somewhere. Maybe the Northwest. Or Mexico.

He knew he couldn't leave any physical evidence behind that could implicate him in a crime. The mountaineering hardware they used to cause the accident on the mountain above the ranch would be identified as military-issue, but after that it was untraceable.

Vuko unconsciously lifted his right hand to close the file in front of him and the pain from the rush of blood to the mangled limb made him gasp. The throbbing returned. He picked up the file with his left hand and walked halfway down the hall to where a burnished steel chute ran floor to ceiling. Stamped into the metal above the bar handle were the words: CONFIDENTIAL DISPOSAL. He levered the heavy chute door open with his right elbow and unceremoniously dumped in the legal file. It would be shredded immediately.

What next? He quickly dismissed threats and witnesses, and he could think of only one person who could directly link him to any criminal action and who also understood or suspected the end result of what he planned. And he knew that he would find her at that damned ranch.

Chapter 26

Patricia kicked the horse into a charge across the clearing where Serena stood transfixed, staring as the burning paper curled and died, and the flames quickly marched on the breeze through the brittle-dry grass. In the seconds it took the wide-eyed Frisco to reach the woman, and for Patricia to slip down, the fire danced across the tinder into the scattered sun-bleached bones of dead trees.

Patricia took the only fire tool at hand, her felt hat, and began beating at the foot-high flames as she screamed at the woman frozen behind her.

"Help! Do something! Help me! Grab something, fight it! Hurry!" she cried.

Pushed by the unhindered winds at tree line, the fire rushed forward.

Still bent over, beating at the fire quickly crawling ahead of her, Patricia screamed again for help. Left untethered, Frisco screeched in terror, jittered and then galloped madly away, empty stirrups flapping. The mare passed like an express bus, while Serena stood rooted to the ground, hands clasping her face in disbelief. The wild-eyed horse snapped her into reality, and in shock she started edging back from the flames and thick, hemorrhaging cloud of smoke.

"Noooooooo!" Patricia cried out once more at the other woman, realizing there was no stopping Frisco. Choking on the smoke, she hacked up a scratchy plea. "Here! You've got to help."

Instead, Serena ran. Panicking, she began scrambling up the naked ridgeline, away from the fire. Her hard-soled biking shoes slipped and skittered off the uneven rocks so that she picked her way, arms spread wide, like an escaping prisoner. She ran, unsure if what lay ahead would kill her, but dead certain what was behind her would.

Patricia's heart plunged as she stared at the fleeing girl. To the east, in the direction she and Frisco had come from, she watched helplessly as the horse disappeared into the tall timber, probably headed for the Dolores River.

Patricia turned and took a half-hearted step toward fighting the fire when she heard a WHU-UMP! and an invisible wall of superheated air drove her backward. Decades of wind had blown broken twigs and small limbs out of the forest. A gray petticoat of kindling peeked out for twenty yards from the forest's skirt. The flames followed this tinder like a wide, thick fuse, and then struck the big dead trees. The forest exploded.

"My God," she gasped, putting a sooty hand to her mouth, "look what she's done."

In seconds, the fire swelled into an inferno. It lived off the wood, sucking in the mountain wind and exhaling thick, choking walls of smoke. Then her other senses registered the noise. Her ears identified it as something like a fast approaching locomotive, or waves at the ocean—something untamed and unstoppable. She *felt* the sound, too, an unearthly roar that seemed to make the mountain vibrate. She sensed the energy begin to seep from her limbs. Her will was leaking away. What could she do alone?

She suddenly realized how thirsty she was. Water . . . *Damn it!* Her hide-covered canteen was in her saddle pack—gone with Frisco. She swallowed reflexively and instantly felt as if she had developed a sore throat. She tasted the chalky ash she was inhaling and tried to pull up enough saliva to spit. With a shock, she realized that she might die up here. She tugged a calico neckerchief from a back pocket and cupped it over her nose and mouth.

The saddle pack! The satellite phone is in there, too!

Patricia tried to rein in her wits. *Get a grip. Think this through. I can't stay here, I'll die of smoke inhalation.* Immediately below her, a once-majestic but long-dead pine cracked and crashed to the forest floor, belching a shower of sparks into the air and igniting still more downed timber beneath it. She shuddered in fear, helpless to prevent the destruction unfolding below her.

Follow Frisco. The horse ran in the same direction the wind is driving the fire—east towards the river, and south towards Double Dare Ranch. The mare is closer to the perimeter of the fire so far, closer than the blonde. Patricia glanced upward, searching and finally pinpointing the woman climbing still higher toward the ridgeline. *But she has nowhere to go. If the wind shifts, the smoke will blind her and suffocate her. The horse at least still has a chance to stay ahead of the fire and make it to the river.*

Follow Frisco!

Once Patricia decided, she knew she had to move fast to beat the fire to the river. She hiked her sleeve to look at her antique wristwatch, its silver and diamonds polished to a time-honored brilliance. Maybe unconsciously she wanted to mark the moment. Record the exact minute Ram Mountain, and everything she and her neighbors loved, went up in smoke.

It was 3:05, come-to-Jesus time.

. . . .

3:05—The ranger in the dark brown lookout tower miles across the valley from Double Dare and Two Havens ranches lowered his high-powered binoculars, the white bloom of smoke on the shoulder of Ram Mountain fresh in his mind. "It doesn't look like this one is gonna blow itself out," he said to himself. He quickly turned to the huge square Plexiglass-covered topo map behind him in the center of the tower, found the coordinates for the approximate location, and then pulled a dog-eared sheaf of paper from the shelf below. On it, he knew, were the names of every trained volunteer firefighter within fifty miles. He grabbed his sat phone and started calling the fire captains.

. . . .

3:07—The Mexican's western boots rat-a-tatted across the wooden porch as quickly and urgently as a Flamenco dancer's flourish. Vernard Ramworthy was already looking up from a book when his foreman burst into the house. "What is it, Manny?"

"Fire," the foreman gasped. "Up on the mountain. Above Double Dare, maybe Two Havens, too. It may be a big one."

Ramworthy started dialing his own list.

. . . .

3:08—The day unfolded perfectly for flying, clear and blue as far as Captain Kathleen Ellerman could see from the Boeing 737 at thirty-eight thousand feet. Almost all the way to Las Vegas, their destination. The only blemish was the cloud of smoke swelling over the lower San Juans. The pilot poked the sleeping junior officer beside her and told him to get on the radio to the Durango airport and tell them they had a forest fire in their backyard.

"And tell them not to bother with hoses and pumpers to reach this one," added Ellerman, staring at the white smoke below that expanded like a hot-air balloon. "Just send men and women. Lots of them."

. . . .

3:09—"It's Ramworthy," the rancher shouted into the phone, breathing heavily. "We've got a fire up on the mountain, above your place around tree line, I think. Manny just told me Patricia's up there."

Cutter jerked forward in the rocker on Double Dare's porch, satellite phone poised inches from his ear.

"Lexiiii!" he yelled for the quickest aid nearby. "Find Bobby for me, please. Right now!"

. . . .

3:13—"Cutter, we've got a fire—"

"Yeah, I know, Bobby. You said Serena went for a ride on the mountain. Do you know of anyone else up there?"

"No. You know the ranch is practically empty, the fall slowdown, and—"

"Ramworthy called and he thinks Patricia is up there."

The rock-steady foreman grimaced. "I'll get our stuff." He looked back at Cutter, who knew what was coming next.

"I'm going this time. You're not in any condition to fight wildfire." It wasn't a question.

"We'll both go," he said, and steeled himself to get up. Standing up would be the worst part, he told himself, as he gripped both arms of the rocker and levered himself upright. He was a little pale when he got there.

"You look like shit," said Bobby. "You sure about this?"

"The only thing we're gonna burn on this ranch this week," Cutter said through gritted teeth, "is that damn chair."

. . . .

3:15—The dispatcher's voice crackled over the police scanner in the small cabin in her usual calm but urgent monotone. "Sheriff, we've got a fire on Ram Mountain above Double Dare Ranch. Southwest Fire Control has been alerted. Volunteers are setting up a base at Ram Mountain Ranch. Advise you and Miguel and Hawkeye head there and take command of the perimeter."

"We're on our way," Jeffrey Morningstar's voice came back from his jeep squad vehicle somewhere.

With that, Dolores County's entire available force—three sheriff's officers—mobilized, plus the one on medical leave lying on his couch in the cabin with the full leg cast propped up on pillows.

"Damn it!" Tim Riordan bellowed, and hammered a fist into the cabin's leather couch.

The only ears that his frustration reached, those of a startled black German shepherd nestled asleep under an open window, instantly perked up and she loped to her owner's side with eyes full of questions.

. . . .

3:16—"It's me," she said into the sat phone. "I thought you'd want to know we have another forest fire here, above the ranch. High up, I think. Everyone seems really worried about it. Cutter and his foreman just drove away to help."

"Hmmph. I didn't believe him to walk for a week," Vuko said, disappointed.

"What?" Lexi asked, thinking she hadn't heard him correctly.

But she got no answer. The phone had gone dead in her hand.

. . . .

3:30—The twelfth phone call made by the lookout ranger and his assistant, alerted at her office in town, rang in the Rim Riders Bike Shop. Owner Bryan Boonstra was a fire captain. The assistant figured the local riders would just be trickling in to pick up tire tubes and patch kits and the latest gossip before starting out on afternoon rides as the day and slickrock trails began to cool. She was in luck. Five of the six riders in the shop were firefighting veterans. Two of them were vacationing Hotshots from New Mexico with full fire packs, even some extras, and gear in their truck.

"C'mon, Laura," one of them said to the lone rookie EFFer in the group, "looks like this is the chance you've been begging us for to work a fireline."

. . . .

3:53—With the first season of visitors to Double Dare Ranch slowing, Mouse Patton had earned a day off. He smiled as he cast his neon line into one of the sparkling shallows of Dove Creek, a tributary of the Dolores River a couple miles above Double Dare. He had seen the rainbow trout—it looked like twelve or fourteen inches, at least—swishing back and forth like a rattler over the golden rock bottom of the stream. But just as quickly it disappeared into the coal-black shadow at the bank's edge. The damn fish lurked in the dark now. Mouse concentrated on guessing where it would pop out of the murk, when he heard a series of splashes downstream. He looked up to see a half-dozen mule deer brazenly dash across the creek. He thought it a little odd because deer didn't move much until dusk. Stranger still, a battalion of raccoons, a pair of red-tailed foxes and not far behind a family of wild pigs made up a rear escort. Behind him came an even louder splash. Mouse swiveled in time to spot a small black bear lumbering across the creek. *No way. This isn't right.* He gave up on the rainbow and pulled out his sat phone, quickly thumbing to the ranger station in his address book.

"Hey, this is Mouse. Is there anything going on out on Ram Mountain that would have the wildlife spooked?"

He got his answer and grimaced. "Okay, I'm headed down. I'll meet 'em all at Ramworthy's place."

. . . .

4:01—Serena had never been more terrified in her life. Her heart pounded a staccato rhythm that her churning, rubbery legs tried to keep up with. Every breath felt like she was inhaling coal dust. The fire below sounded like a fully stoked furnace with its hatch left wide open. It was raging, clearly out of control. And it was following her, stalking her for what she had done. It was all her fault. The inescapable reality of what she faced slammed into her: she was alone and she could die here.

That woman who surprised me, she could die, too. She might already be dead. She imagined the woman burnt black, her clothes and hair gone, her skin cracked in bloody, seeping furrows, staggering blindly through the forest knowing she was going to die. *I left her. I didn't mean to, but I don't want to die, too.*

She had to get help. Once she focused, tried to calm herself, she instantly thought of phoning someone. *Do I have it? Did I pack it?* Frantically, she began searching her fleece vest, already powdered with fire ash, probing for the familiar bulk of the satellite phone. Her hands found it in a side pocket, and she flipped the face open. It still had a charge.

Who?

Who could she call? Who would want to help her?

Cutter.

With that thought, a wrenching, panicky sob hit her. What a hopeless, pitiful idea, she thought. He would be the last person to help her after all the havoc and heartache that she caused him.

The thought of the one person who still wanted something from her hit her, and she scratched at the buttons.

"Rad," she screamed when the phone clicked at the other end. "Rad, it's me, Serena. Rad, I need help. I'm in a fire. I'm caught on the mountain. Help me, I'll do anything. Please. I don't want to die . . ."

"Serena, where are you? Where are you exactly?" Vuko asked. His voice seemed controlled, not surprised or shocked at all. He sounded ready to help.

She looked around her, trying to remember the trails she'd taken on the mountain bike, how she'd gotten there. Her tears carved channels out of the grime caked on her face. The billowing smoke hid the fire from her now, obscuring any landmarks. But she knew—she absolutely knew—the flames were there waiting for her as she gauged the distance and how much time she had.

"I'm on the top of the mountain above Double . . . above the ranch," she said, catching herself. She still thought it strange, his warning never to call Cutter's ranch by its name. But she wasn't questioning it now.

"Stay there," he commanded. "I'll find you. Two hours."

"But the smoke, it's choking me," she screamed into the phone. Another waft of brown air engulfed her, causing her to collapse in a coughing fit. She pulled the tall collar of the vest over her mouth and nose, gasping for any relief.

"Hurry," she keened, curled over the rough ground. "Please."

Serena received no encouraging words in return. The signal was gone.

. . . .

4:03—Location, location, location, Vuko thought, relishing his private joke. But he had to hurry.

. . . .

4:10—"Cutter, can you hear me? Ramworthy again, I'm back." The voice sounded tinny and distant over the sat phone's open speaker, as if it were in a hell of a windstorm.

"Vern, I figure we're gonna stage at your place. Bobby's gonna drive me over and we should be there in twenty minutes," Cutter said, his own adrenaline and the unnatural noise causing him to shout back. He hobbled as quickly as he could to the pickup as Bobby manhandled the last of their equipment into the truck bed.

Cutter's hasty climb up into the truck shot a spasm of pain through his back, all the way to his core. But he wasn't about to ask for a time-out. They both knew minutes made a difference in containing a wildfire, and especially in this case, to their chances of saving the two women probably trapped in it—even if Cutter harbored grave doubts about how useful he could be when he got there. The pain arced across his lower back, and he feared he might pass out. The last thing that a fire crew hustling on a long, hard climb uphill needed to worry about was another weak body to pack out.

"Vern," he gasped, "I don't think I'm going to be worth a damn to anyone fighting this fire. My back would just make me a hazard."

Grateful Bobby cranked the truck starter, and Cutter urged him to hurry.

"Hell, I know that," the man's voice came crackling back. "I'm too old and you're too delicate for us to be in the way. Fighting wildfires is work for guys like The Hulk there with you. We can help in other ways. Don't bother drivin'. I'll pick you up in your south meadow in five minutes." He clicked off.

Pick me up? Cutter's eyes met those of the now glowering Bobby.

"What the hell is he talking about?" Cutter asked.

. . . .

4:15—The willing hands of worried neighbors transformed the front yard and meadows of Ram Mountain Ranch into a makeshift staging area. It would serve as a proper Incident Command Center once BLM and Forest Service personnel arrived. A convoy of local vehicles streamed through the gate, careful to follow the hand signals of the sheriff and his deputies. Most of them were local EFFers responding to a neighbor's plight, armed with the tools common to life in fire country—shovels, axes, mauls, Pulaskis, rakes, buckets, hoses. Anything they could quickly grab to fight a fire with. Others brought food and bottled water. An emergency rescue vehicle from Cortez, flashing red and blue lights, pulled in and picked a strategic spot. Folks wrestled with large canvas tents and already women and children were setting up long picnic tables and chairs off the side of the white-boarded house. They had all seen the giant mushroom cloud of smoke building over Ram Mountain. They knew this wasn't just Double Dare's fight. If the wind picked up, it could push the wildfire east where it could jump the Dolores River and even threaten Two Havens. These days, in this drought, a major wildfire immediately qualified as a threat to the entire valley, to every resident and their way of life. Petty feuds were forgotten and disagreements put aside as once again, like all the generations who faced every kind of natural and human-caused disaster, the tradition of survival in the American West took hold. It was grim-faced chaos.

Cutter slid gingerly out of the truck and hobbled toward the meadow. He waved Grateful Bobby to go on, at the same time wondering where the hell Ramworthy was.

. . . .

4:17—A small white helicopter primly touched down in the Double Dare meadow, pelting Cutter with hay missiles. Cutter remembered the little bird he'd spotted the day he and Grateful Bobby visited Ram Mountain Ranch. The blinding reflection of the low autumn sun off the canopy and dark sunglasses obscured the pilot's face, but he immediately waved for Cutter to hurry and get in. Grabbing the flimsy door for support, Cutter started to lever himself inside but froze when he saw the crusty rancher's mane of white hair flowing out from under an Elk Foundation baseball cap and his aviator glasses.

"You going to stand there and stare like I'm some rock star, or are you getting in?" Ramworthy rasped.

Cutter heaved his bulky firefighter's pack into the tight space behind the two seats.

"You can fly this thing?" he asked as he pulled himself into the cockpit. He had to reach down and manhandle his prosthesis to fit into the confined compartment, conscious of Ramworthy's eyes on his leg.

"Sonny, I was plucking your daddy and his buddies out of the jungle behind Japanese lines in the first Sikorskys sixty years ago," the man replied as he jerked the machine into the sky and tore towards the mountain and the smoke above them. Then he smiled and, as if to ease Cutter's wondering look, he added: "I've got skills."

. . . .

4:22—In less than eighty minutes since the lookout ranger first spotted and reported the Double Dare Fire, driven by the Rockies' afternoon gusts, it devoured more than 300 acres of alpine forest and raced a half mile across the mountain. Below the blaze, the tiny community rushed to try and stop it.

Chapter 27

As Patricia clambered across the rugged ridge, she knew her problems were getting worse, not better. On any other day without a forest fire in her face, Patricia knew that she could easily walk out of the geography. She knew the mountains. She knew how to prepare to go into them in any season, because they could kill you. She knew how to survive, and she'd been prepared. But everything she needed was on the back of her horse, miles away by now, at least she hoped. She ignored the annoying strands of gray hair that swayed across her vision from beneath her felt hat, which now sported a burnt hole in its crown. She was too tired to bother.

Still, she couldn't ignore her desperate thirst. Even with her red bandanna tied bandit-style over her mouth, the choking smoke and thin air turned her throat raw. People forgot that most of Colorado was a high desert, a mile closer to the sun than most of the rest of the country. Dehydration could stalk you into an early grave. To reach the river, she knew she'd have to cross the exposed ridge before she could descend into the forest. She already felt like she was drying up. Adding to her fears, in a couple hours when the sun set, the air temperature would begin plummeting—twenty to thirty degrees overnight.

She knew the wind controlled her fate, A couple times already it turned and the fire charged back up the mountain at her, chasing her farther out onto the barren rock on the ridge. As a result, there wasn't much fuel left to burn immediately below her. But she couldn't sit here and expect to be found. So she followed the blackened tree line east in the same direction Frisco had fled, hugging the granite rock field as long as possible in order to be spotted by a search helicopter if one passed overhead.

Usually the fire blew east, toward the Dolores River and beyond it to Two Havens, and south, burning ever deeper into Double Dare land. When the wind turned or paused, the fire also ate its way west, cutting off her only other direction to escape. But when it did, she gained ground on the main fire. She felt she'd inched slightly ahead in her race for the river, so Patricia plodded on. Her knees and back muscles began to rebel from constantly fighting the uneven rock landscape.

She squinted her eyes, trying to pierce the murky haze below. Where the breeze broke up the oppressive gray-brown smoke, she could see the wildfire plowing forward, straining to catch her. The flames were a spectrum of colors: from cardinal and carrot to ruby and indigo to blackish purple. The entire fire seemed to writhe and morph, as if cavorting across the mountainside. The furnace roar obliterated all sound.

Patricia knew it was time. If she was going to bushwhack down into the spruce and fir forest to intersect the Dolores, she had to do it now. She had to stay ahead of the beast. It was her only chance to reach the bare, wet rocks and slapping water, where she could hope to survive.

She grabbed a corner of her denim shirttail, swabbed her swollen, red eyes, and plunged into the forest.

. . . .

Serena didn't know exactly when she first sensed it or heard it. But she did hear it—a low, buzzing sound at first, which got much louder. Enough to stop her in her tracks. She knew it had to be a helicopter. But where? She stared hard into the smoke below her but couldn't pick out anything. Then the buzz burst full-blast and a black copter hopped over the ridge behind her. It picked its way along indecisively only fifty feet or so above the ground, the pilot obviously looking for a flat spot to land. She dove one hand into a vest pocket, grasping for the phone again, frantic that the helicopter wouldn't stop for her. She didn't even consider whom she would call. Then the pilot inside the bird must have seen her, because it came right at her, dropping as it approached.

Thank God!

Like some sort of oversized insect, it touched down a short distance away and the door on the right side opened. A man dressed in camouflage gear clambered out. His clothing perfectly matched the ridge's landscape, and he carried a full pack and some kind of bulky hump on his shoulders. She took a few hesitant steps forward as he reached back for what looked like another smaller pack, shaped like a fat bedroll, but rigid. Maybe it's firefighting equipment, she thought. But one man, even two people, couldn't do anything to stop a blaze this big. Let's get out of here, she thought. But to her horror, the man ran towards her and the helicopter lifted off, peppering them both with dirt and twigs.

As he closed the distance she locked eyes on a face that looked familiar but was smeared with what must be soot and some kind of green-gray grease. Vuko, she suddenly realized, and opened her mouth to ask what the hell he was doing.

But before she could form the words, he dropped the two packs and shoved her to the ground. Her sat phone flew out of her hand, bouncing on the rocks. With his left hand, Vuko reached to the hump on his shoulders and tugged at a drawstring. It released a huge camouflage cape down his back, as large as a tent. Then he dropped to the ground beside her and the packs, and with a practiced flourish he spread the cape in the air, like some grim matador. Then he let it cover them both.

"Move," Vuko snarled, his face thrust in front of hers, his strong cologne overpowering under the tarp, "and I break your neck."

. . . .

Ramworthy's helicopter was a Schweizer 300, a sweet three-placer that could herd cattle like a cutting horse and regularly made the local copter jockeys weep with envy when he hopped over to Telluride or Durango for supplies. Ramworthy and Cutter agreed that their first concern should be to try to find the two women and get them off the mountain. But if they didn't locate them quickly, they knew they'd have to conduct reconnaissance on the fire and radio back to the command center and the firefighters who were already making their way up the mountain.

Once they reached an altitude high enough that they could see the full scope of the fire, both men were shaken by the immensity of it. The smoke cloud towered over Ram Mountain, visible to people along U.S. 491 in Dove Creek ten miles away. In Dolores, even farther away, anyone who wasn't headed to the mountain to fight the fire could smell it. Vehicles and buildings at Double Dare and Two Havens ranches were already dusted with a fine coat of white ash blown by the wind.

They knew from Manny that Patricia rode up the mountain to High Haven, and Grateful Bobby told Cutter that Serena started out on the Say Hey Trail. So both women were headed in approximately the same direction. Hopefully, both reached the tree line where they could escape into the relative safety of the rocks above and be spotted by any aircraft.

Ramworthy banked the copter steeply left to take them to the western edge of the fire just above the ridge. From there, with the wind at their backs, they planned to follow the tree line with Cutter scouring the forest's edge with his binoculars.

"So you learned to fly in the Army?" Cutter asked over the copter's intercom.

"I signed up like a lot of boys right after Pearl Harbor," the rancher replied, keeping his steely eyes on the business below. "I had some education and I passed a few tests, and next thing I knew the Army sent me to training to fly helicopters. They were boxes of bolts, I'll tell you. I was scared to death. But they had used one to rescue a wounded GI in Burma, and soon after that we were pulling our boys off some of the islands taken by the Japanese."

The Rocky Mountain currents bounced the bird down and back up, and Cutter prayed for his stomach to catch up with him.

"This is a joy ride compared to the junks we flew in the Philippines and the South Pacific. I flew eleven missions."

Quite a speech coming from the normally private man, Cutter thought. There wasn't time for more talk. They climbed above Ram Mountain and Ramworthy edged the copter along the tree line. The rotors, with the help of the stiff wind, blew the smoke away from them, but the air was still choking in the cockpit and Ramworthy took them up fifty feet. Neither of the women appeared to be here.

Ramworthy pushed the copter back and forth twice along the tree line for the width of the fire, which now covered more than two miles.

"I'm going to check out High Haven. That's where Patricia was headed, maybe we'll find them between here and there," the pilot said. "If not, then we'll have to see to the fire and head back for fuel. She carries twin thirty-two-gallon tanks, which normally would let us stay up for five, six hours. But these conditions cut that by more than half." Cutter nodded.

They followed the path they projected from the wildfire to the old Victorian. Flames were still several miles from the house. But with a look the two men silently acknowledged that if the blaze reached this far, it might jump the river. Still, there was no sign of either woman. Once, as Ramworthy sidled the copter, slowly dropping in altitude, Cutter thought he saw a flash of an unnatural yellow in the trees outside the fire perimeter. But he couldn't locate it again and he wrote it off to changing aspen leaves. Ramworthy looked at Cutter and shook his head, then heeled the copter back across the mountain.

Ramworthy estimated that the wind speed was about twenty-five miles per hour, and it whipped the fire into something beautiful and terrifying. The rancher guessed it had burnt roughly one thousand acres of BLM land and they hovered as helpless witnesses as it started to invade the northern edge of Double Dare's border. Cutter realized again how timely it was for Ramworthy to pick him up in the copter, freeing Grateful Bobby to help lead the advance line of EFFers against the wildfire. Back at the ranch, he'd left Mouse and Lexi in charge of directing the flurry of emergency measures to try and protect Double Dare structures.

The two men watched in dread as the flames grew and the fire began to generate its own internal combustion, its own wind, churning and driving it forward. It was transforming itself into a perfect engine of destruction. As if sensing its own unlimited power, it poured on speed.

"The wind is likely to build up until at least sunset," Ramworthy said over the radio. "That will make it worse. The fire will start crowning. It'll jump from treetop to treetop."

Cutter had been putting off contacting Bobby, hoping they would spot Patricia or Serena and have some good news. But as the helicopter sailed past the flames, he knew he needed to call now and relay information to help position the crews to fight the blaze.

"Bobby, can you hear me? It's Cutter," he shouted into a two-way headset. "Where are you?"

"Yeah, I'm here," the foreman replied. "Come about another quarter mile the way you're going and you'll be right on top of us. Any luck finding Patricia?"

"Not yet, Bobby. We looked up and down the tree line and went back to High Haven where we think she had been. Nothing. No sign of Serena, either. We're going to re-fuel, then we'll be right back. Look, you're about two miles from the front of the fire," Cutter said as Ramworthy hovered the copter over the EFFers they now could pick out in the trees below. "Stop there and start chopping a fire line, west to east."

Cutter envisioned one of the oldest and most effective strategies to fight wildfires, hacking out a clear space in front of the fire that hopefully would be too wide for it to jump. He knew the distance and he had an idea of the unbelievable force of the wave coming at his friends below.

"Bobby, you'll have to make it at least twenty feet wide, and I figure you've got about an hour before it gets to you."

The radio fell silent and he could imagine his friend doing the math in his head.

"You mean . . .?"

"Yeah. It's coming at you at about three feet per second. It's a bad one," Cutter said.

"Damn. Well, I guess we better get to work. Get back up there in that bird and find those women. They're both tough. But that may not be enough."

"We'll find 'em," Ramworthy cut in, his rough voice seeming to crack a little over the radio. Then he banked the helicopter and shot toward town.

Chapter 28

Minutes after Vuko covered himself and the girl with the ghillie suit, he heard another helicopter—different buzz, whinier—make its way across the ridge towards them. Its slow, deliberate pass directly overhead told him they must be searching for Serena, or maybe some other lost lamb from Cutter's place. Beneath the camouflage, with fire smoke and dust choking the air, he knew he blended into the rocky ridge as neatly as if an artist had painted him there.

He could hear the copter following the tree line and it wasn't long before it dipped east beyond sight and sound. Those aboard would figure anyone trapped on the ridge would try to escape to the river to beat the fire.

From the time he got Lexi's phone call, alerted his pilot and took the elevator up to the roof of the downtown office building where his AStar 350-B3 copter waited on its pad, it had taken roughly two hours for him to fly south. He always kept a set of field clothes and gear, including the special packs, stored in the copter for emergencies. The trip, with only himself, his pilot and equipment, easily fit within the AStar's range.

En route, Serena's phone call made his mission seem only more propitious, as if she was meant to fall into his hands. After they passed over the San Juan Mountains and headed southwest, the immense fire cloud served as an easy landmark by which to pick out Ram Mountain. When the AStar cleared the ridge to drop him, he couldn't believe his luck finding Serena at nearly the exact coordinates that his military-issue GPS equipment captured when she called.

As soon as he'd read the Bureau of Land Management's lawsuit, he knew he'd have to dispose of Serena. She knew too much about him and his designs on Double Dare and his hatred for Cutter. If she survived the fire, law enforcement would certainly question her, and once they began connecting the dots it wouldn't take even this Mayberry outfit long to uncover his past. But he didn't intend to allow anyone that opportunity. Once he'd cleaned up his little mess on the mountain he'd disappear, just like he did before.

He didn't expect any interference, especially with the fire's gloomy shroud covering the mountain. And especially not from Cutter. He knew him well enough to imagine he would try and serve some noble purpose in organizing efforts to fight the wildfire. But physically, Vuko thought with a satisfied sneer, he'd still be hurting too badly after the beating he received to help an old lady across the street, much less stop him.

For an instant, hidden in his refuge of net mesh and rags, the smoke of a charred, dying land filling his senses, a captive body beside him, Vuko felt transported all the way back to the blackened, bomb-pocked farmlands of his Croatia. That was all supposed to be in the past. It seemed he could never escape this business of war, he thought. His military mind told him to kill her and throw her body in the fire where no one would ever find her. *What a body. Too bad.*

He scrambled to his feet, and looked down at the woman.

"Get on your knees," he ordered.

She stared mutely up at him, blinded by the sun over his back. She reacted dully, as if in a trance.

"What?" she said sluggishly.

Vuko didn't hesitate a second. His left arm rose with a quick back-swing and then whipped down, his open hand crashing into the side of Serena's head, lifting her slightly and sending her sprawling backwards. He allowed no time for recovery.

. . . .

Half-unconscious, she felt him jerk her upright by the front of her jacket even as he pulled something metal, sharp and jingling over her head. It scratched one ear, then her cheek and finally bit into her neck as he gave it a tug. Then a dozen spurs dug into her neck as he dragged her to her feet. Without a word, he slowly slipped his right hand, swathed in a thick bandage of the same camouflage colors, through one pack strap—careful not to so much as nudge it, she noticed. Then from his left hand he gently transferred a braided nylon leash to his right, and began working both shoulders into the pack. Serena's eyes followed the leash across the space between her and Vuko. Still in shock, she reached a tentative hand to her throat and nearly threw up. To her horror, she felt a dog's spiked choke collar encircling her neck, the kind she always regarded with disgust when she saw the macho-types walking their rottweilers and mastiffs in Denver's Wash Park. She had always believed the repulsive devices said more about the viciousness of the owners than the dogs.

Vuko reeled the leash in tight and she had no choice but to obey. Once again, he shoved his face in hers.

"Do as I say. Immediately," he said, snapping the collar for emphasis. "I won't waste time with you. Have no illusions that I am not going to kill you. I just don't want to do it here."

She stood in frozen disbelief. She opened her mouth to speak, but she couldn't sort thoughts into words. Tears flowed down her cheeks.

"I . . . I . . . I'm Serena. Don't you know me? We—"

Quickly shifting the leash back into his left hand, he yanked the braid as if he were pull-starting a lawn mower. The barbs of the collar clenched her neck, puncturing her skin with half a dozen points, grinding others into her collarbone and neck.

He reached with his damaged right hand to pick up the second pack—longer, more cylindrical than the squarish first load—and she wanted to cheer when he winced in obvious pain. He switched hands, the leash back in the right hand, delicately.

"Pull on this," he said, menacing the leash, "and I'll hang you with it. You're in front. Keep moving, into the forest, but not too fast. Move out."

. . . .

With the ghillie suit piled and cinched atop his shoulders, Vuko shoved Serena forward with the pack in his hand. He needed to get off the exposed ridge. He was all about expediency now. He knew from experience the dog collar more effectively terrorized and demoralized prisoners than playing with ropes and knots. He preferred the tensile-tough nylon over chain link to eliminate any field sound. Serena already appeared broken, he thought.

He wanted to kill her on the spot. But the wildfire had already eaten its way into the forest below and he simply didn't have time to hide her body on the open ridge. He decided to drive her ahead of him until they reached cover, or he got close enough to the fire that he could throw her somewhere no one would ever find her. *One more loose end knotted tight.* Then he'd implement his escape plan.

He watched the woman gauge his desired pace and he pushed her into a trot. Their boots kicked up tiny storms of ash as they ran along the burnt edge of the forest. Ahead in the distance, the sun inched toward the horizon.

Vuko smirked. It would be the last sunset Serena would ever see.

. . . .

The wind quickened as the day waned. Right now the wildfire was definitely winning, Grateful Bobby thought as he scraped and hacked with his Pulaski at the earth and brush. It was a medieval-looking tool—half ax, half hoe—but still the most effective wilderness weapon against almost anything. The workhorse tool was named after Edward Pulaski, one of the heroes of the Big Blowup of 1910 in Montana, still considered the worst wildfire in Western history.

Bobby wielded the Pulaski like a dinner fork. All around him, hell's fury had been unleashed. The fire crowded them now, and his heart sank to know that his crew hadn't come close to clearing the break they needed to slow it down.

"Okay, back off," he yelled, signaling. "We've done all we can here." The tired men and women quickly retreated in a ragged line, looking back as they went. Bobby grabbed the trunk of a six-inch downed pine and dragged it with him, one less stick of fuel to feed the monster.

He looked up and down the line of volunteers to make sure they were pulling back. The crew did a heroic job just to scramble and get in front of the fire as quickly as they did.

The flames rolled forward, screaming and popping. The first tongues of fire licked at the edge of the break and seemed to pause tentatively, as if not sure whether to proceed. The wind blew small burning brands out of the larger pines and dry aspens that landed in the clear zone and attacked the stalks of grass and brush left behind. Here and there, up and down the line, a fiery, naked trunk gave way to gravity and fell across and bridged the space. The invading fire leapt forward. Pine needles and acorn litter, shucked by squirrels and chipmunks over years, ignited at the bases of trees across the break and instantly hungry pyres reached upward. In minutes the fire breached the break.

As the larger trees succumbed, the flames curled higher and seemed to suck the wind and heat along with it, and the fire picked up its pace.

Their tools over their shoulders, the crew turned and ran. Their first stand against the fire had failed.

. . . .

The wind ratcheted up a notch. Cutter and Ramworthy could feel it as their helicopter bucked and dipped in the quickening currents as they raced back to the mountain. Looking at the blaze, Cutter guessed it had at least doubled in size since they left for fuel.

Bobby had just radioed in that the fire line had broken and they were moving back and down the mountain, giving away some forest in order to regroup and try again. So far the only injuries came when they had to run for it. A woman from the Double Dare staff suffered a deep wound on the inside of her leg when she fell scrambling over a dead log and speared herself on a jagged limb. They rigged a hasty tourniquet and Bobby was carrying her down to paramedics already waiting below. Two others sprained ankles in the evacuation, but they could stay with the crew for now.

Bobby knew better than to ask about Serena and Patricia. Cutter would tell him the moment he knew anything. They stole the few spare minutes allowed them now to hash out their options.

"We spent most of our time scouting the west ridge at tree line," Cutter explained. "We figure they are bound to head east, stay above the fire, and try to make the river. But we didn't see a sign of either one of them."

"Let's find a natural break on the mountain close to Bobby that he can defend and try and hold," Ramworthy said. "Then we'll go back and search the ridge again. There should be a little light still left up there. But it's going to be dark soon and the copter's not going to be of any use to him or the women until morning."

Left unsaid was the given that the crew would have to fight the fire all night with only the volunteers from surrounding counties that could make it to the mountain. State personnel and the smoke jumpers, the West's elite team of firefighters who were trained to deploy anywhere on a moment's notice to fight wildfire, were on their way to the San Juans. But it would take time for them to stage and mobilize on the mountain.

"Bobby, I've got bad news-good news," Cutter offered hopefully. "The wind is going to get nasty. It isn't lying down like it normally does at dusk. A front keeps pushing it. That fire is going to get stronger, so you've got to be careful not to get boxed in anywhere. The good news is the weather geeks are saying it may bring in some moisture, but it won't get here until early morning."

"Well, that's something to look forward to. We'll be all right. I'm more worried about Serena and Patricia. It's strange not to have picked up any sign from them; they're both smart and know how to survive out here. I worry that something is keeping them from getting out."

No one offered any insights for several seconds after that.

"I think I've got a place for you," said Ramworthy, breaking the edgy silence while at the same time gunning the copter into a climb slightly left of their position. "Do you boys know the Blue Lagoon?"

Cutter did, and he pictured the naturally cleared meadow and methodically ran through the terrain, its pluses and minuses as a defensible position. It wasn't perfect. No spot in a wildfire ever could be. But it was close to the crew, maybe only a mile below them, and it possessed some natural advantages for fighting the fire and helping the crew stay alive. It also was about five miles from Double Dare, if the wind continued blowing in that direction, perhaps leaving them a cushion if they couldn't halt or slow the fire at the Blue Lagoon.

They worked out the details of re-supplying Bobby's crew for the night with food, water and equipment. Each man and woman on the line already carried supplies and a personal fire shelter with them in case the fire overran them.

"Bobby, be careful and keep those folks safe," Cutter said.

"You do the same," he replied, the radio chirping out.

. . . .

Moving swiftly over the charred, smoldering ground already gobbled by the wildfire didn't worry Serena. She was in superb physical condition, and she silently bet herself she could out-last this maniac if she needed to, despite the smoke that ravaged her throat. She took bitter satisfaction at the raspy gasps she heard behind her. She had learned the hard way not to turn around. The one time she did, even though it was only to see if Vuko wanted to slow down, she got a shove between her shoulder blades that nearly knocked her in the dirt as he literally ran her down. Only the snap of the tightened leash and the collar's chokehold kept her upright and she lurched ahead of him down the trail they had picked up. He never uttered a word.

Ahead she could see the day dissolving into a glorious sunset, the sky transformed into orange and gray marble by the fire smoke. She wished she could enjoy it. She wished . . .

What happened? What did I do? I didn't betray him. We had a deal, I was going to run the ranch. Why am I here? Is it because I didn't get him more information? Because I didn't sleep with him?

Her mind whirled with endless questions and recriminations as they rushed past the blackened skeletons of trees. Rows of embers gnawed up and down the trunks like termites feeding on the bark.

In the lead, she instinctively side-stepped the crisped corpses of a porcupine, then a fawn deer, and more forest animals chased down by the flames.

How did I let this happen? This collar, this leash. He thinks I'm nothing more than a pitiful animal. What was I thinking? Why did I do it? I failed, that's why. I didn't do anything right: my career, Tim's accident, the fire. My God, I started this. I didn't mean for any of it to happen. Someone could die here. Me . . . I'm going to die here.

Tears streaked her face. She kneaded them away with her palms, smearing her eyes, cheeks, nose, lips with smoke paint. The second helicopter might have been searching for her, Serena thought, but it might not return until morning. She didn't think she'd be around to greet it.

Suddenly, the wind veered again. The smoke bank turned with it. The blackened ground ended and dry grass and pine boughs ahead waved in their reprieve. The wildfire swept down the mountain, momentarily ceasing its traverse across it.

Oh no. He's going to do it now. He's going to kill me. Damn it, I'm not going to die in a fucking dog collar . . .

Serena could see out of the corner of her eye that Vuko still carried the leash in his bandaged right hand. Teeth bared in a snarl, she pivoted and with both her hands grabbed the rope and wrenched it with all her strength.

"Eee-augh," she screeched.

"Aawwww God," he bellowed in pain, his momentum pitching him forward.

Some latent instinct—Vuko's self-defense training, Serena thought wickedly—took over her muscle reflexes and as he stumbled off-balance, she hooked her foot on his ankle and he somersaulted over the trail down the slope, screaming as he tumbled. He instinctively dropped the longer of the two packs trying to try to shield his stitched-together limb, but the other bulkier load on his back made him tumble more. A howl of agony momentarily interrupted the din of the wildfire and Vuko stopped rolling, steadied on his knees, cradling his injured hand. The bandages broke out in red, blotchy blooms.

He stared up the incline in disbelief at Serena, who held the camouflaged cylindrical pack over one shoulder like a baseball batter on deck. Vuko bellowed and charged toward her like an enraged bull.

Chapter 29

The Blue Lagoon, unfortunately, was no pond. It was a local nickname. Not many years ago an avalanche flattened a narrow scimitar-shaped strip of forest and left behind a new meadow. The only water on it showed up during the spring runoff when the snow melted off Ram Mountain and trickled across the meadow, eventually triggering an explosion of natural cyan—wild lupine and bluebells, aspen daisies and columbine. It became a destination for hikers, mountain bikers and horseback riders looking for a place to picnic and marvel at nature's palette, but the only maps "The Blue Lagoon" appeared on were Double Dare's trail guides.

The avalanche's path created, as luck would have it, a natural freeway-sized break in front of the fire. It started in a nearly vertical chute on the mountain, and then followed the terrain, which knuckled to the southwest. As the bare land curved it lost elevation and gradually widened into the meadow. The avalanche plowed the rock and earth a couple hundred yards to form a new knoll that guarded the bottom of the meadow. As Grateful Bobby and his band of volunteers drifted out of the forest, the shadowy moon and the beams from their helmet lamps turned the meadow into a smoky discotheque. They stared at the eerie openness and quickly realized it might not be enough to stop the monster at their backs. Mainly, the meadow wasn't that wide, maybe only one hundred yards at its broadest point, where the avalanche spread out before grinding to a halt. At the bottom of the chute, the neck of the meadow, barely fifty feet separated the stately ponderosa pines swaying and groaning now as the wind picked up. It was almost as if they, too, knew what was bearing down on them.

There was another problem: all of the timber the avalanche had mowed down still littered the Blue Lagoon. From the air the meadow looked like a lumberyard hit by a hurricane. Still, the meadow gave them some breathing room from the fire's rush. But if they didn't clear it of the timber and dried sagebrush, the open land would feed the fire even more.

Grateful Bobby reverently patted a ponderosa with his hand and then stuck his nose into a crack in its bark and deeply inhaled. Always expected, always a surprise, he took in the unmistakable aroma of vanilla. He patted the trunk one more time, then he turned and started shouting orders for the forty or so firefighters to form a tight line along the edge of the meadow closest to the blaze and begin clearing the ground.

They took turns using chainsaws on the logs, then carrying the pieces and countless limbs behind them to the opposite side of the meadow in front of the knoll. The distance from the rocky chute to the foot of the meadow was about half a mile. Once his crew spread out, Bobby realized, they barely managed to cover one-third of the intended fire line. They desperately needed help.

As if on cue, the helicopter carrying Ramworthy and Cutter passed directly over and, pivoting in mid-air above them, turned to shine a spotlight down toward the lower end of the meadow. Bobby and others followed the beam to where it softly lit the forest edge. Bobby didn't understand the copter's maneuver until he saw some movement back in the trees. Then, emerging from the forest like some ghostly army, a mob of men in helmets carrying shovels and pickaxes and rakes on their shoulders marched into the meadow. There looked to be about twenty of them and their leader directed them to join the end of Bobby's line. Giving some final instructions, the sturdily built man, who looked accustomed to giving orders and having them carried out, continued up the line. Some of Bobby's crew greeted him and a few exchanged jokes as he came. Finally, he drew close enough for Bobby to recognize in the hazy light.

"Manny!" he yelled, and dropping his Pulaski he grabbed both shoulders of the Ram Mountain foreman in his thick, inescapable paws.

"Thanks for coming, brother," he said more quietly to the Mexican.

"*De nada. Mi amigos* work in the bean fields during the summer. They have been getting ready to move south, but when I told them about the wildfire *gigante* they offered their help."

"*Muchas gracias*," Bobby said, touched by the action of the men and the few women among them, most of whom he did not know, but who he did know were not always received so well under everyday circumstances in his country.

"*Muchas gracias*!" he bellowed again down the line, raising and shaking his clenched fists in the smoke-tainted air. A few of the EFFers waved hands, and wide brown-faced smiles greeted his cheer. "Now hurry, *mi amigos. Andale*!"

"Bobby." Cutter's voice came clear and strong over the radio. "We're going to make one last sweep at tree line to see if we can't spot Patricia and Serena. We can't do much else tonight. Stay safe, buddy."

The burly foreman looked up quickly at the copter and waved before turning back to his work. The copter banked and sped away into the night.

. . . .

Sunlight had long since faded into darker and murkier shades of gray. But the immense cloud of smoke that blanketed the mountain reflected the glow from the wildfire below. The air looked luminescent. It would have been beautiful, Patricia thought, if it wasn't so terrifying.

She estimated about four hours had passed since the woman started the fire. Her own life literally fluttered at the mercy of the wind. When it died, she walked as fast as she could down and across the mountain, closing the distance to the Dolores River; when it quickened, she ran to get out of the fire's way. Once she didn't react fast enough. Like a flame thrower, a red-orange torrent leapt at her as she screamed and tried to lurch away. Searing pain attacked her shoulder, and she swatted at the smoking denim. Blistered skin wept raw and red through an ash-ringed hole in her shirt.

The fire gathered strength. Below her she could see orange, flickering scouts of flame exploring the dry fuel.

The fire's bedlam smothered some of the sound of her movement and several times she overtook already frightened forest animals by surprise. Crossing over one small knoll she walked into a small herd of a half-dozen mule deer milling in confused panic caused by the roaring fire nearby. Patricia reached out to them, either instinctively or as if offering some expression of pity. The forest teemed with chipmunk chatter and squawking crows and magpies. But it only served as background noise to the ever-present, unending din of the wildfire. Twice in her peripheral vision she caught the fleeting shadows of larger mammals moving, silhouetted by the fire's glare. Deer or coyotes, maybe bears, she wondered, as they disappeared.

Patricia had no idea how big the wildfire was. If she did, she might have given up. The size of the blaze had multiplied ten times since sunset and its glow could be seen from the towns of Dove Creek and Cahone and even Mesa Verde National Park, forty miles away, which knew all about fire devastation.

Keep moving, she preached to herself through a fog of exhaustion. Keep moving.

. . . .

Riding a helicopter, particularly a small one, in the unpredictable air currents of the Rockies, felt something like breaking a horse. Or at least that's what Cutter imagined as he massaged the throbbing lower muscles in his back. The constant jostling the copter took, combined with the tension of flying over fire and straining to spot people on the ground, exacted a numbing toll.

"I don't get it," he said, as much to himself as to Ramworthy. "We should have spotted either Patricia or Serena, at least one of them, by now. We know approximately where they should be on the mountain. With the winds, and the direction the wildfire is headed, it makes sense to think they would be moving east."

"Looking for clear, safe ground," Ramworthy agreed.

"I think something else has happened in the forest, something that's preventing them from getting our attention. And there's one other thing that's bothering me: no weather threatened any part of Ram Mountain today—the sky was clear, that means no lightning." Cutter looked at Ramworthy. "So what started the fire?"

Neither man had an answer.

Cutter knew there must be another way to search, and he had a crazy idea.

When they left Grateful Bobby and the firefighters at the Blue Lagoon, he suggested to Ramworthy that they make one more easterly sweep across the mountain until they reached the Dolores. Maybe the women made it to the river and were waiting for rescue there. They found nothing, and as they neared the river Cutter began looking for clear spots, moving the beam of the spotlight from one piece of open ground to another. He knew that the idea bubbling in his head went against not only every firefighting Standard Order and "watch-out" situation, but ran totally against all his survival training for the wild. Five minutes more thought and the idea still struck him as crazy. But no one else within ten miles could do anything for the two women down there. He knew the BLM and county crews would be mobilized down in the valley in a few hours, but he also knew Serena and especially Patricia probably didn't have a few hours. Ramworthy seemed right in sync with him, edging the copter along so that it tracked with the spotlight.

As they approached the river, the pines and aspens that lined the red and black cliffs above the rushing water began to break, here and there revealing rock outcroppings and sandstone flats. The last time he'd been up on the cliffs was the day he and his crew started blazing a bike trail along the river's edge, and he guessed they were a mile or two north of that spot. Patricia's High Haven was probably another mile farther. Cutter kept the light trained mainly on the west bank, Double Dare's side of the river. In this section there were no river crossings that anyone would think of attempting, especially in the dark. Of course, a wildfire at your back might make the icy water look like a better choice.

Cutter's spotlight hit on a shelf that loomed bare over the river and he moved the beam toward the trees, gauging distance and clearance.

"That might work," came Ramworthy's deep voice out of the darkened cockpit.

"Huh?" Cutter muttered in surprise.

"You're looking for a place where I can put you down, aren't you?"

"Yeah," he nodded. "Can you do it? We've got to find Patricia and Serena before they think they've run out of chances. Or before they do run out of chances. They've got to be near here. I can yell for them down there, or maybe I'll come across them. They easily could have fallen and busted an ankle and can't move. Why haven't they called in on a sat phone? We need someone on the ground for them, and nobody else is close."

"That's what I thought you were thinkin'," Ramworthy said with a drawl. It occurred to Cutter that at age eighty or so, the rancher-pilot had every reason to be feeling a little stress and frustration, too.

"Let's do it," the pilot said as he sidled the copter down and over to the rocky shelf. Cutter pulled on his yellow hard hat and goggles.

The rotor blades on the Schweizer stretched thirteen feet long. If one clipped an aspen it would immediately wrench the copter, and in such close quarters little room existed for maneuvering or recovery. The machine would likely plunge at least one hundred feet into the river. Ramworthy wouldn't get any closer to the trees than necessary. He neatly swiveled the copter so that Cutter's side faced the woods.

"I'm going to put just your skid on the ledge," he said. "It'll give us a few more feet to spare for the rotor. Got your stuff?"

Cutter nodded that he understood and grabbed the survival pack that he'd brought with him when he and Bobby bolted from the ranch.

"Now I don't want you to go and take this personal," he said to Ramworthy, "like I wasn't enjoying the ride and your scintillating stories."

"Scintillating?" The man next to him acted insulted. "Hell, you're lucky I just don't tip this thing and dump you in the river, calling me any such thing."

They both grinned, and Ramworthy turned all his attention to the business of perching the chopper on the side of the cliff. Cutter kept the spotlight trained on the ledge, which was nearly flat but tilted about fifteen degrees downriver. Ramworthy planted the skid on the rock with no more of a jolt than a rowboat bumping a pier, and his passenger braced himself in the open cockpit door.

"Be smart!" Ramworthy yelled over the deafening rotation of the rotors. They were way beyond telling each other to be careful.

Cutter tossed the pack onto the ledge first. He reached down to clear his prosthesis from the cockpit, then he dropped down onto the rough red slab, clear of the copter. He anticipated the carbon-fiber foot, even with its energy-absorbing shaft, skittering out from under him on impact and he tried to roll. But the landing sent arcs of stabbing pain across his lower back. Gasping for breath, he rolled onto his throbbing back. Looking up, squinting through the storm of flying debris, he gave the pilot the universal thumbs-up. Okay. Go.

The copter lifted slightly, then sidled over the yawning river before Ramworthy sent it hurtling toward the town.

Cutter crawled to his feet. Once he could stand upright, just having his feet on firm ground began to give him some relief. Twisting his back getting out of the helicopter had been painful. But it started to feel better as he quickly stretched his muscles on the ledge.

Feeling refreshed, he studied the terrain around him, taking stock and getting a sense of the night. His plan wasn't anything ingenious. From the air he had gauged the fire to still be a quarter mile west of the river at this point. If the wind picked up, if Grateful Bobby's crew couldn't at least slow down the wildfire, it wouldn't be long before it reached the river across from Patricia's High Haven, or even threatened Double Dare. His throat tightened and he found it difficult to swallow. From here he figured to move south, parallel to the river, in a zigzag pattern that he hoped would cross paths with Patricia or Serena.

He and Bobby had scrambled into their Nomex fire-retardant clothing before they ever left the ranch, and he wore heavy, eight-inch-tall work boots with steel toes and non-melt soles and heels.

Cutter grimaced as he picked up the pack and struggled into the straps. Fifty-odd pounds of gear made his back muscles throb, but there wasn't anything he dared leave behind. The pack carried two hundred feet of nylon climbing rope with assorted other climbing hardware, one gallon of water, a plastic ground cover, an oxygen mask and a small tank, dried food that he could stretch for two days, binoculars and GPS, a small shovel, a fire pot if he needed to light a backfire, and at the very top of the pile, the latest-issue fire shelter in its own nine-inch by five-inch mini-pack. His Pulaski was cinched on his back within quick reach. He toggled the two-way radio on the left-front pack strap to make sure it was working and took a pull on the water tube that snaked over his right shoulder from the Camelback inside the pack.

Cutter glanced at his sports watch. Nearly nine o'clock. Time to make myself useful, he thought, as he headed for a stand of pinyon-juniper swaying and groaning before the growing wind.

Chapter 30

Vuko launched himself up the slope faster than Serena could have imagined. His churning feet scuffed up rocks and loose forest debris behind him while he grasped for any kind of hold with his one good hand. But he only made it half the distance when she shifted her two-hand grip on the shaft-like pack, planted her feet for balance, and cranked the mysterious object above her head, ready to swing it against the trunk of a foot-wide aspen tree beside her. The dog collar still stabbed her neck, the leash dangling. All around them now the forest groaned in fiery throes as the blaze crept closer.

"Stop!" she screamed, cocking the pack higher, "or I smash this thing. Whatever it is, I've been watching, and I know it means a lot more to you than it does to me."

Vuko froze in mid-scramble. Chunks of dirt and dead leaves speckled his face, enhancing the camo. She could see he was still coiled to make a run at her.

"Where do you think you're going?" he barked, spreading his undamaged arm wide as if to collect the chaos going on around them.

She took a few steps backward to another aspen, turning her head slightly each way to once again gauge her escape and check her footing.

"You said you were going to kill me anyway, right? I'm taking this thing . . ."

He took quick steps toward her.

"STOP!" she screamed again, bringing the long object down in a fast arc at the tree, checking her swing just before contact as he halted, "or I will bust this thing, I swear."

Vuko pulled up. Like the woman, his eyes seemed to measure the distance between them, weighing his chances. Ticking off his options.

"I'm taking this thing back up to that flat rock," Serena continued, nodding at a sandstone shelf they had just passed about fifty feet up the trail. Aspens, pinyons and junipers lined the way, close enough for her to swing at. Through the screen of trees behind the rock they could both see the fire flickering. Serena's brain raced, trying to calculate how much breathing room she would have—from the fire and from him—when she reached the rock. *This is crazy, but I have no choice.* Anywhere else, she knew he might be able to chase her down. The injured hand would slow him. But she was betting her life that he wouldn't risk her damaging his precious equipment, and the head start would let her escape into the forest and still avoid being trapped by the fire before he could get to her.

"I'll leave this at the rock once I get there. But if you come after me, I smash it. I'll get at least three swings before you can reach me, and I'll tear the hell out of whatever it is."

"I come after you, bitch," he snarled, "to hang you by your collar. But I won't kill you. I leave you to roast when fire gets to you. Have you ever seen human body burn, the fat—"

"Shut up, you one-eared freak," she cried, trembling with the effort to keep control. Then she started backing up the trail, still holding the long pack over her shoulder like she was walking to home plate.

"First the skin blisters, then it cracks open like sausage," he yelled up the hill at her.

Serena, already engulfed by terror, hardly heard him. She wasn't over one shocking moment, and another seemed to fly at her. She whimpered, then cut it off as she backed up the slight grade, never taking her eyes off him for more than a head-turn to make sure she didn't trip. Her hands tightened knuckle-white on the long pack, which was growing heavier by the second.

"The soft tissues split open first," he shouted at her. "Your gut and . . ."

She looked over her shoulder and saw that she was more than halfway to the rock. She wanted to run, but she didn't. She needed the advantage of every foot she could put between them. She knew as soon as she dropped the pack he would charge up the trail in seconds. She prayed that he would be so concerned about his damn pack—*what was in this thing, anyway?*—that it would at least gain her a few more seconds of safety. She was faster than him on flat ground. She might make it.

"Then your eyeballs start to boil. The heat is so bad it . . ." His voice floated faintly now. And she could feel the assault of heat from the approaching wildfire.

She threw the pack down at the rock and ran. She hurdled downed trees, sucked in smoke and gases and didn't notice. She heard his field boots scuffle up the trail. Tree branches whipped her face as she scrambled on a diagonal line away from the two monsters behind her.

. . . .

His chest heaving from the effort to reach her, all of the synapses in his damaged hand exploded in firecrackers of pain. Vuko silently cursed himself for relaxing when he drove Serena through the forest. Watching her edge away from him up the slope, he mentally calculated the distance to her—too much to cover before she could swing the tough but, he knew, precisely tuned equipment against the tree.

The mission is taking too long. But I can't leave her. Shit!

When she dropped the pack, Vuko charged. But he didn't chase her. He bent to pick up the canvas-covered cargo. He'd already decided not to go after her. He needed to kill her, and then to escape.

He looked over his shoulder for her. Serena—*that bitch!*—darted through the smoke and trees like a spooked deer, nearly hidden from him already, only flashes of her pale blue vest giving her away.

He already imagined a new plan. He knew she was running into a dead-end V, the fire forming one tong of the pincers and the cliffs above the river the other tong, and everything in between would be burnt to cinders. The fire would herd her back to him. He was counting on it. He had no choice. He couldn't even take the time to check the gear he recovered. It worked or it didn't. He needed to move, get in position. Quickly.

I can't catch her. But I can hunt her. She just gave me what I need to do it.

. . . .

The Blue Lagoon writhed with heat and smoke and clamor. Grateful Bobby gauged the wind now up around thirty to thirty-five miles per hour and he shuddered to watch it push the blaze across and down the mountain towards them. As he blinked, his eyes stinging from the smoke, the fire jumped forward by a car length. Six feet per second, at least. It was an awesome, frightening thing to witness. The wind also bore the promise of some weather in its gusts, but right now all it delivered was bad news.

Up and down the fire line, though, men and women kept at their backbreaking job. They took turns hacking at the dead grass and yucca that had sucked all the ground water out of the meadow over the summer, and hauling away the broken timber that lay covered beneath the old vegetation to the back of the clearing where a wall of wood grew. Bobby worried about that.

One of the first rules of fighting wildfire warned never, ever, to allow fire to get below or behind you. The simple lesson of his wilderness firefighting instructor echoed in his mind: "There are two beasts in the wild that can run uphill faster than any human: fire and bears. And they'll both kill you."

Looking at the piles mount, though, he told himself once more that they couldn't afford to waste the time and energy to carry the fuel away any farther. They intended to clear a road-size break as quickly as possible that the fire could not jump or blow over. He made sure the crews left gaps between the stacks of logs and limbs in case they needed to run for it and escape.

All around Bobby a steady babble of single-minded work carried on. Advice, requests for help, quickly told stories of old fires, and hurried grunts of "thanks" flew on the wind.

Wildlife streamed out of the forest in front of them, four-legged refugees fleeing their homes. Instinct told them the flames behind them presented a far greater danger to them this night than the humans ahead. Stately bull and cow elk, already skittish from the rifle-hunting season they were trying to survive, crashed through the timber. Beautiful mule deer bucks and prim does appeared from the trees and then dissolved in the night. Raccoons and skunks, marmots and coyotes, porcupines and rabbits and tribes of smaller creatures added to the exodus.

The forest moaned as the fire devoured it. The wind fanned the flames, which roared as they approached. Unseen, ancient ponderosas exploded in the dark. The crackling of consumed and breaking timber was constant and close.

Without warning, a piercing shriek came from the forest at the lower end of the meadow. Three Mexican firefighters scattered in terror. Seconds later a screaming, wild-eyed horse, spraying sweat and slobber, burst from the smoking woods in front of them. Scared out of its skin, the brownish and white paint horse charged into the clearing before slowing and then finally, exhausted, it stopped, head bowed almost to the ground, its chest heaving beneath a saddle, its flanks trembling.

"That's Frisco! That's Patricia's horse," Manny shouted excitedly from down the line.

Ramworthy's foreman and Grateful Bobby both walked quickly toward the mare, which shied and nervously ran a short distance away. As the mare moved, their helmet lights followed her. A wound—not too bad—glistened crimson on one shoulder.

"She looks okay," Manny said. "She's moving alright, she doesn't look injured. Just scared as hell, I'd say."

"If she's okay, then leave her be," Bobby answered. "There's nothing more we can do for her now."

"Anyway, she can run faster than we can," the Mexican observed wryly.

"I'm gonna look where she came from and see if by luck Patricia's in there," Bobby said as he turned and headed for the trees. "Maybe she got knocked off when Frisco came through the trees."

The big man plunged into the woods and instantly disappeared.

"Patricia! Patricia!" he shouted, looking first to his left, unconsciously planning to work his way back to the right in a hasty search. Thick, choking smoke hung in the trees so that he could see only inches in front of him. Knowing his voice rasped weakly in the din of the bellowing fire, he tried again.

"Patricia!" he yelled as loud as he could, his throat hoarse and raw.

He would have to trip over her to find her in here. Well, he'd take that chance.

"Patricia! he croaked pitifully again.

As if he'd opened the door to a fully engulfed room, fire attacked him. Strands of his silky black hair that had worked loose from beneath his sweat-soaked Dolphins bandanna and hard hat caught fire, and tiny flames crawled around his wrist where his denim shirt peeked out between heavy work gloves and his Nomex coat. Beating his head and arm with his other hand, he ran from the heat. Blindly, he stumbled out of the forest slightly downhill from where he'd entered it. His face gleamed black and wet. His hair smoldered. The wind puffed white smoke and ash off of him. Manny ran to him.

Still patting himself down anxiously, Bobby hurried past Manny. "We're running out of time," he said, breaking into a run back to his position on the line.

. . . .

As soon as Serena knew for sure Vuko wasn't chasing her, she stopped to get rid of the leash. After some trouble, she unlatched the dog collar from around her neck, flinching when the barbs pulled out of congealed puncture wounds, and threw it as far as she could. She tried to rub away the memory.

She started running again. But she hadn't covered the length of a football field before she realized she'd underestimated how close the wildfire was. Like a tidal wave, it was gaining height—and power. She gasped at the unleashed fury.

She couldn't be sure Vuko wasn't pursuing her because all she could hear was the approaching firestorm. She knew there was no getting around it. Her only escape route was past Vuko.

Serena hastily backtracked, her swollen eyes wide with fear. She took small comfort in knowing he couldn't hear her. Peering through forest branches whipped by the fire's bellows, she spotted the white beam of what could only be a headlamp. Almost stationary. Vuko. Hunched on his knees, bent over the hard-packed earth where she left him, playing with one of his toys.

. . . .

The pack he'd reclaimed from Serena on the ground at his side, Vuko turned the other larger pack upside down and shook it. A twisted, intertwined puzzle of dull, army-green metal tubes and black rubber thunked onto the forest floor. Quickly, he started unfolding the contraption. In less than thirty seconds, he was making the final adjustments on a Montague Paratrooper field bicycle.

Military troops had been using folding bikes since the turn of the twentieth century. The infantrymen intensely disliked them at first, but the descendants of those early models were commercially competitive. The rigid-aluminum Paratrooper weighed twenty-nine pounds, still more than its weekend recreational cousin. But they were just as dependable. Intent on the equipment, Vuko seated the stem of the saddle and started to tighten its clamp.

. . . .

Not more than forty feet behind him, hidden by the darkness and a thick tangle of untamed forest, Serena watched the camouflage-clad figure. She had an overwhelming urge to simply bolt past him and try and beat him to the river. She could feel the inferno at her back. Her sprint through the forest and the mounting heat from the fire left her dripping sweat, the Spandex bike shirt and shorts oppressively tight. She swallowed again, desperate with thirst, knowing Vuko carried extra water. The forest shook with sound—old timber crashing, limbs snapping, the pop of overbaked pine cones, a hundred lumberyards torched together.

What's taking him so long?

Serena crabbed forward a dozen feet, then froze as he stood and walked around—a bicycle? His backup plan, she thought, as he leaned the bike against his hip and, holding his bandaged right hand upright, reached down with his left for the precious golf bag-sized pack that she so recently held. *What's he got in there—a boat? It wasn't so crazy. An inflatable kayak? Vuko always had a survival plan.*

Carefully, he rested the heel of his injured hand on the right handlebar, swung a leg over the center bar of the frame and pointed the bike down the trail. The front wheel wobbled from one side of the path to the other under his obviously untrained guidance. He hop-stepped one booted foot from pedal to ground, pedal to ground. Steadied.

Vuko was no Lance Armstrong, she could see, as he rolled unsteadily away and melted into the smoke.

Serena understood her predicament: the fire was pushing her closer and closer to Vuko. It cut her off from any route around him. She needed help. She was convinced now she wasn't going to get out alive on her own. Someone had to be searching for her. She needed a signal that could reach beyond Vuko, beyond the inferno that raged around her.

Chapter 31

Weird, Cutter thought. Despite the wildfire and the beating he'd taken from Vuko, he actually felt pretty good. Adrenaline is a wonderful thing, he decided. Maybe the jostling of the helicopter actually helped work out some of the soreness in his back.

He knew the two women must have headed for the river. He started to yell both their names, hoping the wind might carry his voice to one of them. But after only a couple of tries he realized that he might as well be yelling under the down comforter of his bed back at the ranch.

He kept to his zigzag plan. He bushwhacked into the forest for twenty or thirty yards, watchful for movement or a flash of bright-colored clothing in the otherwise black night. Then he turned and fought his way back towards the river until the pines and aspens thinned and he emerged again onto the red rock ledges looming over the fast-moving Dolores. Each time he reached the river, where he imagined the spray and humidity filtered out some of the soot and ash in the air and he could see farther, he took extra time to look downriver first and then up the cliffs. Each time he expected to turn and find one of them standing on one of the flat rocks that jutted out over the flow, safe from the flames.

Instead, nothing.

He kept on for what he guessed was at least an hour before he began to feel a twinge of guilt. He knew the others—Grateful Bobby and Manny and the overmatched firefighters, and Ramworthy—were working into the night, scrambling to throw tiny man-made hurdles in front of the wildfire. At Ram Mountain Ranch, neighbors and town people prepared food and a tent village for the expected arrival of the professional firefighters. Meanwhile, he simply flailed about.

Twice in the forest he saw thick dark shadows run from him. Probably small black bears, he figured, their pre-hibernation food binge on berries and insects now completely disrupted. He knew that all over Ram Mountain the wildlife had to be moving, either running from the flames or, a less hopeful thought, trying to find an escape route through them. He intersected one of the main bike trails that snaked up and down the mountain and he crossed it with a sense of fresh hope. Still, he maintained his sawtooth-like search pattern.

Halfway down the mountain above Double Dare, and having just cleared the forest heading toward the river, Cutter felt the little buzz of anticipation he got each time he approached the open cliffs. As had become his habit, he looked downriver first. His heart pounded at what he saw; it shocked him more than if it had been Patricia or Serena. Never in his last, best dreams did he expect this, on this night.

The small gray wolf, surely a Mexican, was unmistakable as it stared directly up at Cutter. He would never, ever forget the yellow flash of its eyes as everything else around him stopped. For a moment, the chaos of the night faded, and the only sound was his heart crashing against the wall of his chest.

The wolf no doubt picked up Cutter's scent easily on the strong wind, even among the trees. It stood frozen, its left front paw flexed in mid-stride. Its muzzle, topped by a moist nose as black and silvery as water at night, was closed but imperceptibly tilted upward to better inhale the scent of this new danger. Cutter judged it at about ninety pounds.

Man and wolf locked onto each other. Cutter marveled at how handsome its coat was—black along the straight ridge of its back, mottled gray at its neck and along its flanks, charcoal again down its legs.

The wolf—

Clack! Clack!

—vanished.

The harsh, unnatural sound shattered the moment. Cutter never saw the animal move or leave. It was there, then gone. For a bitter second, he thought, gone for him, forever.

He broke out of his daze and listened again.

Clack! Clack!

If he had heard it only once, he might have dismissed the sound as a small rock fall. But twice and it had his attention. He cocked his head, listening intently.

Clack! Clack!

Three times. Instantly, hope replaced disappointment. What the hell was it? Where was it? The hard, rhythmic beat, so evenly spaced, had to be someone signaling.

Why were they signaling? Because they couldn't yell for help.

So they were hurt or trapped?

Where? Cutter slowly turned his head—slightly left, tilted upward—trying to guess where the sound would come from next.

Clack! Clack!

Definitely downriver.

He carefully walked toward the hammering sound, and he stood where the wolf had been. He still couldn't believe what he'd seen. He couldn't stop himself from looking for a paw print or a clump of hair left behind.

Clack! Clack!

The sound got louder. Standing on bare rock, getting his bearings, he looked upriver where his line of sight widened and what he saw took his breath away. Half a mile up the narrow, steep-faced canyon the water glowed like molten gold—black water reflecting the flames from the forest. Distracted by first the wolf and then the rock medley, he failed to notice that the wildfire behind him on the mountain, even in the face of the wind, had finally fanned out to the river as it voraciously followed the fuel. The scene looked even more hellish as thousands of brown bats, maddened by the firelight, wheeled and dove and cried. Cutter watched mesmerized as hordes more peeled away from their cliffside crannies.

As he turned, a stand of pinyon-junipers blocked his way back into the forest. He ducked his head between both outstretched arms, intending to slip between the whipping edges of two trees, when he nearly tripped over a taxi cab-yellow mountain bike lying in the dust. It had to be Serena's. She'd passed this way. It was his first sign of one of the women, he thought, momentarily cheered, as he reached down for the Stumpjumper center bar.

Clack! Clack!

The rhythm taunted him and he turned to continue his climb downriver to wherever it led. Or to whomever it led.

. . . .

The ghost weaving through the forest on the camouflaged Paratrooper bicycle heard it, too. And he knew what it meant. A wicked-white smile gave away his green- and black-painted face.

. . . .

Serena dropped her arms to her sides, the melon-round river rocks pulling on her already rubbery biceps and forearms. She'd picked up the rocks, ironically, from some long-abandoned campfire ring. The nearly perfect spheres had been smoothed by water, so the river was close. After signaling half a dozen times, she started to doubt her signal. *Is this any use?* She absentmindedly rubbed the raw ring of welts around her neck left by the choke collar.

She knew Vuko would keep to the trail. He probably hadn't ridden a bike since he was the school bully. She kept up with him by bush-whacking straight down the mountain's fall line, hurdling over downed logs and dodging rocks, cutting in half at least the distance he traveled. She'd practiced the same mountain-goat tactics for years as off-season ski training to build up her strength and agility. As she scrambled down the slope, she had to grip tightly to hang on to her signaling stones.

Again she felt the fire pushing her. *Her* fire. The flames were unstoppable. She looked back and saw them take flight on the wind now, crowning, leaping from the top of one tree to another—fifty feet, then seventy, then a hundred. It looked like the sky was ablaze, and she had to steel herself not to try and rush past Vuko.

Her worst fear was that she'd get too close, that one of the times he glanced back up the mountain he'd spot her, silhouetted against the crazy orange backdrop. If he saw her, she knew, she was dead.

Someone else *had* to be out there.

Clack! Clack!

Chapter 32

Each one of her senses warned Patricia that the insatiable wildfire nearly had her.

Her denim shirt and jeans, soaked with sweat and seared with holes from falling embers in a dozen places, scalded her back and legs. She constantly patted out the gray tangle of fuses that insisted on igniting around her head, alerted by the stink of her own burning hair. She could no longer taste the brackish ash that filled the air, but it felt like she'd been swallowing flour. The force of sound, loud as the backwash of a jet engine, nearly knocked her down. The wildfire and the gloom of the moon provided ample light to make her way, if it weren't for her sandpaper eyelids, so that she squinted and stumbled forward leaning on a tree limb she had picked up as a staff.

If anything, the fire-crash and bedlam grew, louder, more eager, more sure it would overtake everything, Patricia thought, when her legs would no longer support her and she pitched forward. When she put her hands out, the sensation shocked her so at first that she thought she must have landed onto a forest floor of embers. Numb with fatigue, she realized instead she had walked into the Dolores River. Grateful, comforted, almost too weak to move, she let the water lap at her arms and chest. Slowly, she turned her face to sip the reviving liquid.

In that moment, the wind quickened yet again, blowing flames out of the forest canopy directly over her. Branches snapped and rattled and small brands flew overhead only to die in puffs of smoke in the river.

Gotta move, Patricia told herself. Still half in the water, she crawled farther into the river. Looking upriver, the spectacle delivered only more jarring views: she had somehow found her way back to the pools she and Frisco had crossed—*when was it*?—hours ago? Days?

Across the river, she saw that High Haven was about to be immolated. She couldn't hold back a mournful shriek.

Reflecting the writhing white-gold heart of the wildfire, the river looked like it too was on fire. From bank to bank, the Dolores canyon glowed like a tunnel of stage light. Above the tunnel, the night hung like a blackout curtain. Soon the trees around her became larger and larger torches launching embers like arrows onto brown grass, dead timber and the sun-blanched house. The lovers' porch that hung over the river from High Haven was already engulfed, while fire surrounded and crawled up the carved wooden spindles of the front porch. Somewhere a window exploded as sudden and certain as if smashed by a rock.

Patricia pulled herself up and waded across the river, unsteady as a drunk. She looked again at the opposite bank. She didn't know what she was more surprised by: being alive, or seeing Vern Ramworthy wading out to meet her.

She tried to move toward him, but her legs and feet felt heavy as granite.

"C'mon, hurry," she heard, picking Ramworthy's words out of the tumult, as he waved behind him toward the little helicopter squatting in the road beside High Haven.

"Patricia." He grabbed her by the arms. "Are you alright? I can't believe I found you. I was just making one last pass by the house before I had to quit."

She looked into his eyes, when the strangest thought came to her, the words of a legendary bull elephant from an old African fable she'd read: *"For now, it is enough to say that I am here."* She smiled up at him. "Get me the hell outta here."

As the copter lifted off, buffeted by the wind and thermal currents of the wildfire, Patricia reached one soot-stained hand to the Plexiglass cockpit shell and told herself it would be the last time she saw High Haven.

. . . .

Vuko bumped uncertainly down the forest trail on the bike, sometimes dragging the toe of one foot because he couldn't squeeze one brake handle with his throbbing right hand. The thick camo fatigues and ghillie hump made the heavyset man appear even bulkier as he hunched over the bike, the better to balance the bedroll-like pack on his back. He knew the wildfire was always back there, always gaining, racing toward him. He *felt* the woman there, too, knowing she had to stay ahead of the fire as well and that eventually she'd get flushed out and he'd finish her. Then he'd get the hell out.

Half an hour later, Vuko rolled out of the forest onto a wide red rock ledge overlooking the river. To his left, upriver, the water came into sight around a canyon wall that danced with the fire's reflection. The canyon spread slightly and the late-season flow of the Dolores shrunk to reveal a naked riverbed choked with rocks, mostly fist- and brick-sized stones, but dotted by enormous boulders large enough to hide a person. The flat shelf he stood on hung some ten feet over the rock field. The river snaked to his right before disappearing around another wall, crashing as it quickly lost elevation. Vuko noticed another bike or game trail followed the rim, probably a continuation of the one he was on. His escape route.

Perfect! This is where she'll come. She doesn't know I'll be here, waiting. She thinks I've left on bicycle, to beat fire. I'll wait for her, right there!

Behind him, pinyon-juniper and tamarisks thrashed in the super-heated wind, awaiting their fate in the encroaching wildfire but for the moment providing a screen of cover for him.

Perfect!

He pushed the bike into the nearby brush and unslung the remaining pack from his shoulder. He laid it gently on the rock floor, and then with his one good hand undid the canvas ties that bound it. Quickly, he unrolled the pack like it was bedding, but inside were nearly a dozen pockets of various lengths and widths, each secured by its own cloth tie. As he worked, he noticed soft flecks of white and black begin to lightly pepper the unrolled pack. He rubbed one with his finger and it left a white smudge on the material. Ash. He looked up into the night sky. With the glow of the fire as a backdrop, it looked like it was snowing. He knew he had to hurry.

From the longest and narrowest of the pockets, Vuko slid a metal tube camouflaged with exactly the same colors that he wore. From another pocket he pulled an unassembled rifle stock of the same tints and hues. Methodically, he assembled the weapon. The AWM .308 rifle system, made by Accuracy International of England, was one of the finest-crafted rifles on the planet. It had a range of 1,100 yards but was bloody deadly within 500. The ammo clips were loaded with Hornady TAP 168-grain plastic-tipped cartridges, which covered 300 yards in less than half a second. At that speed, in less time than it took for the tick of the trigger pull to register with the shooter's senses, the bullet pulverized its target. The Nightforce scope made it an absolutely unfair weapon. Vuko couldn't count the times he'd wished his snipers in Krajina held such a weapon.

"Come for Darko now," he whispered in an accented singsong, instinctively slipping skins into an old, familiar persona much at ease on a battlefield.

. . . .

From the swaying pinyon-junipers behind Vuko, as she tried to calm her heaving chest and control her breathing, Serena saw the rifle.

She watched Vuko as he seemed to make adjustments to his weapon. Obviously, he was waiting for her. *I had it in my hands! I could have smashed it!*

The hunter was so intent that he didn't see what Serena saw upriver behind him—a new white light, from around the bend: a beam, focused, probing, bobbing from the forest to the riverbank and back again. A headlamp. It had to be. And as the form wearing the yellow helmet slowly came into focus through the swirling fire smoke, it looked familiar. The slightly off-kilter, stiff-legged step . . .

Cutter!

Stunned, desperately wanting to believe what she thought she saw, Serena half rose from her protected crouch, ready to scream as loud and as long as she needed to get his attention.

I can't. He'll turn and shoot me!

At the same time, the soldier—that's how she thought of Vuko now—jammed an ammo clip into the rifle, chambered a bullet and stood, filling her view.

Chapter 33

Just past midnight—nine hours since the lookout ranger first reported the Ram Mountain Fire, and five miles west across the mountain from the Dolores River—the only people fighting it were falling-down exhausted. The wildfire was in their faces now, screaming and bellowing at them at the very edge of the Blue Lagoon. One of nature's most awesome forces had crept up to man's insignificant line in the sand, and they were all about to find out if that line meant anything.

As they stopped and leaned on their shovels, Grateful Bobby and Manny knew the crew was in danger. There was too much dead timber, but they had to fight. Just five miles to the southeast, Double Dare Ranch stood next in line.

The volunteer crew never intended to fight the fire up and down its perimeter, or to knock it down. It had grown too big for that hours ago. But the meadow gave them the best chance to at least slow down its march across Ram Mountain until the Hotshot crews and heavy air tankers could hopefully reach them the next morning. It better be the next morning.

Grateful Bobby was more worried that the fire might surround them—the wildfire fighter's worst nightmare. The men and women had done an amazing job of clearing the meadow of fuel. The ramparts of piled timbers and branches, old fence posts and even the remains of an ancient buckboard wagon rested at the back of the meadow as testament to their work.

But the woodpiles continued to worry Bobby. As the grinding labor took its toll, and more and more fuel stacked up, the piles got closer and closer to the front line of the wildfire. The stacks of deadwood formed a shallow horseshoe behind them.

The Blue Lagoon remained an oasis, if a slightly singed one, in the center. They were barely holding the fire back. The awful wind, ratcheted up to forty miles per hour, blew thousands of tiny firebrands out of the trees, each one capable of sparking fire. With each burst of missiles, the crews chased them down and slapped them out. All the while, though, the fire feasted on the west and east sides of the horseshoe. Bobby was so tired he couldn't see straight, but he'd seen enough.

"Manny . . ." he said, before breaking into a hacking cough. "Manny, we've got to get out. We can't do any more. If those piles catch fire, we'll all cook like turkeys in here. You warn your people on that side, I'll take this side. Run, *mi amigo*."

Both men started off in opposite directions. The tireless giant yelled back, "We've got to get everyone past the piles and over the knoll in back. We can run for it from there."

WHU-UMP!

WHU-UMP!

Like two firework caches, the last pile of wood at each end of the horseshoe exploded, lighting up the meadow. Every man and woman in the Blue Lagoon stopped in their tracks, holding their hands up to protect their eyes from the waves of heat that buffeted them. And then for the second time that night they all ran, this time for their lives.

WHU-UMP!

A third stack of wood ignited. The piles, like a line of Viking funeral pyres, were stacked so close together that a chain reaction was inevitable. But Bobby had instructed the crews that no matter what, they had to leave a gap in the middle of the piles so that they had an avenue of escape. The gap was about the width of a good-sized house. The fire would eventually easily bridge that distance. In the worst conditions, it could jump interstates. In 1994 at Glenwood Springs, Colo., flames driven by the wind jumped the Colorado River and Interstate 70 to form the fatal South Canyon Fire that surprised and killed 14 experienced firefighters. Bobby only hoped they left the gateway wide enough.

WHU-UMP!

WHU-UMP!

Just as the first firefighters were sprinting through the opening, two more piles ignited. The small knoll was just beyond the line of timber piles. It formed the rear boundary of the meadow, on ground fifteen to twenty feet higher, and those who scrambled to the top stopped to look back and yell for their weary friends and neighbors to join them. It was like many another Friday night in the fall when they would all cheer for the Dolores Bears at the weekly high school football game. Only on this night, if they didn't make the run, they wouldn't live to see their families or their town again.

The wind seemed to have risen yet another notch and it carried a hailstorm of embers across the meadow as the firefighters streamed through the gap. Grateful Bobby, Manny and three other crewmen—the two New Mexico veterans and the young woman with them, Laura—brought up the rear.

WHU-UMP! WHU-UMP! WHU-UMP! WHU-UUUMMMMP!

The remaining piles suddenly exploded like a string of land mines, as if reluctant to let the last of the firefighters go. The fire now fully engulfed the meadow. The concussion knocked the rearguard of five to the ground as they passed through the gap. On the knoll, the waiting firefighters cried out at the awesome sight. Terror-stricken, most fled over the knoll into the relative safety of the gulch on the other side. A handful instinctively started forward to help the fallen, but they were driven back by the sheer power of the heat rolling towards them at nine feet per second. The fire bellows behind roared end-of-the-world loud.

Bobby and Manny and the others were on their feet, helping each other, their clothes and hair smoking. They knew they had only seconds left. There was no longer time to run.

"Get to the knoll! Get in your shelters! It's our only chance," was all Bobby had time or the breath to yell. They lurched and stumbled toward the tiny knoll. The soft forest ground, pummeled into powder by the stampede that had preceded them, gave way beneath their boots and they clawed their way on hands and knees.

Pinyon-juniper, gambel oak and a few ponderosas, spread out with ten to twelve feet of space between trees, cluttered the knoll. Flames crawled up and down most of them. The five wildfire fighters frantically dug in their packs for their aluminum-covered shelters. Folded to about the size of a dictionary, they wrenched them free and thrashed with the pull straps. The shelters were shaped like sleeping bags and were capable of reflecting ninety-five percent of the radiant heat that reached them. They weren't entirely fireproof, but they were the final refuge for the firefighters.

"Man, I've never had to use one of these damn things," Bobby gasped, struggling to open the shelter as the wind threatened to whip it from his grasp. There was no hiding the fear and doubt in his voice. He remembered from his training that some of the South Canyon firefighters had died in their shelters.

"They work," shouted one of the New Mexico firefighters, just pausing to yell from the last foot of open bag before sealing his shelter closed. Thick, black smoke and leaping flames choked the knoll. Even though the five shiny bags were all within inches of each other, none of the firefighters could see one another. The voice of experience was their only reassurance. "They'll take up to five hundred degrees. Stay down. Try not to panic. I'll call you all when it's okay to get out."

Bobby never heard another word. Inside his shelter, he felt instantly claustrophobic with his nose pressed against the aluminum skin. Even in the dense smoke, the smell of new packaging and the glue that bonded the shelter's layers heating up was pervasive. To Bobby, it sounded like a great storm outside. Or like the time he'd pitched a tent one night not knowing he was twenty feet from a railroad line, and later in a dead sleep he felt the ground begin to tremble, then shake, and within seconds an east-bound coal train had jolted him awake.

The firestorm was coming. Sweat and fear poured off him in the confined space. *I'm lying in a cheap, aluminum-foil coffin and I'm going to die.* He heard a primal scream from close by, he thought, until he realized that it was his own final, defiant, terrified way of kissing his ass goodbye.

Chapter 34

Clack! Clack!

Cutter cleared the canyon bend separating him and the exasperating signal—what else could it be?—expecting to quickly home in on the clatter and find one or maybe both of the women injured, unable to call for help any other way.

"Patricia? Serena? Anyone?" he yelled, his voice sounding tiny in the face of the terrible sight before him. Skyscrapers of flame towered over the riverbed, only a hundred feet or so from ledges that overhung the rock banks, much closer than where he'd come from. The spectacle intimidated him, terrified him with the realization that no one could survive such a force on foot, alone. *How do I get myself out of this?*

He dismissed the thought and did the only thing he could—tried to locate the source of the signal. He strained for the sound of the two-beat rhythm. He yelled again.

"Is anyone out there?"

. . . .

Tinny fragments of words carried down the canyon and Vuko snapped his head toward the sound. It was upriver, not behind him. Not Serena. Then he spotted the uncertain weaving of the headlamp, too. *Who the hell . . .?* It could only be one person. As hard as Vuko tried, he couldn't block out the image of his former protégé: Cutter!

Suddenly, what he'd written off as a total failure of a mission seemed salvageable, an outright success even. He'd take the kill he planned, but also a second one that would avenge eight years of shame. He savored the sweet nip of adrenaline he got when he thought of beating Cutter into the dirt a few days ago. But that wasn't enough. It wasn't nearly enough to make up for his disfigurement, for stealing the idea of Double Dare, for sabotaging his plans.

The bitch could wait. He experienced another push of adrenaline. He jerked into action, with the promise of a much, much bigger prize.

The headlamp across the boulder field made a perfect target.

In one swift, practiced movement he wound the rifle sling, its length measured to an exact fit long ago, around his left elbow, and dropped to one knee at the rim of the ledge. He rested the same elbow on his left knee as an added shooting brace. He figured the shot to be less than fifty yards. Child's play. His right hand started to curl in a familiar embrace around the trigger when he realized the bulky bandage prevented his index finger from fitting into the trigger guard. He pulled the rifle down in frustration, set it upright, leaning against one shoulder, and began to unwind the bandage and free his hand. Cutter disappeared behind one of the rocks. He'd lost his shot.

Throughout the night Vuko had been able to ignore the pain in his torn hand as he busied his mind with details and strategies. When he grasped the bike handlebars on the jolting ride, that had hurt—big time. But he had a high pain tolerance and he forced himself to focus on the smoke-shrouded rocky trail. Now, again, as he wrestled with the bandage and his mangled paw met the fresh air, he winced as the flow of blood surged and pain got his full attention.

His hand now free, he slowly, tentatively, tensed and moved the muscles and fingers in his lacerated hand. The dog's teeth had gouged out furrows, and dried blood and meat instantly cracked anew, and firelight shined in the open wounds. Despite the damage, the hand worked. It would do for now.

He whipped his eyes back to the river. He seemed unfazed by the fire that howled less than a hundred feet behind him and the cliffs overlooking the river as he again set up the shot.

He brought the rifle to his shoulder and nestled his cheek into the green, fitted plastic stock. His right eye centered in the night-vision scope. Cutter's head filled the reticle. Vuko mindfully placed the calibrated crosshairs on the man's ear. *Paybacks are hell.* He blinked once.

Breathe, breathe, slow, hold it . . .

Dare this, Cutter.

. . . .

Serena knew she had to move. Trapped between the wildfire and the soldier, it wasn't too difficult a choice. No one ever ran into a fire.

And then there was Cutter.

She burst from her thin veil of cover without a sound and crossed the few yards between them like a linebacker squaring up for an open-field tackle. At best, she thought, her advantage of surprise and mass would knock him over the side of the ledge. At worst, she realized, her momentum would send her with him.

. . . .

Vuko didn't hear her charge, but he felt it. War—and the memory of war—conditioned the mind and muscle reflexes in many ways. The hair rising on the back of his neck gave him a split-second to brace himself.

She hit him with her shoulder lowered, like the boys had taught her in their Sunday afternoon football games. But he was solid and planted. Pain lanced across her neck and back.

He instinctively coiled every muscle in his body to absorb the blow, and it saved him from being bowled over the ledge. The woman rocked him. His arms shot out to purchase balance and he fumbled his grasp on the rifle. The trigger had only a hair's play and the crash of the .308 gunshot and its echo across the canyon in crackling waves silenced the fire for a moment. Serena's weight and momentum hit him high. Vuko hunched his back and exploded upward with his legs, and Serena went airborne over him. For a millisecond, he had a glimpse of flying blonde hair and clawing hands. Vuko grabbed for the rifle—gone!—but in the same instant a noose tightened around his neck and slammed his face into the ledge. His nose exploded with pain. His forehead cratered on shards of chipped sandstone.

The ghillie suit.

Somehow Serena had managed to snare some of the netting as she sailed over him, held onto it when she fell, and now the tough, knotted cape and her dead weight were strangling him to death, cinching his face and neck to crimson and then purple.

. . . .

Like a human pendulum at the end of its arc, Serena's body slammed into the sandstone and red dirt wall. The impact knocked her out for a moment, and her fingers slowly, grudgingly gave up their death grip on the mesh. Her body stretched full length, her feet already brushing the river rocks, she slumped like a bag of dirty laundry at the base of the ledge.

. . . .

Cutter flinched at the unmistakable crack of the rifle blast. He stared across the boulder field at what looked like a man staggering to his feet, back-lit by hell. *Who?*

"My God," he murmured as his eyes grasped the entire river canyon from bank to bank. Not only were flames climbing into the sky, higher than the trees on his side of the Dolores, but they were leaping across the river—twisting, orange and violet wraiths that shimmered in the gaseous light and seemed alive and evil. Glowing embers sped through the air like bottle rockets while white ash floated and danced on the wind. Even the river couldn't hold the wildfire at bay. Cutter grimaced as he thought of Grateful Bobby and the other EFFers across the mountain as he stood transfixed by the apocalyptic display. And what about Double Dare?

Something else stirring beneath the ledge caught Cutter's eye. Another person, Cutter thought in disbelief. It had to be Serena. Or Patricia.

"Cutter." A woman's weak cry drifted across the rocks. He dropped what he held in his hands and ran for the sound.

. . . .

Vuko struggled to his feet, ripping the ghillie suit loose from his neck, gasping for air. He sucked in a mouthful of ash—but cold, too? His face glistened with moisture. *The woman, the rifle, I can still . . . No. It's over. Get out. Now.*

He couldn't believe the disaster his mission had turned into. Not only had he lost his chance to eliminate Serena and—damn!—Cutter, too, but now he stood weaponless, exposed. Attempted murder, assault, conspiracy and bribery were just a few of the crimes they could pin on him. His ranch, his dream, his power—gone. The disappointment and humiliation of losing it all fell on him like a sudden madness. He felt physically ill, weak, used up.

And his crimes here were the least of his problems if anyone looked deeper into Radic Vuko's past. If they found Darko Magyar.

He surveyed the hellstorm swirling around him. The wildfire screeched at the forest's edge behind him and launched its firebrands, which reached the few pinyon-junipers and aspens that followed the cliff edge downriver. The smoke became indistinguishable from air. It was thick and vile and all that was left to breathe.

Goddamned Cutter thinks he's going to stop me. Thinks he's going to win. I can't let that happen. They haven't caught me yet, and they don't know about Darko yet.

Vuko plunged into the nearby trees. Beating away the flames that reached out for him, he backed out, pulling with one hand the Paratrooper mountain bike. The aluminum frame felt hot and the front tire smoldered. But it seemed usable. He took one last glance at the ledge, glowered at the sight of the other man hobbling across the rocks toward him, and he pointed the bike down the hard rock trail along the river.

. . . .

"Serena!"

Cutter yelled her name as he closed the distance and he could make out the young woman's athletic body. It couldn't be anyone else.

"Serena, are you hurt? It's me, Cutter."

And yet when he reached her, extended his hand to steady her shaky attempt to stand, he wondered how he recognized her. Her tawny gold hair partly hung in bedraggled strands around her face, which was streaked with soot and sweat. The hair on one side of her head actually looked like it had been chopped off until he realized that the frizzy ends were burnt black. Her biking shirt and shorts were stained and torn. Her right leg was caked black, and when she took a step, she limped and her leg glistened ruddy and bloody in the fire glow.

But what scared him was her response. Instead of reaching out to him, Serena backed away. Slowly, eyes locked on him, she edged to her right, as if looking for a way around him. One arm outstretched as if to hold him at bay, she turned and took another crossover step toward the river and stumbled.

"Serena—"

"He . . . we . . . I . . . ," she stuttered, pointing at the ledge above them. "Vuko—"

"Vuko?" said Cutter, stunned at the name. He looked at her like she had lost her mind. Or he had.

A giant ponderosa pine crashed out of the fire, fully consumed. The massive, upended trunk formed a fiery bridge over the trail as its halo of upper branches tipped into the Dolores in a whirlwind of sparks and steam. Branches from one side of the once-majestic prince of the forest stretched from the water like grotesque charred arms.

"He chased me in the fire. The fire . . . I . . . " She whispered the last word, the wind snatched it, and she rushed on. "He came in the helicopter, I thought he was going to save me, but he hit me, he choked me.

Like a dog." She rubbed her neck with one hand, where he could see a necklace of raw welts. She continued to skirt around him.

"Wait a minute. You brought Vuko here? Why—"

"He made me. He didn't make me, but he promised me I would run Double Dare if I helped him. We had a deal. The old lady on the horse surprised me, I didn't mean to—"

"Patricia? You saw Patricia? You're sure? Where?"

"Up there," Serena said, pointing back into the fire, up the mountain. She took another step, toward the water's edge, away from Cutter. "Vuko's out there. Somewhere."

Cutter didn't know whether to believe her or not. None of it made sense. But hearing her mention Vuko's name made it all click into place with a grim certainty. He reached for her. She jumped like a startled deer.

"Where's Patricia now? Did she get out? Is she all right?"

"I don't know."

Patience wearing thin, Cutter started toward her. Serena shied toward the river again.

"She tried to fight the fire but it got too big, too fast. I ran. She headed to the river ahead of me. I should have stayed with her. But that bastard chained me up. Vuko tried to shoot you. I stopped him. Please, don't hate me, Cutter."

Her eyes darted to the ledge. No one. She shielded her eyes against the firelight. Without another word, she pointed at the canyon wall upriver.

Cutter followed her gaze. A two-story-tall, misshapen shadow moved across the red rock wall. But it looked like it had wheels. At the base of the wall, Cutter watched a thick, hunched figure on a bicycle disappear into the scattered pines and aspens in the direction of Double Dare Ranch, the only part of the forest untouched by the fire.

"Stay here!" he ordered. "You'll be safe here in the rocks. Get behind one of the big boulders."

Instead—her eyes flashing from his to the wall of flame rolling at them, then back to him—Serena took short, uncertain steps toward the river.

"It's here," she said. "The fire's gonna kill us. Get in the water."

"Serena, stay here!" he said sharply, then started back in the direction he'd come from across the rocks.

"I can't," she screamed. "Cutter . . . I started the fire. I didn't mean—"

Her confession stopped him like he'd run head-on into the canyon wall. It nearly dropped him—he forgot to mind his right leg and stumbled over a rock. Vuko. Everything pointed at him. It astounded him how much damage the man committed—Tim's fall that night on Moccasin Ridge, the Double Dare takeover, poisoning Serena's life, at least a hand in starting a wildfire that could yet be a killer. He stared at her in disbelief.

"He's not gonna do this. He's gonna pay," he said, and ran as fast as his legs would take him.

"Cutter?"

He ran back to the riverbed, reached into the scorched brambles, and dug out the taxi-yellow Stumpjumper, glad that he picked it up. The fire had baked it black in a couple places, but otherwise it looked in good condition. He noticed the pedal clips and realized his heavy work boots, encumbered by Sasquatch, weren't going to work too well with those. He'd only be able to grip the pedals with a little pressure. It wasn't like he had options.

Cutter swung onto the saddle. Normally a motion as natural to him as pulling on his socks, it sent a bolt of bright, screeching pain across his back and streaked through his knees. In just the few minutes of standing still with Serena, his back muscles had tightened. He clenched his eyes shut, staggered by the attack, and willed it to pass. Slowly it subsided. When he could open his eyes again he stood slumped over the handlebars, gasping for breath. Sweat covered him, cold and clammy.

He took a last look over the bluff down to the river and the rocks where he'd left Serena, the wind biting in his face. He thought he could see a dark shape breaking the reflection of the fire on the water, but he couldn't be sure it was Serena. He didn't have any time to worry about her. If she waded into the Dolores, she was safer than he was.

As he looked up into the black night, white flakes swirled madly in the firelight. He felt their cold sting on his face. It wasn't ash falling anymore, or at least not all of it. It was starting to snow, he realized. And blowing in pretty good from the look of it. No telling in Colorado if it would last five minutes or a day. No matter, it was a blessing as long as it lasted. But if it did continue to snow, he thought, as Sasquatch's hard-soled boot slipped off the glistening pedal clip, it was only going to make what he had to do even crazier.

He stood on the pedals and launched himself after Vuko.

Both of them knew the military man wasn't any mountain biker. On the other hand, Cutter was an expert. Even if he no longer biked as much as he used to before Double Dare, he still made time to scout a new trail or to personally test the bike challenges. Muscle memory quickly took over, and once he adjusted his boot pressure to the swing of the pedals he could concentrate on keeping his weight back, knees churning. He ducked under the huge burning ponderosa splayed over the trail, picking an opening where the limbs beneath had snapped off in its crash, but still had to fight over the scattered slash. Then he stood on the pedals and began to eat up the trail's twists and turns.

. . . .

Vuko expected Cutter to find a way to come after him. If he somehow found Serena's bike, it would be that much quicker. Maybe they could still finish the war between them.

In the meantime, he struggled to stay on the Paratrooper. The trail remained mostly level at the start, but the green-black river immediately plunged deeper into the canyon. As a result, the rim rock he sweated over steadily skirted higher and higher above the water. Then, with the river at least a couple hundred feet below him, he guessed by the hushed flow, the trail tipped downward. Not consistently steep, but in an undulating, twisting theme park dive. His worst problem by far was gripping the handlebar with his damaged right hand and working the brake lever cabled to the rear brakes. Every time he had to squeeze the lever, searing pain engulfed his hand, as if it were stuck in a waffle griddle, and he had to back off and rely more on the left lever that controlled the front brakes. That held its own danger.

Figuring he held only a quarter-mile lead, at best, on the man behind him, Vuko pushed the bike beyond his capabilities. He coasted—too fast—into a switchback, strangled the front brake with his left hand, only to feel his momentum rush forward and the back wheel lift off the ground. The bike launched him over the handlebars in an almost perfect somersault—what experienced riders refer to as an "endo"—and spit him into a thicket of gambel oaks off the side of the trail. The stiff, pointed oak leaves raked his face and left hand, as once again he tried to cushion his right hand in the fall. Every movement made the mangled limb throb and feel twice its natural size. He didn't have the luxury of time to inventory the fresh gashes and bruises. He limped to the folding bike that lay twisted in the trail, re-locked the frame, and stiffly tried to push it with his legs back down the trail.

The two riders left the wildfire behind them, although they could still hear the shriek and moan of the burning forest. At the same time, the light grew dimmer and it was all each of them could do to pick out the trail ahead and pedal and react. The path had probably first formed as a game trail years ago and snaked around bushy pinyon-juniper and straight, slim aspens roughly spaced every eight to fifteen feet as it followed the Dolores. Local riders had discovered the place years ago and, as they tended to do, kept the stash of outrageous downhill fun to themselves, or at least until the secret got out. Then thanks to the trail's notoriety, knobby tires began beating the path into dust.

It's a damn maze, Vuko swore, as he fought to avoid the trees and negotiate the banked switchbacks.

. . . .

It reminded Cutter of a skier's slalom course. Then he remembered where he was. Just above the spot where Vuko and his goon confronted him and his trail crew in what seemed like years ago. *The Mars Slalom.* All the better, thought Cutter, as he swung to the rhythm of the trail, letting the bike's suspension and his knees and arms absorb the track's surprises.

The false foot attached to the titanium leg pylon had taken some getting used to, years ago, when he first started riding again after the climbing accident and amputation. He had to adapt to an entirely different feel on the right pedal. In the process, his riding style became based more on the rhythm of his bunched upper leg muscles than by pure thrust against the pedals.

He had to be gaining, Cutter thought instinctively.

Snowflakes twirled from all directions in front of him, so that he couldn't tell the wind direction. Suddenly, he heard the clink and rattle of a loose chain in the derailleur on the bike ahead of him, the telltale sound of a rider in the wrong gear, and he knew he had almost caught Vuko.

Cutter hadn't given a second's thought to what he'd do when he overtook his former employer. The mentor who was now his enemy. Now the unending night of tension, worrying over Double Dare, and the drama on the mountain poured energy and purpose into Cutter. He flew down the trail. He leaned into a sharp downhill right turn, using only a little brake, and deftly controlled the skid of his rear tire as it sidled over loose gravel. Ahead he looked down a straight chute of a hundred feet or so, and at the end the rear spokes of a bike winked and disappeared around the next bend.

I'm gonna ride right up his damn back.

"VUKO!" he yelled as loud as he could, as he turned the bike loose and hurtled down the straightaway.

. . . .

The challenge from Cutter didn't surprise Vuko. He knew Cutter was there. He knew he was no match for Cutter on a mountain bike. While he had a few yards' lead he looked for a clear spot to stop, and then he'd beat the fucker to death this time, he swore. Even with one hand.

But he hadn't gauged his speed well coming out of the chute. He realized too late he was wheeling too fast for the next right turn and he slammed on both brakes. Slick from the falling snow, the hard rubber brake pads squealed. Vuko's hand exploded in pain and his momentum caused him to lunge forward. The S-turn gave him no warning and the trail snapped hard-left in front of him. He knew it was too late to make the turn.

He had no control over his mangled right hand. As he blew past the turn, he looked down in astonishment at his bloody fingers, which numbly remained curled around the rubber handgrip until they were smashed between the handlebar and a stout aspen. The tree trunk wrenched the handlebars hard right and steered him straight toward a precipice. Below, he saw a smoky abyss with no bottom. One second his brain registered the sound of rubber tires crunching over loose dirt and rocks; in the next second, he heard only the gentle breath of emptiness. In helpless flight, he kicked his legs to try and separate himself from the bike, exactly why, he didn't know. Instead, he only tangled the bulky fatigues in the frame.

Falling took forever.

It gave Darko Magyar time for one final life-summoning reflection. Or so he thought, four seconds before he stained the unyielding rocks of the Dolores River.

. . . .

Every other time Serena slipped into the Dolores River it had been for fun, it occurred to her. On this night it would be because she was terrified.

Standing ankle-deep in the river, she gazed in horror at the cliffs, where shadows cavorted on the canyon walls, as first Vuko and then Cutter tore across the rim in a crazy chase before disappearing.

Downriver she watched a doe lead a frightened fawn into the water. The river looked like it was burning, too, a mirror of the hellfire that surrounded them.

Everyone had left her. The forest was dying all around her. *What else was a girl to do?* The ditzy phrase sounded like surrender under the circumstances.

After standing in the frigid water, her feet felt frozen solid. If she walked out into the current, Serena knew this would be the most important river run of her life.

Chapter 35

Cutter had heard the squeal of Vuko's wet brakes. After swiveling his bike through the S-turn, he expected to find him just ahead where the trail opened up again. But no bike tread creased the snow-coated path ahead of him. He got off the bike and walked back; his eyes searching the trail. Midway through the S-turn he found what he was looking for.

The Mars Slalom ran so close to the edge that he missed seeing Vuko's tracks where he rode through the tight chicane. Vuko had obviously veered violently.

Cutter found a fresh, golden, horizontal scar on an aspen at the edge of the trail at handlebar height. It was no elk rub. Below it, a faint depression of crushed grass pointed at the river. Cutter looked over the cliff, but couldn't see anything. So that was the end of Vuko, he thought. They would have to come back for the body in the morning but he wouldn't hurry. Going back for Serena and catching up with Grateful Bobby were much more important.

Double Dare Ranch lay only a couple miles down the trail—that was good and bad. Good that he only had to ride a short distance, as the muscles in his back flared anew; bad that the ranch still lay directly in the path of the wildfire. He couldn't guess how many times he'd squinted up into the night sky, but he did it again and snowflakes, driven by the wind, stung his eyes.

Will it be enough to stop the fire?

He took care negotiating the rest of the tricky path—thank God he followed his instincts and never opened this section to the public—until he crossed the Say Hey Trail. He made a sharp left turn, his rear wheel almost skidding out from under him in the snow slop. He steered out of the turn, shifted his weight to compensate, and then quickly clicked the gears higher and higher as he made up time on the familiar trail. He came out behind the softball field less than half an hour later.

The ranch appeared empty and silent, that is until his front wheel hit the gravel yard and the still-rowdy wind carried the crunchy sound to Maggie curled on the ranchhouse deck. The copper-colored dog greeted him boisterously, obviously feeling better after the beating she had taken. He could see lights on in the house.

Coasting only on the left pedal with his one good leg, Cutter jumped off the bike and let it fall in the path, one wheel continuing to spin. He burst through the sandblasted glass front door, unlocked as usual. He nearly collided with Lexi.

"Cutter!" she cried, jumping up to throw her arms around him. "Oh, I've been so worried about you. What happened?"

"I'm okay," he said, still trying to catch his breath in between the dark-haired beauty's frantic kisses. "Lexi . . . Lexi, I've got to hurry. Have you heard from Bobby? I've got to try and help them. There's so much to tell you, but it will have to wait."

Untangling her arms from around his neck as gently as he could, he moved urgently into the adjoining great room. He plopped on one of the oversized couches and began hitching up the right pants leg of the bulky Nomex overalls he still wore, struggling to get at the prosthesis. "I'm sorry, but could you run and grab me some stump socks for my socket, please? I lost my pack."

The Australian shepherd half-jumped into his lap with her front paws, eager to join the celebration. "Lexi, could you please take Maggie with you, I just don't have time . . . "

He heard the woman's leather soles clomp up the stairs, followed by the dog's paw nails clicking across the hardwood upper floor. He rolled the pants leg high enough to expose the prosthesis, wriggled the carbon-fiber socket off his leg stump and started to set it on the floor next to him.

Cutter heard the front door open.

"C'mon in. I'm in here," he yelled, guessing it was one of Double Dare's ranch hands. Cutter focused his attention on massaging his chafed limb.

"Where's Vuko?"

The unfamiliar voice, slightly accented, immediately got Cutter's attention. The visitor was still out of sight, in the foyer.

"Dead," he replied in the same instant the stranger rounded the corner and their eyes locked.

Bug Eyes!

"Nooo!" the man screamed in anguish, as he launched himself across the room, his arms reaching for Cutter. His right hand aimed an eight-inch serrated field knife at Cutter's throat.

Cutter pushed himself up on his left leg, at the same time bracing his right hip against the heavy piece of furniture. He grabbed the only weapon within his reach—Sasquatch—and as a pure reflex held it up in both hands as his only defense. The knife blade glanced off the casing of the carbon-fiber socket Cutter held with his left hand and clattered to the floor.

Somewhere off in the distance—maybe in a different world, Cutter thought—he heard Lexi's high-pitched shriek.

His attacker's eyes bulged madly as he lurched to reach the blade. Again, Cutter's reflexes took over. With his right hand, he smashed the other end of the prosthesis—gun metal-blue titanium ankle, machine-pressed carbon foot, steel-toed leather boot and all—into Bug Eyes' face. The cartilage in Bug Eyes' nose snapped like a wishbone and his face exploded in crimson. Cutter immediately levered the artificial limb back and slammed the other end into the opposite side of his head. The empty socket didn't carry nearly the same weight or effect, but it was enough to rock the man. Bug Eyes dropped to the floor, half-conscious.

Cutter collapsed on top of him, pinning both shoulders with his knees. One hand clenched the hair at the back of the man's head, forcing it to the floor. The other held Sasquatch high in the air, poised to swing again.

"Tito?" Lexi's voice sounded small, disbelieving over his shoulder. "Tito? Is it really you? Here? Alive?"

Tito? Tito? This goon is Lexi's brother?

The smaller but compactly built man moaned, both hands holding his nose. But as his senses came back to him, he tried to buck Cutter off his chest.

"He says Vuko is dead."

"Darko?" Lexi cried out.

"No," said Cutter, now using both hands on the titanium shaft of the prosthesis across the man's neck as he fought to control him. "I don't know any Darko. Vuko is dead."

"Darko. Vuko . . ." The stranger tried to say more, but his strangled words came in a gurgled mush.

Even though he had the upper hand, Cutter struggled to hold the man down. The search on the mountain, his attempt to reach Serena, the chase with Vuko, and finally the draining fight had utterly exhausted him.

"No!," Lexi cried, clutching her head with both hands. "Not our uncle. He can't be dead," she sobbed.

Cutter stared in shock and confusion at them both.

"Yeah. He's dead—whoever he is. And together the three of you may have killed my friends," he shouted, before he drove the prosthetic foot into the man's barely comprehending face again.

. . . .

She rushed to the limp body, reaching out to cradle him.

Cutter took the opportunity to hop, still on one leg, to the front porch, grab some orange hay bale twine and quickly begin to tie Bug Eyes tighter than a branding calf.

"My brother. My little Tito," Lexi cooed as if she were rocking a baby.

Cutter kept trying to figure it out. "You told me your brother was killed in the war in Krajina?"

But studying their faces, so near each other, he immediately saw the shared features, the shared blood. And the shared anguish.

"That's what Darko—or Radic, I don't know which one—told me when he brought me to America. After my mother—his sister—was killed in the war."

"He is . . . was the same man," said the foreigner, crawling back to consciousness again. "Darko Magyar and Radic Vuko."

Realizing he was bound hand and foot, he began to struggle again and explore with his fingers for some way to escape.

Cutter tapped him on the back with the prosthesis, made eye contact. "Leave it! Or I'll reset that nose for you . . . How did you get here?"

"Darko found me in our homeland," he glared, "after a long search. He brought me here, after Lexi, but he would never let me see her. He trained me in all ways—language, fitness, combat, weapons. I flew him here from Denver in a helicopter to the top of the fire. I was to pick him up here when he came off the mountain on his bicycle. But I wanted to see Lexi, too. I didn't know you were here."

"*Uncle* Vuko," Cutter repeated, still in disbelief. "So you've been with him all this time," he accused Lexi. "He sent you to Double Dare."

"*Da*," she whispered, not even registering the lapse into her native Croat. "I thought it was strange that he told me never to mention his name to you. But he had private businesses, secret clients that he would never talk about. I thought it had something to do with his work. I never knew he wanted your ranch. That he would harm you."

"But you were spying on me for him, Lexi. How could you do that?

You had to know—"

"I did . . ." She looked up at him through tears, her eyes as black and bleak as the night. "I thought I loved you. But I came to realize I loved my family more. He was my blood. Tito's blood."

Cutter reached over to Bug Eyes—he couldn't think of him any other way—and cinched a knot tighter, drawing a grunt from the body.

"I've got to go help Bobby." Cutter rolled a fresh, slightly thicker sock over his stump, then grabbed Sasquatch and jammed it onto the leg, sealing the suction fit. He rolled over onto his knees, then stood, testing the artificial limb. "I don't know what happened at the Blue Lagoon, or how far the fire has spread," Cutter said. "I don't know where Patricia—"

"She's safe. Ramworthy called. He found her at High Haven and brought her down in the helicopter a couple hours ago. She has some burns, but she's okay."

"That's terrific." Cutter couldn't hold back a fleeting smile of relief, for the first time all night. Then cut it short. "I've gotta go. Lexi, you can't let this . . . this Tito go free. I don't care if he is your brother. He was with Vuko. He did stuff for him. I'm sure they rigged the fall that almost killed Tim Riordan. He's a criminal, do you understand?"

He held her by both shoulders and probed her eyes with his. "I loved you. But not now. I can't. You can stay a while, figure things out. But if you let him go, you better go with him."

He dropped his hands.

She still hadn't moved when the truck wheels shot gravel across the yard. The red dog rode shotgun. *I'm not leaving anything else for the Magyar clan to try and steal.*

Chapter 36

Take one mountain of fire.

Add a thick coating of powdered white ash and dying red embers.

Lower the air temperature to around thirty degrees and lightly dust the mountain with two inches of flaky Rocky Mountain moisture.

Then gradually raise the temperature so that by five o'clock in the morning the smoking mountain is back up to about forty-five.

Mix well, Cutter thought wryly.

And there you have nature's recipe for Ram Mountain Gumbo, which is how he thought of the snotty, muddy sludge that he and the nine other bone-tired men and women slogged through. The thought of any recipe always made Cutter think of Lexi, and for the hundredth time since he tore out of Double Dare Ranch, he wondered if she would be there when he got back.

As he struggled through the muck, he replayed the night's events in his mind.

When Cutter reached Ram Mountain Ranch, Ramworthy told him what had happened at the Blue Lagoon and that no one had heard from Grateful Bobby or Manny. He planned to grab a couple hours' sleep and as soon as there was light he would get the helicopter back up and help direct a search. Then word came that most of the fire crew had made it off the mountain. Sheriff Morningstar hastily organized the search group and they ran to their pickups to find Bobby and Manny.

They found the worn-out fire crew where they had stumbled out of the forest onto an old hunting road halfway up Ram Mountain. They told the rescuers how they had escaped from the meadow and made it over the knoll. The sudden snowstorm hadn't reached that part of the mountain until they were nearly halfway down. They thought Bobby and Manny and the others were right behind them and that the wildfire was still heading down the mountain.

Did Bobby and Manny make it? No one had seen them since, but that had been a few hours ago.

Now Cutter, Ramworthy, Nipsy, Bryan Boonstra, Sheriff Morningstar with a deputy and three Dolores County emergency rescue personnel, and one member of the escaped Blue Lagoon fire crews were less than half a mile from the meadow and racing for it as fast as the sloppy slopes would allow. They carried rescue gear, including oxygen, in backpacks, and their boots carried at least an inch of mud. Before they left the ranch, the sheriff turned his back to them and tried to discretely cram black plastic body bags into his pack as well, but they all saw him do it. The rescuers worked their way upward, quiet, keeping their thoughts to themselves.

Morning light crept softly into the San Juans. Cutter and the rest of the group knew from some flames that still lashed parts of the mountain that the wildfire wasn't out, or even contained yet. Taunting them, though, the dawn slowly revealed the snow's magical effect. It looked as if the gods of the ancients of the Southwest had come during the night and laid a thick white blanket over their mountain and snuffed the fire out. Ram Mountain stood covered in darkness one minute and shrouded with a dense fog the next, the result of the snow condensing above the hot ground. Alpenglow washed the mountain in lavender light as the sun peeked over the horizon. The earth steamed all around them, giving the mountain the eerie look of a cemetery from an old horror movie, Cutter thought. Just as quickly, he remembered their mission, and pushed that image away.

Bobby and the others had to be alright, Cutter thought. He slipped, shooting both hands out to stop his fall, and saw them disappear in the mud. He was beyond exhaustion.

"That's it! There's the knoll," shouted the firefighter from Bobby's crew. He pointed up through the blackened, smoldering tree trunks to where the mountain folded and leveled for a stretch, a hundred yards above them. "They were up there on top."

Cutter led the group up the incline. He thought this close to the meadow they might run into stragglers, that maybe those who were left decided to wait for morning light before climbing down.

As he neared the crest of the knoll, Cutter felt his heart pounding. He imagined that as soon as he could see over the knoll, there would be Bobby and Manny, probably sitting on stumps or gathering up their tools for the hike down.

The knoll was barren. Charred and smoking tree trunks stood out starkly against the snow- and ash-covered hill and meadow beyond. The black and white scene exuded the cruel beauty of an old battlefield photograph. Not a single leaf or green thing remained.

Without a word, Cutter pointed to a small dip in the terrain where five mounds of snow huddled together like an awkwardly organized graveyard. He and Ramworthy looked at each other and ran ahead of the others to the piles. As they got closer the rising sun glinted off the shiny aluminum corners of what they all quickly recognized as firefighter shelters.

"Bobby?" he called softly, going to one mound clearly larger than the others. He brushed the snow from what he now dreaded really might be a grave.

"Manny?" the white-haired man whispered, prodding and shaking one snow-mantled bundle after another. "Manny?"

Nothing stirred.

Rescuers kneeled beside each mound, scratching in the mud and snow for the shelter handles, and upon finding them, peeling open the bags, praying to find life inside.

"Get oxygen on them," the paramedics ordered.

"This one's breathing!" someone reported from one shelter.

Cutter uncovered the shelter and found Grateful Bobby curled in a fetal position, his yellow helmet askew on his head. Ash peppered the long, fine ponytail, which reeked of the unmistakable odor of burnt hair. The big man didn't move. Cutter tossed the helmet aside and rolled him over, then quickly stretched an oxygen mask over his smooth sooty face.

"Bobby! Bobby!" he yelled, shaking him gently. He knew all too well about his friend's medical history. It would be the unkindest trick and ultimate tragedy if such a good man died because his heart was too big.

"C'mon, Bobby. Breathe! Breathe!" Cutter commanded.

All five firefighters were unconscious. Overcome by smoke inhalation, at least. The medics scrambled around the bodies.

One of the New Mexico Hotshots stirred first. Then another. Laura, who had come to the Disappointment Country bargaining for no more than a weekend of tough mountain bike rides, still lay motionless as the paramedic tried to force oxygen into her lungs. He quickly pulled a syringe and clear vial from his pack and tried to pump life into her veins.

Ramworthy knelt with Manny lying backward in his arms while one of the paramedics adjusted the oxygen mask covering his mouth and nose. Suddenly, the Mexican foreman flailed to life, screaming as he tore the mask away.

"Aieeee!" he cried, covering his eyes from the blinding reflection of the sunlight off the snow.

"Aw, hell, he's alright," laughed Ramworthy. The old man wiped something from his eye while the Mexican continued to flop around like a trout, swearing in Spanglish.

Cutter stared down into Grateful Bobby's face and then looked up and beyond at the long recline of Sleeping Ute Mountain to the south. He prayed that Bobby was only sleeping, too, like the great Ute. He looked down and was rewarded by a flutter of smudged, blackened eyelids. Then another. And then Long Water came to life.

"Hey Bobby," said Cutter.

The Indian covered his eyes from the bright light. He looked like he'd crawled out of a coal mine. He reached on his own and tugged the oxygen mask down.

"Cutter," he sighed. "Man, am I glad to see you." He squinted hard against the glare and looked around like he'd just landed on a strange planet. "What is this? What happened to the fire?"

"It snowed two inches early this morning," Cutter replied with a grin. "Perfect timing for the first snowfall of the season."

"I thought we were cooked. The fire blew right over us. I was scared to death. It was so hot in this thing, nothing to see, sweating like a pig. All I could picture was me with an apple in my mouth. It was loud. Like the ocean loud. I guess once it burned all the timber it wasn't quite so loud. But it was still so hot inside I didn't want to open the shelter 'cuz I figured everything was still burning. Then I guess I passed out. How are the others?"

"Manny made it. And two more. There's a girl . . . we can't wake her up."

"Did you find Patricia? Serena?" Bobby said breathlessly. "Did you get 'em out?"

His friend and boss looked him straight in the eyes and nodded.

"Yeah, we got Patricia. She's okay. Bumps and bruises and some burns." His face changed. Tightened. "I found Serena, but then we ran into Vuko—"

"Vuko?"

"He was gonna kill her. Shoot her with a rifle. Maybe both of us. Bobby, you won't believe this, she said she started the fire, that she had some deal with Vuko. It's a crazy story."

"Do you think the cryptobiotic lawsuit drove him over the edge? Made him try this stunt? What were the federal penalties, anyway? I know it's fragile stuff, but I never knew roughing it up could put you in jail?"

"There are no enforceable environmental penalties on private land. That's a Western myth. But the BLM isn't so forgiving."

"Where's Vuko now?"

"Dead. I wasn't gonna let him get away, not after all this. After he tried to shoot us, we got into a mountain bike chase—" Bobby's jaw dropped open as he listened to his friend—"I know, I know . . . He rode off the edge of that trail we built up there. Mars Slalom. Would you believe it?"

"I told you that trail was gonna put a scare into someone some day. I didn't know you'd let me pick the guy," he said with some satisfaction.

"I had to leave Serena at the river. I think . . ." Cutter looked down, his mind seeing the troubled woman wade into the frigid current. "I'm afraid she may have tried to swim out. I've gotta go back and help look for her."

The medical crew took turns working to revive Laura. Finally, half an hour after they found the snow-shrouded shelters, they pulled hers closed again. The loss pressed upon all of them. Somberly, the survivors began to tell how the Blue Lagoon came to be burned totally black. Despite spending the night on the mountain, no one seemed in much of a hurry to leave. It felt like a holy place now.

Then, while the whole group sat in the mud as the sun climbed over the knoll, Cutter told them his story of the Ram Mountain Fire and a lone wolf and a dead bastard named Radic Vuko.

Chapter 37

They spent the second day of the Ram Mountain Fire on search and rescue and recovery.

Grateful Bobby and Manny and the tiny band of firefighters were able to walk down the mountain on their own. Walk was one word for it. Most of the time they were all sliding on their butts as the temperature rose into the sixties and the mountain turned to mush. Maybe some other day it would have been fun. But most of them hadn't slept in thirty hours and had spent the time in between either fighting wildfire or running from it.

When they reached the road they were caked from head to foot in red and black sludge. They threw themselves into pickups, some having to help others to get into the cabs. They sat there huffing and heaving until three of them summoned the strength to drive back to Ram Mountain Ranch.

At the ranch, even though rescuers and rescued alike could barely stand, they insisted on sharing the duty of carrying Laura's body through a somber gauntlet of neighbors and fresh volunteers to one of the county emergency vehicles.

Overnight, while the EFFers and Cutter and Ramworthy did what they could on the mountain, BLM personnel and the Hotshots arrived. An Incident Commander, or IC, officially took over management of the wildfire. The Hotshots, the Forest Service's best-trained wildfire fighters, came up from New Mexico and quickly deployed along key stretches of the fire line. The IC, a veteran who had fought western wildfires from Missoula to Mesa Verde, intended to debrief the local crew. But as Cutter and the others struggled with the body bag and then stood back wearing vacant, exhausted stares, instead he shook their hands and helped those he could stagger across the yard to collapse on cots set up under the huge field tent.

. . . .

The search and rescue effort shifted to Double Dare Ranch. Only Cutter knew, though, as the caravan of sheriff's vehicles and local pickups passed through the mammoth log front gate, that he was still looking for two women, not just one.

He knew Serena was in the gravest danger, and in the minds of the weary men sitting beside him, they needed to find her as quickly as possible. The survival rate when spending a cold night lost in a dark canyon was low. Factor in the wildfire, a madman, and a rogue snowstorm, and the odds against survival started compounding like bad debt. But, as they steered into the ranch yard, Cutter strained for the sight of Lexi while all the others were looking for Serena.

Lexi was gone, and so was Tito. Even though he prepared himself to find the ranchhouse empty, the disappointment and sadness of her betrayal crushed him.

A note he found on the kitchen counter made it official.

My dearest Cutter,

Please try to forgive me. Tito is the only member of my family left alive. I cannot walk away from him. Tito knows what he did was unforgivable. But he is not the kind to go to a prison. We will lose ourselves in your big country for a while. Maybe some day we will return home to Krajina.

You and I—we have not been close for some time. You are more in love with your ranch than you ever were with me.

I left a few things for you in the refrigerator. It will last a while, if you don't let Grateful Bobby know, until you can find another chef. Say goodbye to Bobby and to Double Dare for me.

Do vidjenja—Goodbye.

Lexi

He was sad she left and angry her mercenary brother got away. He was the kind, Cutter thought, who would cause more trouble someday. For someone. After all, he had learned from the worst.

Aimlessly, he opened the door of the stainless steel refrigerator. It was packed wall to wall with Lexi's gourmet food, everything wrapped to last and labeled in her tidy girlish handwriting. He let go and the huge door closed with a hush.

"Where's Lexi?" asked Mouse, wandering into the big kitchen.

Cutter looked blankly at the river man.

"I don't know," he replied honestly.

. . . .

Cutter suggested to Morningstar that he allow Mouse to lead the river search and rescue with him. No one knew the Dolores or river water better, and no one wanted to find Serena alive more than Mouse. If and when they came upon Vuko's body, they'd take care of that, too. But the main mission was to find the beautiful, enigmatic ranch guest.

When Cutter shared Serena's confession that she had started the fire, it shocked them all. Patricia confirmed that she had startled her on the ridge, and wondered aloud that maybe Serena hadn't intended to drop the fateful scrap of burning paper that ignited the mountainside. Double Dare Ranch had escaped two takeovers: Vuko and the wildfire. The blaze blackened Ram Mountain from alpine tree line to within a mile of Double Dare. After it incinerated the Blue Lagoon, it marched another four miles before the freak snowstorm finally snuffed it out.

Cutter, Mouse and two emergency medical techs started their search down the north-flowing Dolores at the riverbend where Cutter had left Serena. The closer he led the rescuers to the rocky spot beneath the ledge where he had tried to talk to Serena, the more he believed they might find her waiting there—resting in the shade of the big boulders, assured that once the snow put out the fire, that someone would come back for her. Standing on the little spit now, Cutter pointed out their footprints in the few clay gaps between rocks, but they found no other signs of Serena. Cutter thought it odd, though, that a few prints came from out of the water.

The others continued to scour the site, looking for clues.

Curious, Cutter rock-hopped back to the cliff wall, looking up at the ledge every few yards to get his bearings. Satisfied he found about the right place, he started looking for Vuko's rifle. What the hell, it was a piece of evidence and would help confirm his story of what happened. He weaved in and out among the giant boulders, searching them from every side, peering down into any crevice into which the rifle could slip. Ten minutes later, his search was rewarded. He found the rifle wedged between two rocks, leaning against the wall as if some hunter propped it there while he took a leak. Both front and rear scope lenses shattered when it impacted the rocks. Otherwise, except for some deep scratches in the stock and barrel, the weapon was intact and probably would fire. It was grim testimony to its reason for being—to survive the most brutal terrain and conditions and still deliver 168 grains of copper-coated oblivion to anyone its owner wanted dead. He worked the bolt-action, and with the whisper of vault tumblers, it ejected a spent brass cartridge. Cutter slipped it in his pocket. After all, the bullet had been intended for him.

"Death from afar," he said aloud, remembering the chilling words printed on a black T-shirt Vuko used to wear around the ropes course. He shook his head and started back to the river.

Mouse and the others each took a turn hefting and inspecting the sniper rifle, but they were all anxious to press the search downriver.

They walked along the river's edge in the canyon's shadows. Mostly, they looked with their eyes downriver, straining to be the first to spot the young woman. When the Dolores crashed through two sharp canyon bends, Cutter pointed above to where the rocky rim jutted over the river.

"That's Mars Slalom up there, where Vuko went flying."

They hadn't hiked much farther when Mouse's trained eye spotted something foreign—purple and green and meaty-looking—trapped in the rocks.

The river master gulped. He didn't want to find her like this. He'd fished dead bodies from the water before and it wasn't pretty. He didn't signal to any of the others that he saw something and walked at the same pace toward the lumpish object.

A body floated half in the water. Or at least what once had been a body. It was tangled grotesquely in the frame of an Army-green mountain bike. One arm must have been broken in a dozen places to be able to wrap around the stem of the frame like that. As he looked closer, he saw it was wedged between the frame and the tire. The river had ripped the clothes from the upper torso. Camouflage cargo pants still hung in tatters from the legs; a bike chain gruesomely braided one of them. Not enough remained to identify the face, but it couldn't be anyone but Vuko. Looking back to where Mars Slalom hung over the river, Mouse estimated body and bike bashed against the rocks for nearly a mile. They looked like it.

Cutter and the other searchers saw Mouse inspecting something, his hands on his knees, and they quickly joined him, and just as quickly wished they had not. One by one they peeled away to retch in the rocks.

Minutes later, they dragged body and bike—no one wanted to try and separate them—out of the water and wrapped them in black plastic ground cover. Then they started to look for Serena again, praying they wouldn't find her like Vuko.

. . . .

A preliminary report estimated that the Ram Mountain Fire destroyed approximately 10,000 acres, more than fifteen square miles, and twenty-four hours later it still awoke and flared in spots.

From the time Ramworthy's helicopter touched the ground at the command center, Patricia fretted over the fate of her High Haven. There wasn't much doubt that the house had burned. She still held hope that some of her cherished heirlooms might be retrieved. Whether any treasures survived depended on which force of nature won the battle in her front yard—wildfire or snowstorm.

After a few hours of much-needed sleep, Patricia couldn't bear waiting any longer. She asked if Ramworthy was around to fly her up to the house; he was away, helping ferry crews to put out the most stubborn hotspots.

She discovered Grateful Bobby asleep in the back of a pickup on a stack of sun-warmed hay bales they planned to dump in the over-cooked forest for four-legged survivors. She couldn't resist tickling his nose, not altogether hidden by his tipped hat, with a stalk.

"Bobby," she whispered. "Bobby, will you please drive me up to High Haven." Minutes later, the pair climbed into Patricia's battered jeep and set out in the same direction she and her paint horse had traveled, what seemed like a lifetime ago, but was only the day before.

The snow melted away in the air super-heated by the sun and steaming ground. A muddy mess of a road led to the stately Victorian, but the four-wheel-drive vehicle made it passable. Patricia's hopes rose the higher they traveled up the mountain in green forest. But once they crossed into the blackened wasteland and fire ash fluffed into the air by the jeep filled their noses and throats, their high spirits turned somber. The only suspense was to see if the fire had left anything untouched.

"Awwwww," Patricia cried softly as they crested a hill with a view of the black, caved-in, smoking ruin.

"Patricia, I'm so sorry," Grateful Bobby said. "C'mon, maybe we can still save some things." He edged the jeep closer, driving over what had been split-rail fence only the day before.

"I left a lot of me in there," she said. Then, hopefully, "But there's only one thing that I really care about."

Grateful Bobby waited for her to say more, but she only stared ahead at the nearly perfect square of charred wood.

"My things were over there," she said, pointing to a little mound of jumbled black beams and siding in what once had been a corner of the house. The siding was nothing more than charcoal in the shape of what used to be boards, and it crumbled to the touch.

Wearing leather work gloves, Bobby muscled the larger beams and posts aside easily and Patricia dove into the debris. The teak bed frame and dresser had disappeared, burnt to cinders, she guessed. All that remained of the stained-glass lampshade, shattered by the heat, were jagged shards of soot-covered glass. The boxes of books and photographs made a tiny hill of ashes and scraps of brown-edged pages and blistered film paper.

At the bottom of it all they found the antique steamer trunk. The fire had eaten holes in the leather sides. But the corners that anonymous old craftsmen reinforced a century ago with heavy brass had stood the fire's test and held the giant box frame together. Patricia knew she had locked the great brass clasp. She brought the key with her, just in case, but she imagined the lock was melted shut forever. She began digging through the sides with her hands. In seconds, Bobby found himself balancing keepsakes in his huge paws that she passed back to him. Silver forks and spoons. Ornate jars. A jewelry box inlaid with mother-of-pearl. Then Patricia turned and gave him the perfect gift—a smile from her soot-painted face.

She stood up brushing litter from a leather picture frame.

"It's the only picture I have of my two husbands together," she said earnestly, as if she was about to share a great treasure with him. She blew ash off the glass, cracked by the fire's heat.

Grateful Bobby stared at a photograph burnt a mellow brown by sunlight years before. In it a startlingly lovely Patricia Keeney, a teenage sprite in a sundress, linked arms between two young men. In the photo, she looked up adoringly at the ruggedly handsome one in an Army pilot's uniform that couldn't be anyone but Vernard Ramworthy. Her other hand clasped the arm of the younger of the two, looking out from owl-framed glasses, a Kodak camera around his neck, as if he were her best friend.

Grateful Bobby's eyes bore into the photo as if determined to unlock its secrets, until he gave up and turned to Patricia with a you've-got-to-be-kidding look on his face and the question poised on his lips.

"The other man is Vern's brother, Lloyd," she said, cheerful as she took things from his hands and headed for the jeep. Looking over her shoulder, she added, "It got complicated after Vern and I divorced. It's a long story."

. . . .

Miles downriver from where they started their search, the rescuers turned back. Cutter and Mouse agreed it was unlikely they'd find Serena alive now, unless she was injured and lying behind one of the car-sized boulders lining the river, in which case they might see her from the opposite angle. But they knew they had conducted a thorough search. The woman must have taken her chances and ventured into the frigid current. Cutter shuddered as the image of Vuko's broken body invaded his thoughts. If they didn't find her now, then the river probably drove her under and held her body.

Cutter was physically exhausted and emotionally empty.

"It's terrible what happened to her," he said, breaking the fragile silence between them. It wasn't necessary to say her name. "How do such young and talented and vibrant people get so down on themselves that they become destructive? To themselves as well as those around them."

"Do you think she intentionally started the fire?" Mouse asked. "That was destructive, all right. It could have killed people." Meeting Cutter's look, he added, "Lots *more* people."

"Patricia has doubts that Serena started it intentionally. She also saved my life. Vuko had that scope on me. I had no idea he even knew Serena until we got into that fight by the river. He threw it in my face like he thought it . . . like she meant a whole lot more to me than she did. I think Lexi thought that about Serena, too. Am I that naive, Mouse?"

"Everyone thought she was hitting pretty hard on you, Cutter."

"Still, someone doesn't gamble with her life like she did. Throw everything away. Vuko did something to her. He was using her. He was like that: he used up people. Serena. Lexi. Her brother. He tried to do it with me when we worked together. We shared a lot with each other. But when I told him I wanted to try and build something on my own, he went nuts, said that I stole all the ideas from him. He dared me, like the neighborhood bully, to quit, and when I did, he swore he'd get even. Serena got in the middle of that somehow. Poor Serena."

"So how do you feel about the ranch now?" Mouse ventured. "There was some talk about lawsuits and that you might cash in? Don't do it, Cutter. You beat him." Nodding over at the black plastic tarp as two EMTs walked in dread to pick up the nasty package and carry it out, he added: "You're breathing; he isn't."

Cutter waved his thanks to the two men.

They reached their starting point. And still no sign of Serena.

"I'm not going anywhere, Mouse," Cutter said. The slightly older man looked hard into his boss's eyes, where he found the same old steel. The same old Cutter.

"I built this ranch out of my dreams. With a lot of help from some damned good people like you and Grateful Bobby and others. The lawyers fought us. The town fought us. Ramworthy fought us until he figured out we aren't here to rape the land; we're here to protect it and use it like it was intended. Maybe not the way he grew up using it, running cattle and living off whatever you could put a barbed wire fence around. But still in a good way. We've been responsible. We've been good neighbors. We've paid our way with sweat and blood and good will.

"Hell," he said, clapping a big hand on his friend's shoulder in a vice grip, "we haven't finished our first year yet. We've still got our first winter ahead of us. I'm looking forward to all those cold-weather challenges we've dreamed up. I'm looking forward to making some turns over on Telluride."

Cutter pointed upriver, past their starting point, in the direction of Double Dare Ranch miles farther south.

"Let's keep on this way for a little bit." Cutter knew that in this section the Dolores changed from a tough dame to babbling past the ranch like an old lady. It stayed that way past where softballs bobbed beneath the Double Dare outfield fence and for a couple miles more until it cut into a canyon and then swelled again, and the whitewater put smiles on the faces of people who loved a challenge. Like Serena.

The two men started to veer toward the bank when something moved and caught the sun's rays and the resulting twinkle grabbed Cutter's eye. He stopped and stared upriver, not far, and Mouse looked where he was looking. Sleeping Ute Mountain loomed in the hazy distance.

Something flashed again. It didn't seem to be in the water but floated somehow above it. Without a word the two men slowly walked back to the river, stumbling every so often on the slick rocks because they weren't watching where they put their feet.

They didn't need to go far to make out the object dancing and winking at them, and to realize they had been searching in the wrong direction. Serena hadn't risked floating the Dolores rapids; she'd hiked its shallows.

"I swear," Mouse said. "that woman leads a daring life."

"Death-defying, is more like it," replied Cutter with a bite of sarcasm in his voice.

Dangling a few feet above the river, as if it were supernaturally suspended in truly thin air, a shiny carabiner and red neckerchief bounced on fishing line strung between willows on both banks of the river. They both noticed something else flapping in the afternoon fall breeze, and light flashed from it, too. Cutter and Mouse splashed into the foot-deep water and raced each other to the fishing line. Cutter's Sasquatch slipped on a river rock and he nearly went down.

Pinned to one corner of the red neckerchief was a 1998 Todd Helton rookie baseball card, skewered there by a sterling silver Double Dare lapel pin in the shape of a four-pointed compass.

Cutter and Mouse knew of only one person who ever owned and held dear the treasure of Cooperstown.

AUTHOR'S NOTE

For those readers who know and love the Dolores Valley, I ask your forgiveness for daring to change it. I moved the location of some real places so that the geography fit the story, and I created some imaginary places in order to better tell the story. However, I kept nearly all of the actual place names to honor the land, its history and its people, past and present.

For the earnest geocachers, Moccasin Ridge does not exist on any map, but its coordinates are real and so are the caches of Double Dare. If you are among the first to find them, you can share the treasures of Cooperstown and Nipsy's Drop. Cooperstown really does lean over the Dolores River, and Nipsy's Drop looks out at Lone Cone Peak.

In real life, I know better than to mess with Mother Nature. But in a novel, it's wicked fun. In September and October, the Dolores River meanders more than it flows. The rock faces towering over the Dolores look like they could be named for ancient Grandfathers, but they are not. Snaggletooth is a rapid, not a waterfall. And the Blue Lagoon is nowhere to be found.

The indisputable fact is that this valley, this river, these red and gray canyons are treasures, no matter the season or the reason for discovering them.

—MM

ABOUT THE AUTHOR

Michael Madigan is the author of two books of non-fiction. *Heroes, Villains, Dames & Disasters / 150 Years of Front-Page Stories from the Rocky Mountain News*, won the 2010 Colorado Author's League award for non-fiction. His Christmas short story *The GyPSy Line* was selected for the anthology *Gem Street*, published in Ireland, and the story was nominated for the Pushcart Prize. His award-winning writing appeared in *SKI, Inside Sports* and *US* magazines and the *Rocky Mountain News* over a 36-year journalism career.

He grew up in the San Francisco Bay area, the son of a lifelong seaman and marine engineer, and the grandson of an old-school hunter and outdoorsman. He was drawn to Colorado in the '70s by a green-eyed girl and the best powder skiing in the world. Once Denver earned a Major League Baseball team, he decided to stay. He has skied, hiked, biked, hunted, snowshoed, snowmobiled, kayaked and rafted across the West. He lives in Arvada, Colorado

Double Dare is his first novel.

You've read about Double Dare's challenges, now try one of your own!

This story is fictional, but the geocaching coordinates on pages 65 and 66 of this book are real—and we've placed real geocaches at those sites. Located at the Dolores River Overlook, these caches are placed on Bureau of Land Management land, and true to the story, there's a cache named "Cooperstown" and one named "Nipsy's Drop." Just like in the book, the Cooperstown Cache contains a 1998 Todd Helton Rookie Card, and the Nipsy's Drop Cache contains a carabiner. To help as many people as possible join in on the fun, we've included ten of each item in the caches, so the first ten people to find each geocache can claim a prize straight out of the pages of this book! It's our hope that these geocaches will introduce you to the Dolores River Valley, the inspiration for this book, and also get you interested in geocaching, a great outdoor activity.

Cooperstown: N 37.8067199, W -108.7931577
Nipsy's Drop: N 37.8076655, W -108.7918455

Double Dare is driven by a strong sense of place. It has just the right mix of outdoor adventure, central character presence and quirky secondary players and sidekicks to make it a must-read.

— Robert Greer, author of the *Los Angeles Times* best-selling C.J. Floyd mystery series

Double Dare builds slowly to an explosive ending, where the characters not only battle with each other, but with a beast of a wildfire that Madigan's prose brings to frightening life. Readers who enjoy outdoor-oriented, adventuresome thrillers will be pleased with this heart-stopper.

— Beth Groundwater, best-selling author of the *Rocky Mountain Outdoor Adventures* series